The Compass Room

A 21st Century Geopolitical Thriller

A Wartmann Thriller – Book Two

Mark James

NORTH ARROW PRESS

THE COMPASS ROOM

Edited by Pete J. Gerardo
www.petejgerardo.com

First edition: 2025

ISBN 978-1-969608-06-3 (Paperback)
ISBN 978-1-969608-07-0 (Kindle Edition)
ISBN 978-1-969608-08-7 (EPUB Edition)

Cover design by North Arrow Press
Interior layout by North Arrow Press

North Arrow Press
Annapolis, Maryland
www.northarrowpress.com
Printed in the United States of America

NORTH
ARROW
PRESS

PROLOGUE

Russian Ambassador Denis Pirog sat at the head of the conference table with his legs crossed. He watched the large flat-screen television mounted on the wall.

Breaking news on CNN.

More US air strikes in Iran. The American president would address the nation about the situation there shortly.

When she came on, the US president sat with her back straight and her face set like a stone. She looked like a schoolmarm.

"Good evening," she began. "Earlier today, I ordered America's armed forces to strike a broad range of military and security targets in Iran. The Iranian government has been nothing but hostile and belligerent following attacks on the USS *George W. Bush*, Naval Support Activity Bahrain, and the Al Qudaibiya Palace in Manama."

Nearly a month ago, the American *Ford*-class aircraft carrier USS *George W. Bush* suffered a catastrophic explosion in the Khawr al Qulay'ah inlet between Muharraq Island and the main island of Bahrain. It sank the next day.

More than 3,000 American sailors perished in the catastrophe.

The Americans blamed Iran.

To make things worse, an Iranian-backed Islamist group—the Islamic Front of Bahrain—set off a car bomb outside the main gate of the US

Naval facility in Bahrain *in the middle of rescue operations,* and attacked the Al Qudaibiya Palace, home of the Bahraini royal family.

It didn't look good for Iran. America was preparing for war.

"We will *never* forget our young sailors who gave their lives serving our country," the American president continued. "We will *always* remember the *Bush.*"

"Our armed forces' mission is to attack Iran's nuclear, chemical, and biological weapons programs, and to degrade Iran's capacity to threaten its neighbors and American forces in the region.

"That operation is ongoing as I speak," she said.

Denis leaned back in his chair and yawned. *Just more chest-thumping by the Americans. You reap what you sow.*

A commotion behind the cameras stole the President's attention as she spoke, and her voice hesitated. The Oval Office camera lights went dark.

Men in suits—Secret Service agents, for sure—rushed into view, but they were silhouettes in the dark room.

"Go, go, go!" one of them barked. He seemed to tackle the seated President, and then rainbow bars with PLEASE STAND BY filled the television screen.

Staff in the CNN newsroom gasped.

Pirog leaned forward.

Interesting.

A CNN reporter now filled the screen, but the sound was interrupted by three squawks followed by a droning tone.

The American Emergency Alert System.

A recorded message followed.

"The United States Northern Command has detected a missile threat to the Washington, DC, metropolitan area."

A ticker in a red banner scrolled across the center of the screen. It read what the automated voice was saying. "A missile may impact your area within minutes. This is not a drill."

The Ambassador stood and the embassy staff snapped into action. "We must get you to the basement, Mr. Ambassador," said a young military aide in uniform.

"If you are indoors, stay indoors," the announcement continued. "If you are outdoors, seek immediate shelter in a building."

"No," said Denis.

Outside, sirens near and far were ramping up, rising and falling independently of each other across the American capital city.

"Remain indoors, well away from windows. If you are driving, pull safely to the side of the road and seek shelter in a building or lay on the ground."

"We go to the roof," Pirog ordered.

"We will announce when the threat has ended," the announcement concluded. "Take immediate action. This is not a drill."

A moment later, Pirog and various aides stood on the roof of the main nine-story building of Russia's Embassy. It was a cool, brisk evening, and the early night sky above was cloudless.

To the southeast, white phosphorous flares shot out from something—a helicopter, perhaps—and took on the appearance of giant angel wings suspended in the night air before they slowly flickered out.

Four more angel wings appeared and Pirog nodded and smiled. He understood exactly what he was seeing.

It was Marine One and a convoy of Raider helicopters lifting off and banking away from the grounds of the White House. They deployed anti-missile chaff countermeasures as they took flight over Washington.

The American president was being evacuated.

~ ~ ~

One mile southeast of the Russian Embassy on the opposite side of the circular compound of the US Naval Observatory was the Embassy of the Republic of Türkiye.

Ambassador Tayfun Ulusoy took a pack of cigarettes from his coat jacket and withdrew a dark brown Turkish cigarette. He lit it up and took a deep drag. He let out a long smoky exhale and looked up at the darkening sky as the smoke slowly ripped apart in the evening breeze.

He savored the lingering aroma.

The air raid sirens were dying down, but the missile warning remained.

Tayfun looked around. He imagined that his fellow ambassadors along Embassy Row, especially those of fellow European and NATO allies, were rushing to their bunkers and basements.

He instinctively looked northwest toward the Russian Embassy. The distinctive all-white building was on the other side of the US Naval Observatory, whose leafy grounds blocked his view. He imagined that Denis Pirog, his Russian counterpart, was right now standing on the roof atop *his* embassy, perhaps with a glass of vodka in hand. *He* wouldn't be in a bunker, no way.

Tayfun snickered and took another drag on his cigarette.

The home of the American Vice President was on the grounds of the Naval Observatory. No doubt, Daddy Longlegs—as the lanky American Vice President was both derisively and endearingly known—was cowering in a fortified bunker beneath the Observatory. The American President, meanwhile, had been whisked away by her Secret Service detail and was probably airborne in some doomsday plane.

An aide stepped forward and handed Tayfun a dispatch. The flash messages from the home Foreign Ministry in Ankara, and Turkish embassies in capitals across the Middle East, were coming fast and furious.

Explosions were reported in Manama, Kuwait City, and Riyadh.

And Washington, of course, was under a missile warning.

It was an eerie moment.

Remember this night, he told himself.

To the north, Tayfun spotted red flares high in the night sky. They grew in brightness. He assumed that he knew what they were. Not flares. Rather, they were re-entry vehicles housing warheads, like the Scud missiles he had seen in Syria.

"Everyone down," Tayfun said. He was calm, and he flicked his cigarette away.

He crouched down to his knees and, with his hands, covered his head.

Part One

BELLUM

CHAPTER ONE

A sleek double-rotor Raider helicopter swooped out of the night sky and landed on the South Lawn of the White House, its side door already open.

The president was shoved into the helicopter and the Raider, now designated as Marine One, lifted off.

It wasn't on the ground for more than thirty seconds.

"My family!" Cynthia protested as the helicopter lifted off.

"A second Raider is right behind us, Ma'am," shouted a young soldier. "They'll rendezvous at Andrews."

Minutes later, the Raider landed at Joint Base Andrews, just yards from Air Force One.

The VC-25B version of a double-decker Boeing 747-8 sat at the end of the runway, ready to roll, its four engines already revved up.

President Belle was practically carried by her Secret Service detail from the Raider helicopter to Air Force One. As she ran up the stairs, two more helicopters swooped down and landed as ex-Marine One lifted off.

Archie Meglowin, America's First Gentleman, departed one of the Raiders and bounded up the stairs to Air Force One with their twelve-year old daughter Katie in his arms.

Oscar Schwartz, the President's National Security Advisor; Martin Hartshorne, the President's Chief of Staff; and Admiral Erik Sorenson, the Chairman of the Joint Chiefs of Staff, raced up the stairs and entered Air Force One after departing the second Raider.

Once Admiral Sorenson entered the aircraft, the door closed behind him and the stairs were pulled away.

The pilot was given the green light, and he took the engines up to full throttle.

Air Force One seemed to sink momentarily as the large aircraft rocketed forward.

No one had sat down yet, not even the President, when the aircraft sped down the runway.

They dashed to their seats and buckled in.

The nose lifted up followed by the body. The bumpiness of the runway gave way to floating on air.

Air Force One was airborne.

~ ~ ~

"Okay, what the *hell* is going on, Oscar?" Cynthia asked. She sat at the head of the Air Force One conference room table, which doubled as a dining room.

She was sweating and almost out of breath.

"Madam President, NORAD and Space Force satellites detected up to 110 individual missile launches in Iran, most of which appear to have been short- and medium-range ballistic missiles.

"However, twenty-six of those appear to be intercontinental ballistic missiles, or ICBMs," Oscar said.

Cynthia turned pale. "My God," she said, her hand going to her mouth.

"Are they nuclear?" she asked.

"We don't know," Oscar said. "Not until …"

Oscar trailed off. He didn't need to finish the sentence.

"Ma'am," said Admiral Sorenson, "I recommend that we go to Defense Condition One *immediately*. This puts all of our armed forces — including our nuclear forces — on emergency alert and ready to deploy at a moment's notice," he said.

"DEFCON *One?*" asked Cynthia. "That's nuclear war!" she protested.

"Not quite. But if any of those ICBMs are nuclear, we need to be ready to retaliate in force."

Cynthia rubbed her eyes and took a deep breath.

"How much time before impact?" she asked.

Sorenson looked at his watch, then at the map on the screen in the Air Force One conference room.

"Seventeen minutes," he said.

"Madame President, we should order nuclear strikes *immediately* on Iranian military bases and nuclear facilities."

It was Daddy Longlegs, the Vice President. He appeared on one of the flat-screen monitors in the Air Force One conference room. In real life, he was sitting in a bunker beneath Number One Observatory Circle in Washington.

"You can't be serious, George!" said the President.

"Well, hell," he said, "Twenty-six ICBMs? Russia made it clear years ago—you don't wait to see if they're carrying flowers or fire. You treat each one as nuclear until proven otherwise." He leaned forward. "That's how grown-ups play the game."

"This isn't a *game*, George, and I'm not starting World War 3."

"Ma'am, with respect, if you don't hit back *right now*, you might as well send them a fruit basket and a handwritten apology." He took a sip from a glass. "We go big or we go home."

"Ma'am," Sorenson interjected, "DEFCON One puts our attack submarines out to sea, ready to respond in ... case. It also puts strategic bombers in the air and our silos on alert."

Cynthia nodded. She looked down at the table, her brow furrowed.

"Okay," she said. "Defcon One. But if those missiles turn out to be non-nuclear, we immediately drop to Defcon Two."

Cynthia pulled her chair back and leaned forward. She rested her cheeks in her fists, which in turn were supported by her elbows on her knees.

Cynthia looked up. "What are the targets?" she asked her National Security Advisor.

"We're not yet sure about—"

The Commander of NORAD interrupted from a monitor on the wall. "Twenty-six missiles total so far, Ma'am, and that number hasn't changed." It was Space Force General Jack "Ripper" Sterling.

"That's a good thing," Sterling continued. "Two missiles appear to have hit Diego Garcia, in the Indian Ocean, and four more are headed to Guam, in the Pacific."

Ripper paused and looked down.

"You said twenty-six missiles, General," Cynthia said. "I count—"

"Yes, Ma'am," Ripper interjected. "The remaining twenty missiles appear to be headed to the East Coast, probably Washington, DC, Ma'am."

Someone off-camera handed Ripper some documents, and he thrust his chest out as he skimmed them. "Ten missiles are headed for DC, and ten to Houston. Washington and Houston," he said, more confident now.

"How long?" Cynthia asked.

"Fifteen minutes, Ma'am."

Cynthia closed her eyes and rubbed her forehead.

DC I get, she thought. *Same for Guam and Diego Garcia.*

"Why Houston?" Cynthia asked, raising her head.

It was Daddy Longlegs who answered.

"It's the heart of our energy sector. If you want to cripple us, you go for oil and government. Knock out the capital and the refineries, and you get us on our knees—or so they think."

~ ~ ~

President Belle waited.

The clock had counted down to zero. The missiles would have hit Washington by now, and in few more minutes, Houston.

"We have reports of impacts in Washington, Ma'am," General Sterling said.

A flat-screen television embedded in the conference room wall was tuned to CNN. They reported up to twenty explosions in the city.

Nothing nuclear. So far.

Thank God.

CNN cut to footage from Houston, Texas. A local news drone captured multiple explosions, all of them unbelievably massive, near and far, as it panned in a circle.

Fiery mushrooms that quickly cooled into roiling, gray clouds.

There was a collective gasp from her staff.

"Were *those* nuclear?" Cynthia asked. They sure looked like it.

"No, ma'am," General Sterling answered on Oscar's pad. "That drone would've been fried."

~ ~ ~

"Do it," the president had ordered.

"It" was an emergency executive order activating the Continuity of Operations Plan (COP) to ensure the continuation of government in the event of extraordinary circumstances—like a nuclear attack on Washington, DC.

Congressional leaders—the Speaker of the House, the Majority and Minority Leaders of both the House and Senate, members of particular Congressional committees, etc., were already being evacuated from Washington as part of the Secret Service attack response protocols. COP authorized the relocation of all of Congress to the Mt. Weather Emergency Operations Center under Blue Mountain in Virginia, twenty miles west of Dulles Airport. The protocols also moved White

House and certain Pentagon operations to underground bunkers at Raven Rock, just north of the Maryland state line in rural south central Pennsylvania.

Air Force One had landed at Pittsburgh International Airport, where several Raider helicopters were waiting, one of them designated as Marine One. Thirty minutes later, they landed at Raven Rock.

President Belle and her family were introduced to their living quarters. And then it was off to the Raven Rock Situation Room for Cynthia.

"What's the damage in Washington and Houston?" Cynthia demanded.

"More than twenty-five impacts, so far, in both Washington and Houston," said Oscar Schwartz, the National Security Advisor. "Probably thirty each," he added.

"So," Cynthia rubbed her forehead, "we're talking sixty impacts? How is that possible?"

Oscar looked to Space Force General Sterling on one of the room's TV screens.

"Ma'am," Sterling said, "it appears that the missiles contained three multiple independent reentry vehicles, or MIRVs, each. In other words, each missile had three warheads, and it seems the warheads were each aimed at individually designated targets."

"So ... what, 30 different targets were struck in Washington?" Cynthia asked.

Her forehead pounded. She rubbed her eyes.

"Yes, ma'am. They appear to have been concentrated on a handful of targets. At least a couple of warheads fell in remote areas. The rest were accurate to within several—something like eight—square miles of their targets. Which means we were lucky. There was no direct hit on the White House or Capitol Building despite multiple impacts in their vicinity. Same for the NSA and CIA buildings," Sterling said.

"Nevertheless, the closest missiles struck within yards of some of those buildings, and shrapnel caused significant damage to many of them, including the White House," Curtis Templeton interjected. He was Secretary of Homeland Security and a former New York City cop.

"Multiple floors of the main NSA building in Fort Meade are on fire. The Pentagon sustained at least one direct hit. Damage might rival 9/11."

"Casualties?" It was Daddy Longlegs. He was calmer now. The Naval Observatory wasn't a target, and the Vice President's official residence had suffered no damage.

"Miraculously, very few. No deaths reported yet, but that can change," Templeton said. "Most people were in bunkers."

"Okay, tell me about Houston."

"It appears all of the missiles aimed at Houston were targeting the big oil refineries down there," Templeton said. "Deer Park, Bay Town, Texas City. Satellite imagery suggests significant damage. Local news reports massive fires."

"Ma'am?" It was Joy Chatterjee, Director of the CIA, on yet another screen. She was in a bunker in Langley.

"Joy, thank God," Cynthia said, relieved to see she was okay.

"Ma'am," Joy said again. "Iran has invaded Kuwait."

"We've lost contact with all of our bases there," Joy continued, "and the Kuwaiti government has also gone dark. It appears that the Al-Diwan Al-Amiri Palace, home of the Emir, was destroyed in a missile attack. Our embassy reports Iranian soldiers in the streets."

"Satellite imagery reveals several miles-long convoys stretching from Basra to Kuwait City. And … the convoys have crossed into Saudi Arabia."

"*Goddamn it,*" Daddy Longlegs exploded, "This is *exactly* what I was talking about. We need to strike and we to strike *right now.*"

"*Jesus,* George!" The President gave Longlegs a withering look.

"What about the 82nd and 101st Airborne Divisions en route to Kuwait?" Cynthia asked.

"We had to divert them, Ma'am," said Bernie Mentzel, the Secretary of Defense. "They've landed at Ramstein Air Base in Germany."

"We've also lost contact with our base in Bahrain." It was Admiral Erik Sorenson, Chairman of the Joint Chiefs of Staff, speaking now. "Our embassy in Manama reports multiple air and missile strikes in the vicinity of the Navy base, as well as the Al Qudaibiya Palace. Along with Al Udeid Air Base in Qatar, and our bases in Kuwait, they appear to have been targeted by Iranian missiles."

"Madame President," Longlegs interrupted, "if I may—"

"Shut up, George," snapped Cynthia. "Continue, Admiral Sorenson."

"Saudi Arabia was hit, as well. Air or missile strikes in Riyadh. And the Space Force reports that five Saudi air bases, along with their King Khalid Military City and Eskan Village army bases, were targeted."

"What are our options, Admiral? Can we strike their convoys?" she asked. The President looked to Daddy Longlegs. He nodded approvingly.

"After the strikes on our bases in Kuwait and Qatar, and on Diego Garcia and Guam, our only air assets in the region are the *Obama* and *Doris Miller* carrier strike groups. Those Iranian convoys are almost certainly employing advanced S-500 Russian-supplied antiaircraft systems."

"We can strike," Admiral Sorenson continued, "but it would be limited in scope and probably wouldn't slow them down much. Very risky. We wouldn't necessarily have command of the skies. It would be high risk with low payoff."

President Belle nodded and sighed. She leaned back in her chair and closed her eyes as she thought.

She rubbed her temples. "Tell me about the missiles."

~ ~ ~

"Uncle Zayne, Uncle Zayne, you must come out!" Ilyaas, Zayne's sixteen-year-old nephew, was excited.

"What is going on, Ilyaas? Is everything okay?" The bright-eyed boy was in a state.

"Come out, Uncle, you must come outside! The whole city is out. Iran has struck the Great Satan!"

Zayne Awada lived above a small pawn shop and a larger thrift clothing store, both of which he owned.

His brother Haidar lived a few blocks away in an apartment above a corner halal café that he managed for Zayne. On occasion, young Ilyaas operated the cash register and cleaned tables there.

It was a family affair.

The "Great Satan"? Oh, no. Not you, Ilyaas. Not you.

A flash of anger crossed Zayne's face. *Manage your boy, brother. We agreed that this life is not for him.*

"What is going on?" asked Zayne's wife.

"I don't know. It was Ilyaas. He's excited about something."

"Ilyaas?" She was confused. It was after one o'clock in the morning.

Zayne stepped out onto the small balcony above his shop. Ilyaas was right. The street was full of people. Young men jumped up and down and sang. Boys set off firecrackers. Young men on mopeds held fountain fireworks aloft as they rode. Cars blared their horns.

It was pandemonium.

Zayne dressed and went down into the street. He was immediately greeted by jubilant young men.

He shook hands and smiled as he worked his way through throngs of people to the other side of the street. The next block was no less crowded. Indeed, the whole city *was* out.

All of Paris. Ilyaas hadn't exaggerated.

Zayne made his way to his cafè. The light was on. He pounded on the door. After a moment, Haidar opened it for him.

"Ilyaas called me," Zayne said. "What is he doing up at this hour?"

Haidar shrugged. "What can I do? He has a strong will."

"What is going on?" Zayne demanded.

"What do you mean?"

Zayne turned his palms up in incredulity. "There's a million people outside."

"You don't know?"

Zayne shook his head with impatience.

Haidar snickered. He waived Zayne in.

Haidar poured a glass of tea for Zayne and himself, then reached for a remote behind the counter. He lit a cigarette, and turned on the small television perched in a corner above the tables.

Al Jazeera. Missiles falling on Washington, in America.

Iranian missiles.

Outside, the celebrations continued. With the firecrackers and improvised fireworks, it sounded like World War 3. And it wasn't just Paris. Cities all across the Middle East and North Africa, from Rabat in Morocco to Karachi in Pakistan, and in Europe from Paris to Brussels to Frankfurt to Malmo, in Sweden, had erupted in raucous, joyous celebrations despite the wee hours.

Zayne gingerly sipped his tea. He was deep in thought.

CHAPTER TWO

The night had bled like a cut. The blue hour had come and gone, and so had dawn. The sun had risen above the horizon, casting the morning dew in a soft mist of yellow, orange, and blue.

Back on the roof of the Russian Embassy, Denis Pirog looked out, bleary-eyed, on Washington. Situated on Mount Alto, the third highest point in the city, the Embassy overlooked the federal district, which stretched southeast to the horizon.

Several plumes of smoke punctuated the morning haze at varying distances, betraying the trust of the early morning. Most of the plumes were whitish, which he imagined meant that the fires there were largely put out during the night or otherwise under control.

The biggest plume of smoke was darker, though, and billowing. It was dead south, right in the vicinity of the Pentagon. *That* fire had not been extinguished, it seemed, at least not entirely. Thick dark smoke with streaks of whitish gray—an indication that firefighters were at least making progress—billowed high into the mid-morning sky and drifted eastward across the Potomac, shrouding lower DC.

A slight pungent odor permeated the crisp morning air. Multiple helicopters circled above the city. *Military.*

Denis wanted to dispatch couriers to explore the city and report back, but Washington was on lockdown. He would get a better idea of the state of the city by watching CNN.

But they were so shrill in their reporting. Other networks were no better.

Denis took a deep breath and headed back inside.

"Last night was unprecedented in the history of this nation," a young African-American reporter said. She was calm and collected, unlike the television pundits reporting from the Washington and Atlanta studios of CNN, and the New York City studios of other outlets.

Denis had never seen her before.

Bernice Hamdawana had worked through the night, covering the missile strikes from the streets. Perhaps it was fatigue that made her so calm, but whatever it was, she had a stilling effect on Pirog.

She is going places.

"Various ICBMS have struck the nation's capital. Upwards of thirty strikes across the region have been recorded. None of the missiles, I repeat, *none* of the missiles, were nuclear, nor were they chemical or biological in nature," Bernice reported.

"All of the missiles were conventional. Further, the missiles were accurate insofar as landing in the metropolitan area, but by all accounts—except for a strike on the Pentagon—the missiles appear to have missed their presumed targets.

"One missile, apparently targeting the CIA headquarters in Langley, fell in the Potomac and caused no damage. Another missile, targeting the National Security Administration in Fort Meade, landed in a parking lot, destroying vehicles and damaging the facades of buildings, but the NSA reports no injuries or deaths.

"It is unknown if there are casualties at the Pentagon, but we can report that most of the on-duty personnel were in bunkers."

Yuri Panchenko, Major General in the Main Directorate of the General Staff of the Armed Forces of the Russian Federation, which was still known by its Soviet-era acronym GRU, came to the doorway. He was unshaven and gruff looking, his tie loosened and collar opened. He had pulled an all-nighter, working encrypted phone lines and cables.

Yuri and Denis made eye contact.

Denis stood and stretched. His staff stood as well. He had gotten the on-the-ground report from the city that he had wanted, more or less, courtesy of CNN's new star Bernice Hamdawana.

Other pundits chimed in now, but their contributions were shrill and almost certainly false. The fog of war was a real thing.

Although the warheads may have missed their primary targets, some had fallen on populated areas. There were certainly casualties, but the sensational numbers tossed out by temperamental reporters were not believable.

"Walk with me, Yuri," Denis said as he put on his coat. Yuri turned back to retrieve his own. He tidied up and straightened his tie.

The two men stepped into the brisk cold morning, walking at a leisurely pace. They were closely trailed by two young *Spetznaz* special forces soldiers serving as the Ambassador's body guards.

All four men were sharply dressed in crisp, gray suits.

Wisconsin Avenue bustled with vehicle and pedestrian traffic most days, but not today. The street was eerily devoid of its usual vibrancy. Denis spotted a solo pedestrian, a young woman walking her dog—a happy and rambunctious labradoodle straining against his leash—across the street.

"News?" Denis asked.

"There is nothing new on the *George W. Bush* front," Yuri said. "We just don't have any insight, and neither does anybody else, for that matter. Our sources tell us that the intelligence agencies of the West—the British, the Germans, the French—they are all desperate for information.

"And, by the way," Yuri continued, "so are the Iranians. Even *they* seem to be confused. But the Americans are adamant about Iranian involvement, even if they have no evidence."

"Can you blame them?" Denis asked. "I mean, after everything?"

Yuri grunted.

"Well, the ship and her crew are lost now," Denis sighed. He was almost mournful. "Whatever secrets she has, she has taken them with her to the bottom of the sea."

Three thousand sailors lost. *Of course* the Americans were losing their minds.

The men continued along Wisconsin and entered the High Street section of Glover Park. Most of the shops were closed.

"Beijing's Guóānbù presented an Iranian white paper to us this morning written by an Iranian Rear Admiral, Hashemi Ghavam. It is their blueprint," Yuri shared. "To the letter."

"Oh?" Denis said, and looked to Yuri with his eyebrows raised. Then he looked down at his feet in thought as they continued to walk, his hands clasp together behind his back.

"Hashemi Ghavam is certain that the Americans will go to war against them," Yuri said. "He wants to deny them the space—their staging grounds—to build their forces and launch their attack."

Denis stopped and looked at Yuri. He didn't say anything right away. His brow was furrowed in thought.

"So that's why they staged the Friendship Games in Basra," Denis said.

Just days before, Iran and the Basra Governate of southern Iraq had hastily announced a Friendship Games between the two countries to showcase their growing ties. But it wasn't a bunch of athletes that had converged on Basra, but Iranian troops. Nearly 100,000 of them.

He snickered and started walking again. "And we all thought it was a defensive move, to be a stumbling block for the Americans. But it was a staging ground of their own."

"A preemptive strike," Denis continued. He spoke with a tone of admiration.

"Why didn't we see it?"

"No one saw it," Yuri said. "At least, not until they moved into Kuwait last night. It was all about the element of surprise. That was everything, and they are moving fast."

Denis shook his head, and the smallest of smiles crossed his face.

He stopped again. He surveyed the street around them and looked up at the cloudless sky.

"Tell me about the missiles," he said.

~ ~ ~

"Iranian copies of North Korean Hwasong-18 ICBMs," said Joy Chatterjee, Director of the CIA. She spoke from a bunker beneath the George Bush Center for Intelligence at Langley.

The President had asked the night before, but information then was speculative, and the information today was only a little better.

"Are you fucking kidding me?" seethed Daddy Longlegs. He was there in person now, having flown up from Washington before sunrise. Now, he sat with his arms folded across his chest. His demeanor was defiant.

President Belle shook her head.

"When in the world did Iran acquire ICBMs?" Longlegs fumed.

It was a rhetorical question for now, Joy knew, but it was a question she would have to answer shortly. Her team—the multi-agency Iran Desk, dubbed the Sean Connery Fan Club because of the late James Bond actor's resemblance to Ayatollah Ruhollah Khomeini, the founder of the Islamic Republic of Iran—was already scouring through reams of data to see what they could find and what they may have missed.

"We are working with the Space Force and the NGA to determine that, sir," Joy offered. "We'll know soon."

"Casualty updates for DC and Houston?" Cynthia asked.

"It appears that one or two missiles fell on or near the GWU campus, not far from the White House," answered Curtis Templeton, Secretary of Homeland Security. He was in a bunker of own in Washington. "No residence halls or dormitories were affected as far as we know, and it was after hours, so, miraculously, we don't have any reports of injuries or deaths so far. In terms of federal institutions in Washington, the extent of damage is surprisingly mild, almost negligible."

"Governor?" asked Cynthia.

Texas Governor Bill Sanchez and his ten-gallon cowboy hat filled one of the screens on the wall.

"Ma'am," Sanchez answered, "in the Houston area, Iran targeted multiple oil refineries: Baytown, Deer Park, Harrisburg/Manchester, Texas City, and Port Arthur.

"As in DC, the missiles weren't all that precise. But when it comes to oil refineries, you really don't need to be. All of the targeted refineries suffered major damage, according to initial assessments. They are all on fire. There have also been multiple secondary explosions after the missile strikes.

"As for casualties," the governor continued, "several refinery workers were killed, and scores injured."

After the governor, Martin Hartshorne, the President's Chief of Staff, spoke up. He was the meeting's unofficial conductor.

"Ma'am, I have Dr. Emily Yorke here, chief economist at the St. Louis Federal Reserve. I'll let her speak to the significance of the Houston attacks."

"Go on, Dr. Yorke," Cynthia said.

"Ma'am," Yorke began, "roughly one-third of the world's liquefied natural gas and a *quarter* of world oil consumption, including 35% of the world's seaborne oil shipments, exits the Persian Gulf through the Strait of Hormuz *each day.*"

Yorke cleared her throat.

"With the presumed closing of the Persian Gulf due to the outbreak of hostilities there, even if temporarily, oil prices have risen a thousand-fold. Oil supplies had already been constrained by the wars in Ukraine and Moldova—"

"Please, Dr. Yorke," Cynthia interrupted. "I don't have time for a lecture on global economics."

"Right. I just wanted to lay out—"

"It's okay to get to the point," Cynthia said. She *tried* not to be short with the economics professor.

"Right," Yorke said, adjusting her glasses. "The Houston area alone accounts for roughly 22% of crude oil production in the United States. That is not insignificant. The attacks covered the gamut of refineries in the area, so, in combination with the presumed closing of the Strait of Hormuz, we can expect oil prices to—"

"What will prices be at the pump?" Cynthia asked.

"Twenty dollars a gallon by end of the week, Madam President," Yorke said, "if not sooner."

The room erupted in heated discussions until Martin Hartshorne smacked his palm on the conference room table.

"Bernie," Martin said, as in *your turn*. As the meeting's conductor, Martin was like a prosecutor calling defense witnesses for cross-examination.

Bernie Mentzel, the President's Secretary of Defense, shared high-resolution satellite photos that showed much destruction at the Navy base in Bahrain. Ships alongside piers resting on their sides. Burning.

Satellite photos of the air base at Al Udeid in Qatar showed blackened pockmarks and bomb craters along its multiple runways. What were once maintenance hangars were now blackened smudges on the ground.

Same for the air bases in Kuwait.

Daddy Longlegs sat stoically with his hands clasped before him on his desk, but his eyes darted from screen to screen, photo to photo.

Daddy looked down to a satellite phone handset next to his clasped hands. He had tried multiple times to call Raymond Cole, the young Undersecretary of Defense for Intelligence and Security, whom he had dispatched to Kuwait to be his backdoor conduit to the military commanders there.

Guilt tugged at him.

Ray had to have been at Ali Al Salem Air Base when the attacks occurred, and Al Salem was now a smoking ruin. Daddy was certain that Ray's plane hadn't diverted to somewhere else because he wasn't answering his calls. And you don't just not answer calls from Daddy Longlegs.

The satellite phone buzzed and Daddy's heart nearly skipped a beat.

He snatched it up.

"Longlegs," he growled although he kept his voice down so as not to interrupt Mentzel.

It wasn't Ray.

"Mr. Vice President, this is General Alexander Pitts of Central Command in Tampa, Florida."

Daddy leaned back in his chair and let out a deep sigh.

Cynthia looked to Daddy. "It's General Pitts, Central Command," Longlegs whispered.

The President held up her hand to quiet the room. "Does he have news?" she asked.

"All!" Longlegs barked, "I am putting you on speaker."

"Yes, sir," Pitts answered. "A contingent of some 400 or 450 Marines and Navy SEALs fled Bahrain by ship this morning and landed in Qatar. They reported air and missile strikes on their base in Bahrain. Multiple ships in port were hit, several sunk. "It's Pearl Harbor all over again. Heavy casualties."

"We're looking at satellite images as we speak," Longlegs said.

"The soldiers and SEALs left Bahrain because Iranian troops were at the front gate," Pitts continued. "The base commanding officer was negotiating a surrender to the Iranians."

Hushed murmurs filled the room.

"Ma'am?" interrupted Lynn Benjamin, the Secretary of State. She was on a video screen from a bunker beneath the State Department in Washington. "Our embassy in Manama is reporting Iranian troops and tanks on the streets there. It appears that Bahrain has fallen."

The room erupted with renewed, and heated, discussions.

Longlegs sighed. At least they were getting a better picture of what was actually happening over there.

"Madam President, Mr. Vice President?" asked General Pitt.

"We're still here, General," Daddy said. "Go on."

"More alarming news, I'm afraid. The SEAL commander reported that Iran is flying stealth aircraft," Pitts said.

Daddy leaned forward.

Did he say stealth aircraft?

"General," Longlegs asked, "what *kind* of stealth planes?"

"The SEAL commander said that the stealth planes looked like American F-35s. But they were black, with Iranian markings. Also, they were twin-engine. F-35s have only one.

"Sounds like they were Chinese-made FC-31 Gyrfalcons," Pitt continued. "The stealth aircraft were able to take out radar and air defense systems in Bahrain and at Al Udeid in Qatar before Iran followed up with ballistic missile strikes."

"Son of a bitch," said Longlegs. There was a hint of admiration in his voice.

It was beginning to make sense.

So *that's* how Iran was able to catch the Saudis, Kuwaitis, Bahrainis—hell, *everybody*—off guard. Including the United States.

Secret stealth planes from China.

Longlegs tapped a finger on the table as he thought.

Secret ICBMs, copies of North Korean missiles ... *Well, I'll be damned.*

~ ~ ~

Time seemed to be moving fast, and Raven Rock was too cramped for Daddy Longlegs. Besides, he had work to do outside the bunker.

As for the President? *Stay put.*

He didn't want her putting up roadblocks at every turn, not with the stakes as they were. She simply didn't understand geopolitics and all that it entails, and whenever he tried to bring her up to speed, she cut him off.

Cynthia Belle was a billionaire hedge fund manager before she was elected President. She had no prior experience in government.

She was black and glamorous and considered smart as a whip. Maybe she was … when it came to investments. But in Daddy Longlegs' experience, investing wasn't much different from gambling. Some people got lucky; most people didn't.

For Cynthia, her beauty and her luck were a winning combination. It didn't hurt that American politics was dysfunctional. The two parties had become so divided, and the divides between them so deep, that Cynthia was able to step in and capture the middle.

It took a lot of persuasion by people like Daddy Longlegs to get her to run. He knew he was going out on a limb, but he had also found Cynthia to be smart. *Quick* smart, the kind that played well in politics. She might be inexperienced in government, but that's where Daddy Longlegs would come in.

And it worked. If only barely.

Cynthia had lost the first four Republican primaries, though each of them were close. But things had evened out on Super Tuesday, and it was a slugfest from there. Daddy Longlegs and other legacy Republicans stumped hard for her, and they ultimately eked out the party's nomination for her.

Cynthia chose Daddy Longlegs as her running mate to plug the "inexperience" hole. That was the deal from the start. The general election was another slugfest, but independent voters put them over the top.

And yet, the two of them never really got along. Longlegs shook his head, and the wisp of a smile formed on his lips.

Neither liked being told what to do. Cynthia was frustrated at nearly every turn as she tried to pass legislation—or, rather, as *Daddy Longlegs* tried to get legislation passed. It was up to *him* to negotiate, coddle, cajole, or browbeat members of a divided Congress to get her priorities through.

It was an agenda that turned out not to be so centrist after all: a highly controversial practical elimination of capital gains taxes, a massive corporate tax cut, and a lowering of the income tax threshold, all of which particularly benefited the wealthy.

It was standard conservative fare. The budget deficit soared.

Cynthia's poll numbers suffered nearly from the start. They were losing voters registered as independents. They were *especially* losing Democrats who had crossed party lines to vote for her "outsider" credentials.

Daddy Longlegs couldn't care less about tax cuts. Cynthia was a hedge fund manager, after all. The fact that she was conservative, well, who could have imagined such a thing? But so long as the economy didn't crater and the world didn't blow up—foreign policy was Daddy Longlegs' forté—they would probably do just fine in the next election.

But the world *did* just blow up. And the economy was likely to blow up right behind it.

Daddy gazed out the window. They were flying south over Frederick, Maryland. The small city quickly gave way to agricultural fields—probably soybeans and corn for livestock.

It looked bucolic and rustic. Peaceful.

That's what matters, he reminded himself.

Right there. That's what matters.

~ ~ ~

Daddy Longlegs' helicopter touched down on the grounds of the Naval Observatory in Washington. Carolyn, his wife of nearly forty years, awaited him in the residence foyer.

Daddy stooped low and she hugged him tightly. "You look tired," she said.

"A bit," Daddy admitted. "Lots to do."

"Well, not before we get some food in you. And I won't take no for answer."

Care turned on her heels and headed for the kitchen. Daddy followed her like a puppy. He leaned against the doorway and watched, arms folded across his chest. Care placed bread in a toaster and opened the fridge. She withdrew various items: mayonnaise, a can of crab meat. After years in Washington, Daddy had grown to love Maryland steamed crabs, crab cakes, and just crab meat in general.

She was efficient.

After a moment, the two sat at a small kitchen table. The kitchen itself was cozy.

Daddy took a bite of his toasted crab meat sandwich and grunted. "So good," he purred.

"How is the president handling things?" Care asked. She sat across from him and watched him eat.

"She blames me," he said after wiping his mouth, then took another bite.

"Were you wrong?" Care asked. "About Iran?"

Daddy finished his sandwich, wiped his hands and mouth with a napkin, and leaned back in his chair. He looked at Care.

"I don't think so," he said after a moment.

"You don't think so?"

"It's just—" Daddy looked down at the table and frowned. "We should have been prepared for a contingency like this. We might have ..." He shook his head. "I don't know. We might have rushed things."

Longlegs lowered his head in further thought.

"I might have been arrogant."

"I know you to be *confident*, Mr. George Wartmann," Care said. *"Daddy Longlegs,"* she added. There was sternness in her voice. "There's a difference."

Care let Daddy absorb her words. Then, "What could you have done differently? What *would* you have done differently, given what we now know?"

Daddy let out a long sigh and whistled. "You sure cut to the chase," he said. He smiled weakly. He looked down at the table and tapped a finger on it.

He replayed everything in his mind. News of the USS *George W. Bush* aircraft carrier blowing up and sinking in the Persian Gulf.

Iran was clearly responsible even though evidence would be hard to come by with the ship sitting in pieces at the bottom of the sea. Tensions had been running high between the US and Iran for years, nay, *decades*, before the disaster.

And then an Iranian-backed terrorist group, the Islamic Front of Bahrain, set off a car bomb at the Navy base's front gate even as rescue operations continued for sailors of the *Bush*.

He had immediately insisted that force protection troops be deployed to the Persian Gulf. He then embarked on a diplomatic mission to Europe to rally support for a unified response to Iran's aggression.

While he faced some resistance there—France and Italy hid behind the lack of direct evidence and the weapons-of-mass-destruction fiasco in Iraq *more than three fucking decades ago*—he was able to secure the backing of Germany, Poland, and the United Kingdom.

Iran had made some moves of their own: the Friendship Games.

It was so obviously a ruse. And within hours—at Daddy Longlegs' insistence—more than twenty U.S. Air Force C-17 Globemaster cargo planes ferrying one hundred 82nd Airborne paratroopers each, had lifted off into the midday sky at Fort Bragg, North Carolina. Five hundred miles west of Fort Bragg, another twenty or so C-17s lifted off from Fort Campbell, Kentucky, ferrying over 2,000 101st Airborne paratroopers. Another series of C-17s, ferrying units of the 24th Infantry Division, Mechanized, followed the 101st.

All of them were literally *in the air* when Iran struck, forcing the deploying troops to divert to Ramstein Air Base in Germany.

Finally, Daddy Longlegs spoke.

"Given the information I had, no, I don't see where I could have done anything differently."

"The only thing," he added, and paused. He tapped his finger again on the kitchen table.

"Our troops were on their way when Iran launched their invasion. If we had deployed those forces just a few hours earlier …"

Daddy Longlegs' eyes narrowed, and he looked to Carolyn.

"Well, then," Care smiled.

Daddy nodded his head. He smiled back with tired eyes.

The head of Daddy's Secret Service detail came to the kitchen doorway. "Mr. Vice President, ma'am, we need to get to the basement. Another missile warning."

~ ~ ~

"Can you believe that guy?" Harvey Hubble asked.

"What guy?" Harv was speaking with John, his brother-in-law.

"You know, Daddy *Long*legs. "

"What about him?"

"That guy started the damn war without evidence of Iran's involvement in the *Bush* disaster!"

"True," John said. He paused for just a second. "Are you watching the Phillies game?"

"Just like Bush!" said Harvey. "I mean, WMDs—*Hello?* And now missiles are raining down on *us!* And it's about time, too. When are these guys gonna learn? You keep starting fights overseas, eventually you'll get your nose bloodied!"

John laughed. "Yeah, true."

"I mean, *geeze.* Right?"

"Exactly—hey man, I hate to do this, but I've gotta run in a minute. I called to tell Karen 'Happy Birthday'."

"Oh right, let me get her."

"Hello?"

"Hey Karen. *Happy Birthday!*"

"Oh gosh, thank you——"

"Here's Teresa." John passed the phone to his wife.

"How's my favorite Birthday Girl?"

"Oh hi, Teresa. Gosh, thank you both for calling …"

CHAPTER THREE

Daddy Longlegs sat quietly this time.

The president raised the defensive posture of the country back to DE-FCON One again—temporarily. *Of course.*

The president's cabinet and advisors waited in silence. Would any of *these* missiles be nuclear?

Longlegs was stoic, his arms folded across his chest. He was back in the bunker beneath the Naval Observatory. CNN was on one of the monitors displaying a four-way split screen. The New York City skyline was on one, while the others showed reporters on location in Battery Park, Brooklyn, and Harlem. Occasionally, the screen would shift to show reporters standing in the Bronx and Central Park.

Air raid sirens blared across the city and scores of people scurried into subway stations.

Fear on their faces.

This can't go on. This can't be a daily occurrence. She's got to see that.

The meeting was a rehash of the previous night's. Updates on assets and materials.

Daddy studied the principals. There was a lot of sweating: Bernie Mentzel, the Secretary of Defense; Lynn Benjamin, the Secretary of State; Admiral Erik Sorenson, the Chairman of the Joint Chiefs of Staff; Joy Chatterjee, Director of the CIA; Oscar Schwartz, the president's National Security Advisor; Curtis Templeton, Secretary of Homeland Security; Barbara Hahn, Administrator of the Federal Emergency Management Agency; and a slew of administrative staff and advisors.

Perspiration on foreheads. Fidgeting. Excessive checking of notes and the whispering of staff in their ears.

"All reports are in," Mentzel shouted above the din of ongoing conversations and murmurs. "No nuclear detonations."

"Thank God," breathed Barbara Hahn, visibly relieved.

Some of the principals and many of the young staff erupted in applause.

Applause!

Daddy Longlegs hid his disgust behind a mask of stoicism. Missiles had just rained down on American cities for the second night in a row, yet they are *applauding* because they happened not to be nuclear. *This time.*

Fools.

"*You've* been quiet, George," President Cynthia Belle said. She was looking at Daddy Longlegs on the screen.

The crowded situation room at Raven Rock grew quiet.

Daddy raised his chin. He unfolded his long arms and deliberatively placed his palms on the desk in front of him.

"The 82nd and 101st Airborne Divisions, and the 24th Mechanized Infantry Division, were all diverted to Ramstein Air Base in Germany in the middle of last night's attack. We need to get them to Saudi Arabia as soon as possible.

"We need to go on the offensive. Call up the reserves—*everyone*—freeze all military leave, evacuate dependents from the region, deploy anti-missile systems in CONUS and forward bases; and—" Daddy took a deep breath, "bomb the goddamn living daylights out of Iran starting *five minutes ago.*"

Now *all* the faces at Raven Rock were stoic, except for the President's.

Cynthia chuckled. "Thank you for your candor, Daddy, as always," she said.

Bernie Mentzel, the Sectary of Defense, spoke up. "Madam President, Mr. Vice President, Lynn and I are working to do just that."

"Saudi Arabia has gone completely dark," Lynn chimed in, "but we are making multiple inquiries across a range of channels, including the CIA."

Joy Chaterjee, Director of the CIA, spoke up. "Madam President, Mr. Vice President, about Saudi Arabia …" Joy motioned to a young aid and whispered in her ear. The young woman walked to the wall of television screens and switched one of them to Al Jazeera.

"CNN and American news media are dedicating their entire coverage to the missile strikes on CONUS," Joy said. "Al Jazeera and other regional media have been reporting—"

A collective gasp filled the room.

"We can't confirm anything yet," Joy said.

On Al Jazeera, a live camera was trained from a distance on the walled Al Salam Royal Palace in Jeddah, on the Red Sea coast of western Saudi Arabia. It was the middle of the night there, and the palace lights twinkled gold. Flashing red and blue lights of emergency vehicles filled the grounds.

There had been a shooting hours earlier, according to a ticker at the bottom of the screen.

More: the King of Saudi Arabia and his Crown Prince were dead.

~ ~ ~

"They say that it was General al-Mutairi, Commander of their Army," Joy said. "He was about to be sacked by the King for readiness failures after the Iran attacks. They took heavy losses."

What in the name of—

"Who's in charge over there?" Daddy asked. He was exasperated.

"We don't know."

Jesus.

The room was once again enveloped in a din of conversations and reactions. Everyone had an eye on the President, though, who continued to watch the Al Jazeera report.

Cynthia pushed her chair away from the table and brought her elbows up to rest on it. The room quieted down.

Cynthia looked to Daddy Longlegs. She displayed just the slightest of body language to indicate that she was, *maybe*, in agreement with him. Turning to Bernie Mentzel, she said, "Make it happen. Full mobilization."

Then she turned to her press secretary. "I need to address the nation about these missile attacks and the shit going down in the Gulf."

Cynthia slapped a hand on the table and shook her head.

"What did they think was going to happen?"

It was a rhetorical question.

"What is the status of our Aegis Ashore systems?" Daddy Longlegs asked.

Aegis Ashore is the land-based anti-ballistic missile system modeled after the ship-based Aegis systems deployed on more than a third of the US Navy's *Arleigh Burke*-class destroyers and about half of its *Ticonderoga*-class cruisers. Aegis Ashore was the same physical platform built for a ship but was instead fitted atop a concrete base in the shape of an *Arleigh Burke* destroyer.

Why reinvent the wheel when the ship-based model was a proven platform?

Two Aegis Ashore systems were built: one in Słupsk, Poland, and the other in Caracal, Romania. Both were under the command of NATO.

A third system was under construction on Guam.

"Like our ship-based platforms, Aegis Ashore is effective against short- and medium-range ballistic missiles," Vice Admiral Baltzer Oberkirsch answered. "The missiles that targeted the East Coast were *long-range* ICBMs. Although they went practically right over Słupsk,

Słupsk isn't programmed to defend against the higher altitudes of long-range ICBMs. They are programmed to intercept missiles that threaten Western Europe specifically.

"But after last night's attack, we ordered that the Aegis Ashore platforms in Poland and Romania be re-calibrated to intercept missiles from Iran that appear to be aimed at CONUS."

The room went quiet for a moment as the principals absorbed Oberkirsch's words.

"Will they work?" asked Daddy Longlegs.

Oberkirsch shrugged. "We'll see."

The admiral didn't sugarcoat anything. Daddy liked that. But it didn't absolve him of answering tough questions. Not in a time like this.

"What about our sea-based Aegis systems?" Daddy asked. "Where the fuck are *they* and why aren't they stepping up?"

Oberkirsch took a deep breath before he answered.

"Sir, our ship-based Aegis systems are split between ships currently deployed and ships undergoing either post- or pre-deployment maintenance schedules. Active ships with Aegis on board are currently deployed to the Pacific and Mediterranean.

"We have three ships—two *Arleigh Burkes* and one *Ticonderoga*—that are in early pre-deployment workups. After last night's attack, we are in the process of updating their coding, and recalibrating and testing their systems.

"It takes time, sir," Oberkirsch added. He seemed defiant—no, *tired*—in his answer.

"That's what I want to hear," Daddy quipped with a quick encouraging nod. "When do you think they'll be up-and-ready and on-station?"

"Our sailors are scrambling," Oberkirsch said. "Three, four days."

He is covering for his ships, Daddy thought. *Any admiral worth his salt would.*

"*Yesterday,*" Daddy scolded. "We need those goddamn ships on station *yesterday,* do you understand me, Admiral?"

"*Yes,* sir," Oberkirsch answered. His eyes were narrowed into a defiant squint.

Daddy continued to grill. "Where are we with Patriot missile systems?"

"Two systems each are being set up at Fort Meade outside of DC, and at Aberdeen Proving Ground, northeast of Baltimore. They should be operational within hours."

"Anyway to make them visible? Say, park one right in the middle of the National Mall, or even the Ellipse? Hell, even Central Park in Manhattan. Give people a sense of security," Daddy offered.

"I like that," the President said. "Do it."

"Yes, ma'am."

"Okay, we need to get ahead of things, as Daddy said." The President turned to Bernie Mentzel. "I want options."

"We have only *one* option," Daddy Longlegs interjected. "We need to re-establish the principle of *deterrence.*"

"It's too late for that," Cynthia said. "That ship has sailed."

"Not for Iran, Madam President, but for the rest of the world. For Russia. For China." Daddy leaned back in his chair and draped one leg over the other. "As for Iran," he continued, "we've allowed them to yank our chain for fifty years, and look where it's gotten us. We need to make an example out of them."

~ ~ ~

Zayne pretended not to notice Juliette, the blond French girl, gushing over Ilyaas. The two were hanging around each other more and more of late. He watched out of the corner of his eye.

But it wasn't the girl he was watching. It was Ilyaas. He watched Ilyaas absorb the girl's adulation. And he wore it well. He was passive, almost dismissive. The subtle tilt of his head, the sideways glance, the easy smile. Zayne was proud.

Ilyaas was no longer a boy. He was growing into a confident young man.

He could be happy here.

It was okay for a young Muslim man to take a non-Muslim woman for his wife.

Not the other way around, of course.

Zayne glanced over at Haidar.

His brother was behind the counter, counting packs of cigarettes and taking inventory. But he had paused. He, too, was looking at the young couple. But his eyes were vacant. Like a predator's. He bit his lower lip.

Haidar was looking at *her*.

Zayne shuddered.

He walked to the young couple, breaking Haidar's spell. Zayne handed Ilyaas a fifty euro bill. "Go get some ice cream," he said, smiling. "It's on me."

Ilyaas blushed, just a little. Juliette giggled. "Thank you, Uncle Zayne," the boy said, taking the money. He looked to his father. Haidar nodded his approval, though his face now wore a scowl.

As the young couple left, Zayne looked to Haidar.

"I must get back," he said.

But Haidar had already resumed counting.

Zayne watched him for a moment, then left.

As the door closed, Haidar paused again and looked up. He took a deep drag on his cigarette as his eyes lingered on the front door.

~ ~ ~

Kyle Cropper bobbed in the water, his eyes trained on the horizon. Bumps indicated an oncoming set, and Kyle turned his board and paddled. Water sprayed in his eyes. The wind had turned, and the ocean had become choppy.

He missed the first wave, and so much the better. It was a closeout, but it left a clean surface for the next wave, and Kyle paddled methodically, picking up speed. The back of his board rose as the wave caught up with him. Two more strokes, and Kyle placed his palms under his chest and swung his feet up beneath him, replacing his hands. He was up and looking down the line, already leaning forward on his front foot.

It was a nice waist-high wave with good energy, and he raced along the face of it before shifting his weight to his back foot and turning his board into the oncoming wall of water. He snapped to the left with his arms and hips, spraying water like a Japanese fan, and raced back down the line.

He got one more turn in before the wave's energy was spent.

Kyle lay on his board. He, too, was spent. His arms were heavy, and the dull ache in his neck and shoulders was satisfying. It was the good kind of ache, the kind that comes after a hard workout.

Another wave with energy crashed behind him, and Kyle paddled to pick up speed ahead of the whitewater. It enveloped and lifted him as he paddled. He leaned forward and rode the whitewater on his belly all the way to the beach, leaning left, then right, then left again, steering toward the board bag he had left lying on the beach.

It was a good ending to a good session. Most days, he waited for that last clean wave, long after he was spent. When it finally came, he could barely paddle, and if he was lucky to catch the wave, it wasn't clean, and it was usually over before he could do anything with it.

And then came the long paddle back to the shore—the paddle of shame. This happened more often than not.

Kyle gathered himself and his board, and staggered up and out of the surf. No easy task when you're exhausted. His head was perched over his shoulder as he exited the surf. *Never take your eyes off the ocean.* His father had drilled that into him and his brother. You never take your eyes off the ocean, lest it surprise you with a rogue break.

He unhooked the board's leash at his ankle while facing the ocean.

Another surfer clumsily exited the surf a block away—his chin perched over a shoulder, eyes on the water.

"Thanks for coming out," Kyle said, as the surfer approached.

"Of course," Jack answered. He held his board snug against his hip amid a gust of wind. "I'm surprised you're in town." He still wrestled with the wind. "Figured you'd be in a bunker somewhere."

"Not me. That's for the leadership."

"And here I thought being a Senator comes with all kinds of perks. Do you have time for the Cap'n?"

"Always."

~ ~ ~

Colonel Haim Levin and his *Aman* team—Aman is Israel's Military Intelligence Directive—were ghosts in the desert.

They had shadowed the Iranian Army's progress as they swooped southward—all the way from Kuwait and into the UAE. They had witnessed what appeared to be everyday traffic of tractor trailers and private cars getting caught up in the advancing Iranian Army's convoys.

What happened next was confusing.

The trucks and cars had stopped in front of a large car mall composed primarily of SUVs, halting much of the Iranian convoy.

Jets swooped down, bombing and strafing the convoy.

They were American F-35s. It was a turkey shoot, as the Americans liked to say.

The occupants of the trucks and cars, meanwhile—some 400 armed soldiers—had sped off into the desert in commandeered SUVs from the car lot.

They were Americans, Levin and his team surmised. *American special forces.*

~ ~ ~

Haidar stayed up while his wife went to bed. It was his routine.

He went downstairs to the cafè. The street outside pulsed with life—pedestrians, young revelers, mopeds buzzing by. The small bell above the front door rang every time it opened. It was constant. Patrons came for a myriad of small things: cigarettes, vapes, Makla chewing tobacco, or some baked goods: baklava or pastries.

Others sat quietly, sipping tea or coffee, or engaged in low, intense conversations.

The café was cozy. For many, it was a brief respite from the liveliness on the other side of the door.

Most were regulars, whether patrons or deliverymen. Case in point: Ahmed Farooq, a burly man with a bushy black beard, carried in boxes of restaurant supplies on a hand trolley. Plastic bags, cups, food containers, utensils, and the like.

"How is the kitchen?" Ahmed asked when he spotted Haidar sitting in a corner sipping tea.

Haidar only nodded, and Ahmed went about his business. *No response means all clear.* Ahmed pushed the trolley into a storage room in the back and stacked the boxes neatly.

On his way out, he stopped and used the WC. While in the bathroom, he pulled out a slim wooden panel at the base of the wall, revealing an open slat. He retrieved an envelope from his overalls and stuffed it into the opening, then put the panel back into position.

He washed his hands and left. Just a delivery man making routine deliveries.

It was almost midnight when Ilyaas came in.

"Hello, father," he said.

"Did you have fun tonight?" Haidar asked.

Ilyaas tilted his head. His father had never asked him that before.

"Yes," he said. "We had a good time."

"Why don't you date a nice Muslim girl?" Haidar asked.

Ilyaas snickered. He didn't expect that.

"I dunno," he said, smiling. "I like Juliette."

Haidar leapt to his feet and smacked Ilyaas across his face, sending the boy crashing to the floor.

"She's a whore!" Haidar bellowed. *"She is not Muslim. And you are not French."*

He stepped over the startled boy and went upstairs.

Ilyaas stayed on the floor, leaning on an elbow. He touched his mouth where his father had hit him. Blood.

He stared at the red smear on his fingers. He rubbed it between his thumb and forefinger as he tried to understand what had just happened.

CHAPTER FOUR

Clearly, the Americans were on the run.

Levin phoned in his team's observation. Their mission was to shadow *Iran's* Army, not the American special forces who were suddenly on the scene.

But it wasn't long before paratroopers—probably *Iranian* special forces—were spotted far to their south in the direction that the Americans had fled. According to his map, the paratroopers were landing so close to the border with Oman that it was hard to determine if they were landing in Oman or the UAE.

The bulk of Iran's advancing Army, not its special forces, had bypassed Abu Dhabi. They were now east of Dubai and accelerating toward Sharjah.

It was apparent that the Iranian Army was moving to pinch off the entirety of the UAE.

Levin reached for his satellite phone to call in his latest report when …

A new sun materialized almost straight over their heads.

"Get down!" he shouted, burying his face in the desert sand. Although his eyes were closed, he perceived another flash of searing light.

~ ~ ~

Major General Ari Benjamin, Agency Executive of Aman, paced back and forth at the Operations Center in Jerusalem. So far, Colonel Levin and his teamed had phoned in at precisely the prescribed intervals.

This time, they were late.

"Sir." A young cryptologist alerted him that Levin was reporting in. He handed Ari a headset.

It sounded like a hurricane.

Clearly something had gone gravely wrong.

Levin had to shout at the top of his lungs, but Ari still had a hard time hearing his words.

Ari straightened as Levin shouted his report.

His head dropped as he listened. He sighed audibly into his mouth-piece.

"Thank you, Colonel," he said. "Come home."

He removed his headset and looked to the young cryptologist.

"Get me the Prime Minister. It's a national security emergency."

~ ~ ~

Back in Washington, Daddy Longlegs was up at five o'clock in the morning. By six o'clock, he was out the door of Number One Observatory Circle, the official residence of the Vice President of the United States.

Every day. It was his routine, rain or shine, and now, it turns out, in war or peace.

The Secret Service was well-versed in his routines, and their protection protocols and "what if" scenarios were well-practiced. Not that it made their job any less harrowing on any morning of the week. But they were professionals. Every day was treated as though today was *the* day.

The day of an assassination attempt. Or an accident. The VP getting run over by a car. Or having a hard fall, heart attack, or some other medical emergency.

An armored ambulance discreetly shadowed the VP as he performed his morning jog. Longlegs didn't even know it—well, as far as *they* knew—and his Secret Service detail liked it that way.

The good thing about Daddy Longlegs' daily runs is that they were so early in the morning, either before sunrise or right after, depending on the time of the year. That meant that the leafy, rustic Rock Creek Trail, which ran right by the Naval Observatory, was usually devoid of anyone but the most dedicated of runners, hikers, or bird watchers. On most mornings, in fact, nearly everyone that the Vice President might encounter was a Secret Service agent.

Daddy cherished his morning runs. *This* was where he got a lot of his thinking done.

As he ran, he went over everything. *Again.* He couldn't be sure, but it seemed to him that he had gotten through to the President.

Daddy crossed under the Massachusetts Avenue Bridge and, a moment later, jogged along the ravine that cut just south of the Italian and Danish embassies. He slowed to a walk astride the stone bridge in Dumbarton Oaks Park, which marked the end of his six-mile run.

He rested his hands on his hips as he walked, and took deep breaths. The air was fresh and full of morning dew. His fingertips tingled with the usual flood of endorphins—the runner's high. At sixty, it was still a thing, and Daddy was grateful. It's what kept him continuing *wanting* to run.

A young Secret Service agent in a sweatsuit, who had trailed him the entire way, jogged up alongside him, handing Daddy a small bottle of Gatorade.

"Morning, Tommy," Daddy said. The kid was a running fanatic and rail thin. He ran two or three full marathons a year. Daddy couldn't help but be a little jealous.

"One day I will outrun you," Daddy said.

"Yes, sir," the kid said, and sauntered back to take his place several feet behind Longlegs.

In other words, *not a chance.* Like, *ever.*

The kid was right, of course. *But don't think I wouldn't break your legs first.*

Daddy smiled to himself.

Daddy came upon a set of stone steps nearly hidden by lush foliage. They led out of the ravine up to Observatory Circle.

After a quick shower at the VP mansion, Daddy Longlegs rode in an armored SUV to the campus of George Washington University, just a few blocks from the White House.

The moment he stepped from the SUV, he was surrounded by reporters covering rescue efforts.

"Mr. Vice President! Mr. Vice President!"

Daddy walked to a National Guard soldier, who saluted him and lifted police tape for Daddy and his Secret Service detail to step under. He walked on without answering any questions.

"Welcome, sir." It was an Army officer—a Colonel Hathaway, according to his name tag—who stepped up to greet the Vice President. The order of tidy city blocks, stately government buildings, streets, sidewalks, restaurants, trees, cars, people—all of it—seemed to have been wiped away. It was as though Godzilla had stomped through DC, his tail indiscriminately wiping out whole city blocks as he waddled past and breathed fire.

Left behind were smoldering piles of rubble and twisted rebar. They seemed to have been piled atop two or three square blocks in the middle of the city. Even the street grid here was gone, replaced by upturned earth, debris, and a large crater in the middle of everything.

It looked like Gaza City during the Hamas War, and the air was pungent.

"Jesus," Longlegs breathed. "What am I looking at, Colonel?"

Colonel Hathaway pointed to a stories-high lump of shattered concrete and twisted metal. "This is the International Monetary Fund complex. Or was. And that," he said, pointing to another giant pile of rubble, "was the GWU law library."

"Casualties?"

"I know it seems impossible, but none so far. But we have a lot of buildings and rubble to comb through."

"How is that even possible?"

"The strikes happened after hours, so we don't think there were many people, if anyone, in either building."

Firefighters and rescue teams with dogs worked over the remains of the law library as Longlegs and the colonel looked on. Longlegs insisted on staying back and watching from a distance. He didn't want to get in the way of the rescuers, and he didn't want to slow them down.

His phone buzzed in his breast pocket. He ignored it.

"One of the several Iranian warheads aimed at the White House landed here, obliterating the IMF complex, along with GWU's Lerner and Stockton Halls and the Law Library," the colonel continued.

The scale of destruction was really hard to believe.

Longlegs' phone buzzed again, and this time he took it out. He realized that it was the satellite phone that he kept for in-the-field contacts— military, intelligence, etc. His regular cellphone was in his other breast pocket.

"Sorry, Colonel," Daddy said, then answered the phone. "Longlegs," he barked. It was General Pitt in Tampa.

"Say that again?" Longlegs seemed alarmed. "Jesus," he breathed.

"Okay," he said, taking a deep breath. "I'll do what I can. Keep me posted, General."

His secret service detail rushed forward. *"Sir, we have to go!"* an agent shouted, grabbing his arm.

Daddy didn't protest, but ran with his detail as they kept him covered. He was shoved into his SUV as reporters scrambled to take photos. The SUV sped away.

Within minutes, Daddy's convoy turned onto Massachusetts Avenue and sped, with sirens blaring, back toward Naval Observatory One. When they blew past the Japanese embassy on the left, and the Turkish embassy on the right, Daddy leaned forward and shouted.

"Turn up here, at the Islamic Center, turn right."

"Sir, our orders—"

"Do it, goddammit!"

They were just a half mile from the Naval Observatory, but Melvin Bauer, chief of Daddy's Secret Service detail, obliged, and the convoy turned onto the leafy, residential Belmont Avenue. It was just ten minutes past 7:00 a.m., and if much of the neighborhood wasn't already awake, they were now. The sudden convergence of police vehicles with sirens blaring made sure of that.

"Stop here!" Daddy commanded, and the convoy halted in front of the Embassy of the Sultanate of Oman.

It was a stately redbrick home with white window panes framed by black shutters. The house was largely hidden behind mature elm trees and an elegant redbrick wall with a black ironwork fence perched on top. The brick wall was broken by an arched, iron-gated pedestrian walkway at the center, as well as a driveway closed by a larger iron gate on the right.

Daddy stepped into the crisp morning air and waited outside the walkway gate. His secret service detail took up positions around him. Police closed off the street.

There was a commotion at the front door of the house. The door opened, and a man stuck out his head and saw the police cars and Daddy Longlegs standing at the walkway entrance. He went back inside. Another man stuck his head out, then another.

Finally, a man came out dressed in a robe and slippers. He walked briskly to the walkway gate.

The man was twenty years Daddy's junior, with thick black hair. His robe and slippers appeared to be laced with gold.

When he saw Daddy Longlegs standing there, his eyes went large.

"Mr. Vice President!" he gasped. He hurriedly unlocked the gate. "Please, please, won't you come in?"

"Mr. Ambassador," Daddy said, nodding. "Thank you for inviting me."

~ ~ ~

Halif bin Theyazin. He looked like his elder brother Haitham, the Sultan of Oman. Halif was only a couple of years younger than the Sultan.

Halif barked orders in Arabic to his staff, then smiled broadly at Daddy. "Please, please, we have tea, coffee, whatever you like."

"I can't stay long," Daddy said, "as you can imagine." He nodded to one of the flat-screen televisions—there were several in the house. Each of them was tuned to Al Jazeera, and Daddy could see the breaking news that General Pitt had shared.

The video on the screen was from atop a skyscraper in Dubai, facing inland. The sky was dark and ominous. An angry sandstorm was about to swallow the city. Daddy was reminded of the occasional Arizona haboob, but this sandstorm was larger and angrier by orders of magnitude.

Beyond the gathering storm stood two giant geysers of sand whose peaks were so high in the atmosphere that they were lit by an unobstructed sun. The tops of the geysers were golden orange blobs while the pedestals of sand on which they stood were being slowly obscured by airborne dust.

A ticker below the video feed ran continuously:

"... Possible nuclear explosion in desert outside Dubai ... Burj Khalifa on fire ... Possible nuclear explosion in desert outside Dubai ..."

If it was a nuclear explosion, then clearly there were two, given the two separate geysers.

Daddy turned to Halif. "I have a personal favor to ask of the Sultan."

~ ~ ~

Mornings were still chilly this time of year. Low 40s, sometimes 30s, or even lower. It was hard to warm up after an early morning dawn patrol.

Kyle peeled off his wetsuit as quickly as he could, which wasn't fast enough in the cold air, and changed into a T-shirt, sweats, and a hoodie, all while covered by a beach towel. Shivering, he tossed his wetsuit, booties, gloves and board into the back of his pickup truck, and clamored into the driver's seat. He turned on the engine, cranked the heat up to high, and rubbed his hands together.

He was still shivering as he waited for the heat to take hold.

Kyle closed his eyes and relished the stoke. This was the surfer's high. He savored the dull ache in his shoulders and arms. He savored the scent of salt water and sand, and the feel of them, in his hair and on his skin. Waves and rides played over in his mind. At least two were the epitome of perfection, and he smiled.

He looked out his passenger side window and saw that Jack was changed and ready now in his own truck. Jack gave a thumbs up. Kyle backed out and led the way.

Minutes later he pulled into Captain's Corner, and Jack pulled in right behind him.

A handful of pickup trucks with surfboards sticking out of their beds, and a couple of cars with boards strapped to their roofs, were parked in the lot. Now there were two more.

Captain's Corner was a dive of a diner, owned and operated by sixty-five-year old Teddy Walston, an old surfing buddy of their father's.

Teddy's father was a retired Navy captain, and Teddy had named the restaurant in his honor.

Teddy was like an uncle to the Cropper boys.

An opening in the wall between the kitchen and the service counter allowed customers to see the cooks at work. Likewise, Teddy could see who came and went, and he instinctively looked up whenever he heard the door's bell ring.

He did a double take. "Well, I'll be," he said. He was in the midst of frying eggs and bacon, and couldn't walk away from the kitchen. "Hey Chris!"

Christopher Cropper sat in a corner, sipping coffee and working a crossword puzzle. He wore glasses perched on the tip of his nose.

Christopher glanced up and peered over the top of his reading glasses. He looked at Teddy, following his gaze to the two men who had just come in. His eyes smiled. Kyle and Jack walked over and joined him.

"Hey Dad," Jack said. "Look who's not in a bunker."

"Glad you're still in town," Chris said. "But shouldn't you be heading back to Washington?" He seemed amused. His eyes were still smiling.

"Nope," Kyle answered. "The leadership are at Mt. Weather. All business is on hold for now. I can work out of my OC office and be back in DC in a couple of hours if they need me. Perks of living on the Eastern Shore."

"And you two surfed, no less," Christopher said. "Goddamn if I didn't raise you two right."

"Glad you're still home," Christopher continued. "It's probably way safer here anyway than in DC."

Christopher paused. "You're earning your keep now, son," he said. He offered a crooked smile. "Bout fucking time."

Jack snickered.

"You're the one who pushed me into politics," Kyle countered.

"Don't blame me or your mom," Chris answered. "You knew what you wanted."

Kyle snickered now. "Yeah, guess that's true."

Jack remained quiet. Both had attended college at Johns Hopkins in Baltimore, and both had returned home to continue to work for Christopher. But while Jack had majored in business, Kyle had majored in Political Science and International Relations. It was clear that something to do with diplomacy or geopolitics was his calling, and he was dithering it away.

Four years after college, Kyle was married, and his first child was on the way. So Chris pulled him aside and laid down the law. It would be his last year working at Cropper Construction. Although he was a hard worker, the business was Jack's domain, not Kyle's.

His dad was right, of course, but Kyle was silently resentful for a time. Quite so. And in a panic. His own father was pushing him out of the family business. What would he do?

His path became obvious when a large client refused to pay what they had agreed to. It turned into a prolonged battle, and Christopher faced the specter of multiple lawsuits when he couldn't pay his workers on time. The whole business teetered.

Kyle hated to see his father work under so much pressure. He wasn't young anymore. And the Mayor and representatives of the Town and County Councils were all indifferent.

It wasn't the first time. Businesses had failed to pay on time before, and some had even skipped out altogether. But their contracts weren't as big as this one. Somehow, Christopher had managed to carry on.

At twenty-six, Kyle ran a passionate campaign for a seat on the Town Council. Someone had to look out for the little guy, the myriad sweat-equity contractors like his dad, and mom-and-pop businesses.

The small business community rallied around him, as did the tight-knit community of local surfers. It was rare for one of their own to run for office, so they showed up on election day to support him. Kyle won his seat by a record-setting margin.

Four years later, he was Mayor of Ocean City, Maryland.

His record as mayor was mixed. Some accomplishments were highly controversial, like narrowing the lanes of the busy Coastal Highway to accommodate a bike path and making the downtown pedestrian-only on weekends. Those policies stayed put, however, even after his departure as mayor.

Through it all, he never gave up his passion for surfing.

A statue of a surfer with a wave curling over him adorns the 48th Street roundabout. Forty-Eighth Street is the premier break for more advanced surfers because of its fast, steep break. The statue is of a young Jack Cropper, who turned pro at fifteen. But because Jack and Kyle look alike, the statue is popularly known—wrongly—as "The Surfing Mayor."

Ocean City is Maryland's second-largest city in the summertime, and Kyle's impact was well known throughout the state. In his last year as mayor, he ran for the United States Senate.

In a crowded field, the thirty-eight-year-old won over the party apparatchiks and secured the nomination. The general election was a cake-walk, and he was sworn into office in January.

~ ~ ~

Teddy came out of the kitchen to visit Christopher and his sons. He took Kyle and Jack's orders, then looked to Christopher.

"Yours is ready, but want to wait until theirs are ready? I'll keep it warm. Won't be long."

Chris nodded. "Thanks, Teddy."

Teddy glanced up at the television as he turned away. His head snapped back to the TV and he paused.

"What in the world?"

Multiple videos from the Middle East showed two unworldly orange heads of fire. No, it was the sun reflecting off the heads of two mush-room clouds.

Nukes.

The videos were from the United Arab Emirates, and depicted the apparent use of nuclear weapons on advancing Iranian troops outside Dubai.

"Oh my God," Kyle said, standing. "I better go into the office. This is unreal." He headed for the door in a hurry.

"*Kyle!*" It was his father. His voice was like thunder. He stood leaning forward, his palms pressed into the table.

"Be careful."

CHAPTER FIVE

The President was stunned. She sat down in the Raven Rock version of the Situation Room and put her hand to her mouth.

"Did we do that?"

The nuclear strikes were clearly aimed at the Iranian army as they advanced deep into the United Arab Emirates from eastern Saudi Arabia.

"We don't know yet," said the Chairman of the Joint Chiefs of Staff, Admiral Sorenson. "I've ordered all nuclear-armed commands to report in."

"Was it Israel?" Cynthia asked.

"We just don't have enough information yet," Sorenson said. "What we *do* know is that the yield was significant, about 350 kilotons for both bombs. That's big."

"Ma'am," interrupted Oscar Schwarz, the president's Chief of Staff. "The President of Russia is on the emergency hotline."

"Madam President," the President of Russia spoke. *"What have you done?"*

~ ~ ~

Back at the VP mansion, Daddy awaited as a Raider helicopter swooped along the Potomac River.

Where the river bent to the left, the Raider continued straight, right over Georgetown and onto the front lawn of Number One Observatory Circle.

The helicopter landed, Daddy jogged over and climbed in, and the helo—now designated as Marine Two—lifted off.

There was no time to waste.

Twenty-five minutes later, Marine Two banked sharply, navigated the narrow valley between Cacoctin and South Mountains, and landed on the helicopter pad just outside the blast doors at Raven Rock. Daddy was ushered in.

The helicopter, no longer Marine Two after dropping off its lone passenger, lifted off. More helicopters were inbound: national security principals from across the federal government.

~ ~ ~

Buck Arnold sipped coffee from a tall tumbler emblazoned with the Seal of the United States Senate. An Army General from the Pentagon, teamed with an analyst from the National Geospatial Intelligence Agency, droned on about the missile attacks.

The audience comprised the principals of the United States Congress, including Buck—the Senate Whip.

How do you make an unprecedented missile attack on the United States, and evacuations of elected officials to Mt. Weather and Raven Rock, boring?

Leave it to the Pentagon.

The tumbler was hefty and expensive-looking. Buck had already resolved to stash it in his satchel and take it home once the emergency had passed.

If missiles from Iran or wherever don't kill me, boredom just might.

He took another sip and glanced around. Bare, claustrophobic rooms, concrete walls, and dank, cavernous hallways defined the underground facility. *At least the coffee is good.*

Buck took his phone from his pocket to check on emails while the two presenters spoke. The phone buzzed in his hand.

A text message from his Chief of Staff: *A nuclear attack on Iran! Holy sh*t!*

Buck bolted upright and nearly spilt his coffee. Ella Sanchez of Brooklyn, the Minority Leader of the House of Representatives, nearly jumped out of her chair.

"Sorry, General, but that'll be enough."

Everyone was standing now, moving chairs to clear space. Phones buzzed and rang.

"We need a television!" someone shouted.

"Do those work?" Buck asked, pointing to a row of flat screens on the wall. "Let's get them on."

Staff scrambled, and the televisions were turned on. They were tuned to various news channels, including CNN.

The room went silent.

The large screens were filled with the mushroom clouds in the desert outside Dubai. Bernice Hamdawana was reporting.

Gasps and murmurs filled the room.

"Dear God," someone said. "We really did it…"

Buck felt a flush of anger rise from his chest to his face.

She went nuclear.

He caught a glimpse of the House Minority Leader. The two made eye contact. An inferno raged behind her dark eyes.

Ella turned and made eye contact with other Senators and Representatives, both Democrats and Republicans.

She climbed on a chair and stood above everyone in the cramped room. She looked at each person again before speaking.

"This is madness," she said. "They started a war without the pieces in place to wage it. They brought missiles *raining down on our cities.*"

"And now," she nodded to the monitors on the wall. "This cannot go on."

Lawmakers nodded. Some looked away. Many looked stunned.

"The President and Daddy Longlegs must go," she said.

The room erupted.

~ ~ ~

It had been a long day. Shipments had come in. They had to be inventoried and stored. Noora, meanwhile, had worked the thrift store.

Now, Zayne and Noora sat down for dinner. The chicken shawarma filled the room with warm spice.

They ate mostly in silence. Noora mentioned she'd caught up with some friends who'd dropped off a few bags of clothes.

Afterwards, Zayne and Noora made their way into the den. He liked to watch the news for a bit before turning the remote over to Noora.

Zayne settled into his chair, sipped a cup of tea, and turned on the television.

Al Jazeera was buzzing with breaking news: the nuclear attack in the UAE. Multiple videos from CCTV cameras to phone cameras were stunning.

What in the world?

Noora gasped.

Zayne's phone buzzed. He glanced at the screen.

Someone had left a review of Haidar's Café on Yelp.

He tapped the notification—and nearly choked on his tea.

His heart began to pound.

What is happening?

He read the review again:

★ ★ ★ ★ ★

"Let the waters flow under the light of the moon." — *The Commander*

His phone buzzed in his hand. A text message from Haidar.

Do you see what I see?

~ ~ ~

Denis watched Bernice Hamdawana on CNN again. She was in Dubai now. He did the math. She must have been sent to Dubai not long after reporting from the streets of Washington on the morning of the first missile strikes. Thirty-six hours ago.

She must be running on adrenaline.

Yuri Panchenko, unshaven and disheveled as before, entered the room.

"Sir, a communique from Moscow."

Denis looked it over and handed it back to Yuri.

It wasn't unexpected.

"Raisa," he said, and stood. Raisa, his personal assistant, stood against the wall at the ready. Always. She practically blended in with the embassy furniture.

"Pack my suitcase. I am going to Moscow."

~ ~ ~

Daddy Longlegs sat at the corner of the long conference table just to the right of the President.

"Madame President," he said, "I recommend an immediate nuclear strike on Tehran to end the *scourge* of that government once and for all, and to bring this war to a quick end."

"This is about American *lives,*" he said, and then paused to let the word hover over the Situation Room. "Like Harry Truman, you can save the lives of tens of thousands of young American servicemen and women by ending this war *right now, today.*"

On the wall were several monitors, each with news programs from around the world in English: CNN, BBC, France24, China's CCTV, Germany's Deustche Welle, Al Jazeera. Each showed shaky cellphone videos of the ominously dark skies about to swallow Dubai, topped by the two mushroom clouds high in the atmosphere. More videos were coming in, each one as dramatic as the last.

In addition to videos of the mushroom clouds and looming sandstorm, China's CCTV showed stock footage of Chinese Navy ships at sea, stealth fighters in the air, and shock troops conducting live-fire exercises.

A ticker below read:

"... *Chinese military on highest alert ... Russia declares state of emergency ... NATO on alert ... Global markets in free fall ...*"

"God*damn* it, Daddy!" President Belle shook her head. "The whole world thinks *we* nuked the Iranian troops, or that Israel did, and you want me to *nuke Tehran?*"

"I am *not* going to be the first president to use nuclear weapons since Harry Truman," she seethed. "We don't even know who *did* drop those nukes. *That's* our priority right now. We need to know *with certainty* that it wasn't us, and then we need to ascertain exactly who the fuck *did*. Are you with me, Daddy?"

Daddy took a deep breath through his nose.

Things were spinning out of control.

CHAPTER SIX

And it's about to get worse.

Oscar Schwartz ducked out of the roiling discussion to take a phone call. He jotted down some notes, then discreetly disconnected his phone.

He stared down at the table in thought and seemed to be gathering himself.

Daddy Longlegs gestured for everyone to quiet down.

All eyes, including the President's, looked to Daddy.

"Oscar?" he asked.

The National Security Advisor realized that the entire room was now looking at *him*.

"Madam President, I'm afraid I have some more news." He was practically whispering. "I've been getting reports, but I wanted to wait until the US Geological Survey and the Space Force confirmed it. They just did.

"Deep in the desert, east of Kerman in south central Iran, the government of Iran detonated six nuclear warheads in an underground test. The estimated yield of each of the warheads ranged from 60 to 350 kilotons."

The room erupted anew.

~ ~ ~

Ella Sanchez was not taking no for an answer.

The General fretted. He was torn. He had had his orders from the White House to evacuate Congressional leadership to Mt. Weather. There were no orders to return them back to Washington.

"Make it happen, General. Or we will walk out of here and *hitchhike* back to Washington if we have to."

The General looked trapped. He glanced around the room as if looking for the exit.

It's not like I can keep them here against their will. It's a democracy, after all.

He took a deep breath and sighed, visibly deflated.

"Yes, Madam Leader."

~ ~ ~

Aleksandr Perchenko. President of the Russian Federation.

He was short and stocky. A bulldog of a man.

Not small, at least not in the metaphorical sense. Quite the opposite. He was boisterous and spoke in a rapid-fire fashion. In his younger days, when he was one voice among others, no one else could get a word in edgewise when he spoke. There was simply no room. Not only did his loquaciousness fill in the time, his words also stole thunder. They evaporated the floor that others stood upon.

If one were to observe as a disinterested or disengaged third party— something Denis always tried to do in order to steal time to think and get a read on the room—what was astonishing was that Perchenko's brain worked even faster than his mouth.

Where others saw a talking head, Denis saw an intellect that burned super-hot.

He was one big-brained motherfucker, as an American might say.

Denis didn't fly to Moscow. A presidential Ilyushin-96 wide-body jetliner flew him from Reagan National Airport in Washington to Vladivostok, the San Francisco of Russia, on the other side of the Pacific.

6,500 miles.

Despite the thirteen-hour flight, Denis found it difficult to sleep on the plane. An armored SUV awaited him at the airport when he arrived, and whisked him to Vavilov Manor, a traditional, if small, Russian villa.

Denis had never been here before. When he pulled up to the charming yellow house, Denis thought it quaint. In fact, it looked like a nice little bed and breakfast, as Americans would call it.

Except men in sharp suits and dark sunglasses stood all over its garden and grounds, looking this way and that.

Denis was ushered inside, then stood alone in the tiny foyer. He placed his hat on a velvet chair in the corner—the coat rack was full—then folded his jacket over the chair. He clasped his hands behind his back and raised his chin.

As he waited, Denis reminisced.

Aleksandr Perchenko understood that security was of the utmost importance for the Russian state. No other issue even came close.

Perchenko wasn't so much a student of history. That was Denis' forte. But Perchenko's experience as first a *Spetznaz* special forces soldier, and later as a *Spetznaz* officer in a GROM Unit of the Main Directorate for Drugs Control—well, he *lived* Russian history.

He fought in the Second Chechen War as an eighteen-year old conscript before being selected for *Spetznaz* training. He saw action in the Georgian War. Then, in Drugs Control, he battled Chinese Triad gangs in Russia's Far East and helped clear St. Petersburg of Tatar drug gangs. His home state of Krasnodar Krai borders Crimea to the west. To the east, it borders the restive Russian Muslim republic of Karachay-Cherkessia, and Abkhazia, the breakaway republic in Georgia.

Security was not an abstract concept for Perchenko. Russia was besieged by enemies on all sides, both within and without.

And encroaching on its Western Front was the European Union, led by Germany, the most hated of Russian foes since the Nazi invasion in 1941. They swallowed *all* of Central and Eastern Europe after the collapse of the Soviet Union, and were laying the groundwork to swallow Ukraine, Russia's historic kin and ally, before Russia—its back against a wall—invaded.

They—the West—don't have Tatars, Chechens, Circassians, Karachays, Abazins, Nogais, Dargins, Dagestani, Avars, Turks, Turkmeni, Kumyks, Lezgins, Tabasarans, Bashkirs, Chuvash, Kazakhs—the list goes on, and each with their own territorial homeland *within* the Russian Federation. Nor do they administer over 4,500 miles of largely defenseless open steppes from one end of the country to the other.

Only by pushing out to formidable geographical barriers like the Caucasus Mountains to the south, the deserts of Kazakhstan and Mongolia to the southeast, and the Pacific Ocean in the Far East, could Russia develop a semblance of security.

And none of these expansions were offensive in nature. Each was the result of an attack on Russians on their frontier, or the imminent threat of one, which forced them to push the frontier farther and farther from the heartland of Moscow and St. Petersburg.

And in the west, whence came the invading French in the Nineteenth Century, and Germans in the Twentieth, the only option was to extend Russia's frontier to the Carpathian Mountains in western Ukraine and Romania. That would limit an advancing western power to the narrow lowlands of the Polish Plains that follow the Vistula River and its tributaries, especially the Bug River that meanders from Warsaw to the Belorussian city of Brest.

More or less. In reality, the western frontier was all but impossible to seal.

The foyer door opened.

"Please come in, Mr. Ambassador," said an elegantly dressed and wickedly beautiful young woman. Stefania something, the President's personal secretary. She was all of twenty-three years old.

"Why, *thank ya, sweetheart.*" It was a perfectly good American accent, maybe even Texan. Denis winked.

Stefania ignored him. Denis blushed. His heart even raced ahead a bit.

You idiot, he chastised himself. He raised his chin and walked through the door that Stefania held open for him.

~ ~ ~

It was like something out of a movie.

The room was ornate, with busts of Vladimir Putin, Peter the Great, Vladimir Lenin, and Leonid Brezhnev stationed in the corners, astride green plants and vases spilling vines down to the hardwood floors.

Paintings depicted pivotal battles of the Great Patriotic War and the Napoleonic Wars, while cherubs with angel wings and trumpets amid clouds adorned the high ceilings.

A long and shiny Siberian Pine table, with high-backed chairs, stretched the length of the room. President Aleksandr Perchenko sat at one end of the long table, along with military officers and civilian principals of his national security apparatus.

Denis did a double take. At the opposite end of the long table from Perchenko sat Chiang Li, the President of China, along with a half dozen of Li's principals.

The high backs of the chairs made everyone, including Presidents Perchenko and Li, look like children.

Perchenko stood, and everyone followed suit.

"Denis!" Perchenko greeted Pirog with a warm and enthusiastic hand-shake.

It was antipodean to the moment. The room should be somber, but Denis detected an air of … *relief* … as though a long-anticipated moment had finally arrived.

A commotion behind him made Denis turn around, even as Perchenko gripped his hand. The door from which Denis had entered had swung open, and in walked Wu Shuguang, Denis' Chinese counterpart in Washington. He must have been ordered to Russia at the same time as Denis.

Now it was Chiang Li's turn to enthusiastically welcome and embrace his ambassador to America.

~ ~ ~

"I'm sorry, ma'am," the General said. "No one is taking our calls."

"We're getting out of this … *dungeon,*" Ella spat. "Whatever it takes. And if *you* can't do it, *I* will."

"We'll keep trying, ma'am. We'll get you back to Washington ASAP."

Ella returned to the conference room down the hall where many lawmakers had congregated. Some paced. Others feverishly checked their phones.

"No one's answering the General's calls," she informed them.

"Well, we can't *stay* down here," argued a Senator. "We're not *hostages.*"

"Who the hell do we call?" another snapped. "The White House is evacuated, and nobody at the Pentagon is answering."

Ella stood near a folding table covered in maps and half-eaten pastries, speaking into her phone. Her voice was tight with fury.

"Then find someone who outranks the general. I don't care what the chain of command says—this is still a democracy."

In the corner of the room, Buck Arnold sat cross-legged with his laptop open, mumbling to himself as he navigated websites.

Aha: luxury motorcoaches in the DC metro. And there were *plenty*—tour companies that ferried tourists to Monticello or Gettysburg. Another company advertised VIP buses with tainted windows for private security teams.

Perfect.

He selected a fleet of three buses. They were all climate-controlled with reclining seats and onboard bathrooms. Congressional dignity could survive the ride.

He pulled up his SOPOEA credentials from his secure notes and entered the details. When the payment page prompted him for a purpose, he typed:

Emergency return to Capitol for continuity of constitutional governance.

"Hope the auditor enjoys *that* line," he mumbled. He hit *Submit.*

Moments later, he was on the phone with the dispatcher.

She was completely unfazed.

It's Washington, Buck reminded himself. *They probably get all kinds of reservations from governmental agencies. It's probably their core business.*

"Yes, ma'am. Just put in the GPS what I put on the form. I'll have someone meet the drivers at the outer gate."

He hung up and stood, stretching his back.

Ella stopped pacing. "What was that about?"

"Tour buses," Buck said. "From DC. They'll be here in two hours. Air conditioning and leg room to spare."

Ella stared at him.

"You're kidding."

"Nope. I ordered them online and put it on my SOPOEA tab."

Ella blinked.

"That's brilliant."

~ ~ ~

The moment was historic. The fact wasn't lost on Denis. The President of Russia and the President of China together in Vladivostok, along with their ambassadors to America.

Nor could the meeting be more momentous. It had been mere hours since the nuclear attack on Iranian troops in the United Arab Emirates. The Americans proclaimed their innocence. They insisted that they had nothing to do with the mushroom clouds in the deserts outside Dubai.

Who could believe them?

Their denials were laughable. They were already the first and only country to ever use nuclear weapons when they dropped an atomic bomb on Hiroshima, Japan, on August 6, 1945, and another on Nagasaki three days later.

The nuclear bombings killed as many as 250,000 people, almost all civilians.

And here we are again. This time there were in the order of 120,000 casualties, including not only an estimated 40,000 to 50,000 Iranian troops, but an additional 50,000 to 60,000 civilian deaths in the more than twenty villages and desert oases on the outskirts of Dubai.

Neither Russia, nor China, could let such a calamitous and deliberate tragedy go without challenge. America would—*must*—be stopped before the whole world was, literally, destroyed.

CHAPTER SEVEN

What did it mean?

The national security principals heatedly talked about the implications of Iran's nuclear test.

To Daddy, several messages were clear.

First, by detonating *six* warheads, there was no telling how many warheads Iran actually possessed. They had likely been producing nuclear weapons in secret for some time now, probably years.

Second, by testing various yields, Iran demonstrated a mature level of sophistication in nuclear weapons technology.

Third, their ICBM attacks on the continental United States demonstrated Iran's capability to *deliver* nuclear warheads even though those attacks had used only conventional, non-nuclear, warheads. But there was no difference between a conventional warhead and a nuclear warhead in terms of the carrying capacity of ICBMs.

The president slammed her palm on the conference table. "We're *fucked!*"

She looked to Daddy Longlegs. "Do you see what you've done?" the President asked. Her eyes were bloodshot and burned raw with accusation.

"You broke the world."

~ ~ ~

Denis Pirog was back in the USA. It had been the most surreal forty-eight hours of his life. The missile strikes on Washington. The nuclear attack on Iranian troops in the UAE. The emergency recall to Vladivostok of all places. The meeting. The return flight to Washington.

Then came the hour-and-a-half drive up to the Raven Rock bunker in Pennsylvania.

Madness.

He stifled a yawn as he waited. *I will sleep when I'm dead,* he told himself. *If I can be so lucky.*

He wasn't there long when Wu Shuguang, his Chinese counterpart, was ushered in to wait alongside him. He somehow looked refreshed. He wore a smart looking black pork pie hat that blended well with his long gray overcoat. The two nodded to each other. It was a warm and knowing nod. They needn't say anything. The two were now quite familiar with each other after spending hours together at the long table in Vladivostok with both of their presidents. They worked on a joint proclamation to bring the war to an immediate end. *Now, that was a meeting for the ages.*

Denis shook his head. *And this one is sure to top that one.*

Wu grunted as though he had heard Denis' thoughts.

"The President of the United States is ready to receive you." Vice Admiral Baltzer Oberkirsch held open the office door. He was dressed in full combat fatigues.

Wu removed his hat as he and Denis entered the Raven Rock Oval Office. It was a bit smaller than the *actual* Oval Office in the White House, and it wasn't oval. It was completely square, with concrete walls, no windows, and a low concrete ceiling.

Like a prison cell.

The mahogany desk and chairs, elegant lamps, and the blue carpet sporting the Seal of the President of the United States, helped soften the room. Somewhat. But there was no mistaking that they were in a bunker.

President Cynthia Belle stood behind her desk, flanked by Vice President Daddy Longlegs at her left, and Lynn Benjamin, the Secretary of State, at her right.

"Welcome to Raven Rock," she said. Her voice was strained.

Denis casually surveyed the room as Wu Shuguang bowed slightly and shook the President's hand. The small room was crowded with people. Denis recognized each of them: Oscar Schwartz, the President's National Security Advisor; Admiral Erik Sorenson, the Chairman of the Joint Chiefs of Staff; Joy Chatterjee, Director of the CIA; Bernie Mentzel, the Secretary of Defense; Martin Hartshorne, the President's Chief of Staff; and Vice Admiral Baltzer Oberkirsch, the uniformed Navy SEAL who escorted them in. He was the Acting Chief of Naval Operations. And lastly, the President's Russian and Mandarin Chinese interpreters, who stood at the ready.

Daddy Longlegs was formidable in appearance. He looked like a scarecrow the way his long sports coat hung on his tall, lanky frame.

There's such a chill.

It was Denis' turn to greet the President. He, too, bowed slightly and took her hand. "Madam President," he said. "Thank you for receiving us."

"May I?" Denis carried a briefcase that was handcuffed to his wrist. He nodded to the President's desk. The President gave a slight nod of her head.

Denis hoisted his briefcase on to the edge of the President's desk. Wu Shuguang spoke as Denis fetched a key from his pocket and unlocked the briefcase. He retrieved a leather-bound executive binder.

"Madam President," Wu began, "His Excellency Ambassador Pirog and I have been instructed by our respective Presidents—President Aleksandr Perchenko of Russia, and President Chiang Li of China— to personally deliver to you this hand signed letter of utmost importance."

Denis handed the binder to President Belle. The room was deathly silent as she opened the binder and read the document. The silence was awkward, tense.

After reading, the President held the binder out. "George," she said. She wasn't using nicknames for her staff in the presence of the ambassadors of foreign powers.

Hostile foreign powers.

Daddy took it from her. The President turned her back and paced as Daddy read the letter. When he was finished, he handed it to Lynn who, after a moment, handed it to the Secretary of Defense.

Daddy looked into the eyes of Denis.

Denis tried not to avert his eyes, but he quickly looked down at his feet.

It's their moment now, he thought. *Let them grieve.*

In his mind, Daddy summarized the four main points of the letter:

First, the introduction of nuclear weapons made it essential that a cease fire immediately be implemented and respected.

Iran had already agreed to it.

Second, the United States must halt all military operations in the Persian Gulf.

Third, the United States must *not* send a naval expedition to the region.

Fourth, the United States must accept the postwar reality of the so-called Islamic Emirates of Al-Ahsa in Iranian-occupied Basra, Kuwait, Dammam, Bahrain, and Qatar. There would be no return to the pre-war status quo.

Otherwise, the letter warned, there would be dire consequences.

Daddy took deep, deliberate breaths to maintain his composure.

The letter was, essentially, an ultimatum.

After the last principal read the letter, Daddy Longlegs handed it back to President Belle.

No one had said a word.

"Thank you, Gentlemen," President Belle said, and nodded to the two ambassadors. "Your letter has been received and read."

Admiral Oberkirsch opened the office door and ordered armed soldiers to escort the ambassadors back to their cars.

Denis Pirog hesitated, but Wu Shuguang bowed. His face was mournful.

Wu turned on his heels and walked out, leaving Denis alone in the office.

Denis looked to Daddy Longlegs. Daddy licked his teeth as he stared down at Denis. His mouth was turned up at the corners. A smile of blood lust. Daddy appeared ready to pounce and savagely sink his teeth into him.

Denis smiled meekly and followed the Chinese ambassador out the door.

~ ~ ~

Daddy seethed.

"Who do they think they are? We're not done with Iran. Not by a long shot. Hell, we haven't even *started.* "

"What are our options?" Cynthia asked.

The room went silent.

"Not everyone at once," Daddy quipped.

"Madam President, our short-term options are limited," Admiral Sorenson answered. "With the fall of the Gulf States and disarray in Saudi Arabia, we no longer have a rally point like we had in Saudi Arabia or Kuwait in the run up to the First and Second Gulf Wars. Oman might be an option, or Western Saudi Arabia—what do they call themselves now? Kingdom of the Hejaz? But that's a heavy lift for the State Department. We could hit Iranian supply lines and the like, but I'm not enthusiastic about how effective they would be without troops on the ground."

Another person chimed in. "Madam President, we can strike Iran directly. Target their nuclear program, target their leadership."

Daddy Longlegs looked across the room at the speaker. It was Vice Admiral Baltzer Oberkirsch, the Navy SEAL.

My man.

"We can strike Iran's government institutions, military bases, nuclear sites, missile factories, ports, and other targets with conventional or nuclear ICBMs within a few hours," Oberkirsch continued. "We can augment with long range sorties by our B-21s, B-2s, and—"

"*Stop it,*" interrupted the President. "I will not—*will not*—order nuclear strikes on Iran," she seethed. "I don't want to trade New York or Los Angeles or any other goddamn American city for Tehran or Tabriz.

"Do I make myself clear?"

Baltzer nodded. "Yes, ma'am."

An awkward silence threatened, but Daddy Longlegs spoke.

"Where are we with our Aegis ships and Patriot missile batteries?" he asked. "When will they be ready?"

"The AEGIS-equipped *McFaul* is now on station at Navy Yard in Washington, and is operational, sir," Sorenson answered. "The *Cole* is on station in New York Harbor. It, too, is operational. The AEGIS Ashore systems in Poland and Romania have been recalibrated and are up and running. A Patriot battery is being set up on the National Mall, as you suggested, between the Capitol Building and the Washington Monument. It should be operational sometime this afternoon. Another is being set up in Central Park in Manhattan. It will be operational by this time tomorrow."

Daddy nodded his approval. He looked to President Belle.

"Madam President, our anti-ballistic missile systems proved very effective some years back with Iran's attacks on Israel. With our ship-based AEGIS systems and Patriot missile batteries here on the East Coast, and AEGIS Ashore up and running in Europe, plus Vandenberg in California, CONUS is covered. We are ready to defend against Iranian ICBMs. The events of the past two nights are behind us."

"Are you willing to stake millions of lives on that?" the President asked.

Daddy straightened where he stood and folded his arms against his chest.

"Yes."

The President slapped a hand on her desk. "Well, *I'm not*. And I don't want to hear any more about it."

"Okay," said Daddy. All eyes turned back to him. He seemed to acquiesce.

The president was guarded.

"Let us consider, then, what comes next," Daddy offered.

President Belle's eyes narrowed. Daddy remained stoic.

The president nodded.

"This ultimatum by China and Russia is only the beginning," said Daddy. "If we capitulate, then Taiwan is lost. And with it, the entire South China Sea."

Daddy paced as he spoke.

"Our Pacific allies—the Philippines, Vietnam, Singapore—will see the writing on the wall. Australia and New Zealand will be very lonely places.

"Who knows what happens in Japan? Or India? They might have to go out on their own, seek security arrangements apart from us."

Daddy paused and shook his head.

"This is a *bluff,*" he said, and laughed. "A high stakes one for sure, and *bold*—I'll give them that! But a bluff nonetheless."

"I am not going to risk the lives of *millions* of Americans on the assumption that they're *bluffing*," said the President. "The war is *over!*"

"The war hasn't even *begun*," Daddy countered. His ire wasn't entirely directed at the President. He looked at each person in the room, one by one. "We are the most powerful country on Earth. Don't tell me that we shouldn't, or can't, confront this *monstrosity* of a government in Tehran. We have *eleven aircraft carriers*, for crying out loud!"

"We *had* eleven," said Sorenson. "We now have ten. Two—*Obama* and *Doris Miller*—are on station in the Gulf of Oman. *George Washington*, based in Japan, is preparing to deploy, but she is slated to patrol the South China Sea. With China threatening to deploy her entire Navy to head off any expeditionary fleet we can muster, *Washington* will be in the thick of it—and very much alone.

"*Trump* and *Clinton* are doing workups off Virginia in preparation for deployment in the next three months. We could deploy one or both right now. But they won't be at peak readiness.

"Three carriers are just back from deployment. *Ford* and *Reagan* are undergoing extensive upgrades and refits."

Daddy Longlegs scowled as Sorenson continued. He was either unhappy or deep in thought. Or both.

"With Woody Island in the Paracels, and Fiery Cross Reef and Mischief Reef in the Spratley Islands," Sorenson continued, "China doesn't need all six of *its* aircraft carriers deployed at once. These three islands house large airbases, and the Spratleys are smack in the middle of the South China Sea.

"That gives them the equivalent of *nine* aircraft carriers to *our* nine deployable carriers. Three of their nine don't need post-deployment repairs and upgrades—because they are *islands*—and *none* have to deploy thousands of miles from home.

"The Straits of Malacca are well within striking range of the Spratleys and Paracels, and even from Hainan Island in southern China."

Sorenson paused, but only for a moment.

"All I am saying is, if we do this, we will need time to plan, prepare, and train. *D-Day* took months of preparation and practice. We have to consider a whole range of contingencies. This is total war."

Daddy Longlegs continued to scowl as he looked to Sorenson. Then he nodded, ever so slightly.

Sorenson took that as a cue to continue.

"Assuming that we circumvent or otherwise break through the Chinese forces blocking the sea lanes, what is our mission? Who are we liberating? The government of Kuwait was decapitated. The King of Bahrain was presumably killed in the air raid on that SEAL convoy in Qatar. The Emir of Qatar has fled to Oman and otherwise made nice with the Iranians. The United Arab Emirates willfully capitulated, one emirate at a time, without firing a shot. The government of Saudi Arabia doesn't exist anymore. Riyadh is descending into sectarian violence as we speak, and the whole western side of the country has declared independence.

"Only Oman stands, and the evacuation of our soldiers aside, they're desperate *not* to get caught up in the chaos."

~ ~ ~

Daddy Longlegs couldn't stay. Raven Rock wasn't big enough to house both the President and Daddy Longlegs. She had practically ordered him out of the mountain bunker.

The words of British Prime Minister Margaret Thatcher came to Daddy's mind. She was speaking to US President George HW Bush in the hours after Iraq invaded Kuwait: *Remember, George, this is no time to go wobbly.*

Bush had taken her words to heart. He built an international coalition and decisively defeated Iraq in the First Gulf War in 1991.

President Belle, however, was clearly in over her head.

If she won't listen to me, maybe she'll listen to our allies.

Daddy scrolled through contacts on his phone. He found who he was looking for and hit Call. After a few seconds without an answer, he hung up and tried again.

Still no answer. When prompted for voice mail, Daddy spoke. "Jonathan, it's Geor—Daddy Longlegs. Call me as soon as you get this."

Daddy looked out the window in thought. *Who next?*

Baerbock. Gyde Baerbock. Daddy had convinced the German Chancellor to back American actions against Iran. Nearly all of Europe followed her lead.

A modern Margaret Thatcher if there is one.

Daddy hit call and waited. No answer, then the prompt for voice mail.

"Madam Chancellor, George Wartmann here. Please call me as soon as you can."

It was highly unusual, of course, to directly phone the German Chancellor without official clearance, but desperate times called for desperate measures.

Who now?

Why, Jacques Michelet, the *French* President, of course.

Same thing. No answer.

Daddy tilted his head in thought.

Could they be ghosting me?

Marine Two swooped low and did a loop around the Washington Monument.

Daddy had been looking out the window of the Raider helicopter the whole time, but only now saw that the National Mall was filled with black and multicolored dots. People. Lots of them.

What's going on down there?

Only when a Marine Two crew member responded did he realize that he had asked the question out loud.

"Protests, sir," the crew member answered. "Anti-war and, um, anti-Belle."

Of course.

~ ~ ~

"*Geeze*," said Harvey.

"What is it, hon?"

"This guy Billy, remember him? He played second base in high school. Look! He's got *Go Daddy Go* memes on his Dimensions accounts. I mean, *seriously?* You know that guy went to *college?* I mean, *geeze*, right?"

"Did you get milk?"

"I mean, who knew that the little guy at second base—I mean, he was great, such a nice kid—would turn out to be a *fascist?*"

"I don't know. I wouldn't go *that* far—"

"He's posting all these articles from *News America*. You can't get more right-wing than that! I mean, he might as well wear a Nazi *arm* band!"

"We're low on toilet paper, too. We should make a list."

CHAPTER EIGHT

Why am I watching this?

The whole world might be captivated by the news coming out of Iran, but the work of an analyst continues.

Luc Morel stared at the link on his secondary monitor. It had come from one of his sharpest junior analysts. He decided to give it the benefit of the doubt.

The video was a minute long. Clearly, it was generated with AI.

A black flag rippled in the wind. It flickered in and out of transparency, overlaying footage of Paris in flames, then a years-old march in Hamburg. Thousands had chanted, *"The Caliphate is the solution!"*

At the top of the screen was white Arabic script that read *Al-Khilafa al-Islāmiyya fī Ūrūbbā (The Islamic Caliphate of Europe)*.

A deep, distorted voice spoke in classical Arabic with English and French subtitles:

The Commander has taken his seat. France, Belgium, Germany, Sweden—you have no kings, only tyrants. The Caliphate is not coming. It is here. Those who stand with God, rise. Those who doubt ... run.

The screen went black.

It was pure propaganda.

But ... *The Commander. I've seen that name recently.*

Luc emailed his team. "Run a query on The Commander."

~ ~ ~

Luc Morel sat at the end of the table, fingers steepled beneath his chin. A large screen flickered to life as one of his analysts, a wiry young man in a hoodie, stood beside it with a tablet in hand.

"Alright," the analyst began. "We ran a full query on *The Commander* across all flagged platforms—surface, deep, and dark web. We've pulled everything from encrypted Telegram channels, burner Reddit threads, anonymous message boards, and a few Arabic-language sites we monitor in conjunction with GCHQ and the NSA.

"The very first thing that came up was encrypted communications picked up by the Americans in Bahrain last month. There was a lot chatter, some of it signed off by somebody calling themselves The Commander. The Americans were able to trace the platform posts to Tehran.

"The Americans captured one of the perpetrators of the car bomb attack on the front gate of their Navy base. He fingered his imam, but the imam had died—the Americans suspect it was an Iranian hit before he could be arrested.

"The Bahrainis passed along the imam's cell phone. The Americans were able to decipher text communications between the imam and, again, somebody calling themselves The Commander. They traced the origins of the texts to Tehran, as well.

"Beyond that, we've uncovered a range of posts ourselves. *Voltaire*—that's our AI—helped us filter out mundane uses of the term and zero in on correlations with particular contexts or unexplained inconsistencies.

"We've indexed almost 200 discrete posts or references to The Commander over the past eighteen months. Most were easily dismissed with a bit more digging, especially the most recent posts—jihadist fan fiction, role-playing cultists, conspiracy junkies, stuff like that. But early posts raised red flags at the time—and in hindsight, they were right to be flagged."

He tapped the tablet, and several posts filled the screen.

In what the Americans believed was a Hamas-run communication conduit masquerading as a recipe-sharing Reddit thread on Middle Eastern cuisine, "The Commander" posted a cryptic message that was inconsistent with the theme of the thread:

The harvest begins early this year. The stones are sharp, and the orchard's owner sleeps. Cast not one stone, but seventy. May the sun rise red over the citrus groves.

"The message was posted a week before a multi-prong terrorist assault on Israel. Mossad later traced the message back to … you guessed it, Tehran."

Several more platform posts appeared on the screen.

"All of these were similarly cryptic posts by The Commander. This one was to Hezbollah," he said, pointing to one post, "and this one was to the Houthis in Yemen," he said, pointing to another.

"This is the most recent post. It is a review of a Haidar's Cafè in Saint Denis. It was posted two days ago."

Let the waters flow under the light of the moon.

"What does it mean?" Luc asked.

"We're still working on that," the hoodie analyst said. "But, like the other posts, it is inconsistent with the platform, which is why *Voltaire* flagged it."

Luc sat back in his chair and crossed his arms against his chest. He shook his head as he processed the information.

"So, The Commander is Iranian," Luc said.

"Yes, sir. We have a high level of confidence that the posts originate from Iran."

"Is it a person?"

"More like Iranian intelligence. Or, rather, IRGC intelligence."

Luc paused to think.

"Sir?" the analyst continued. "This video—*The Commander has taken his seat* video—is the first public-facing media under that name. The others were buried, posted on narrow platforms with specific audiences. This was loud. It's some kind of signal."

Luc narrowed his eyes.

"To whom?"

The analyst gave a grim half-smile.

"Anyone listening."

~ ~ ~

Now it was Luc Morel's turn under the lights.

He pitched his own presentation to Philippe Karcher, summarizing his unit's findings.

"Initially, we thought The Commander was some kind of fringe fantasist—until this morning's video," Luc said, nodding to his laptop screen where the ICE announcement stood frozen in a paused frame.

Karcher leaned forward. "So who is he?"

Luc shrugged slightly. "We're not sure it's an individual. The Commander appeared sporadically online over the past year—mostly in obscure Islamist forums and end-times message boards. All were traced back to Iran."

He flipped to a slide of a classified SIGINT summary stamped *NSA–Eyes Only*. "American signals intelligence suspects the IRGC. But everything since the nuclear strike reads *Sunni,* or at least pan-Islamic. No overt Shi'a language. No reference to the Mahdi. No praise of Tehran. If this is Iranian, it's an extremely disciplined front."

Philippe squinted at the imagery on the screen. "So, the riots—the pressure cooker bombs—this isn't organic."

"Oh, I don't know about *that*, sir," Luc said. "The nukes in Arabia? I think the protests *are* organic. But whoever The Commander is, he's an opportunist. He's exploiting the situation, and the situation *is* unprecedented. He—or *they*—didn't *cause* the riots, but they are pouring gasoline on it. And they definitely appear to have activated pre-positioned networks that were sleeping."

Philippe stood and paced.

"Is France a target?"

Luc hesitated. "France is a *gateway,* sir. But this is bigger. The ICE video named four countries, all of whom have a significant and restive Muslim population."

"Europe is the target," Philippe surmised.

"It appears that way, sir."

Philippe closed his eyes and shook his head.

"They've declared war on Europe—and they're not even bothering to take credit," he said.

He looked to Luc.

"What's the game?"

~ ~ ~

Daddy looked at the Queen Anne style house. It was the first time he saw the house as *home.* Maybe it was the light. It was approaching six o'clock, and the sun was beginning to set.

Maybe it was the long day. *Or...*

Carolyn stood under the portico, a shawl wrapped around her shoulders. Daddy watched her for a moment, then looked down at his feet and smiled.

It might be the end of the world, but the sun still blinds if you look too long.

After a quiet dinner, Daddy was ready to get back to work. But not before spending time with Care.

Still, his mind drifted.

"Anything I can do?" Care asked. She snuggled against Daddy's chest as he sipped red wine on the sofa. Debussy's *Clair De Lune,* a favorite of his, streamed on the living room stereo.

Daddy smiled, wanly. "Be near me."

"Always," she said. She pulled away and stood up. "If you need anythi—" Daddy pulled her in for a kiss.

~ ~ ~

Back at Raven Rock, Sir Jonathan Galloway rode in a mine car. It was like being at Disney World.

But the deeper into the mountain he went, the more constraining things became. The walls were closer and closer, the ceiling lower and lower.

Anyone making policy down here, well, they wouldn't be operating in the most stable of environments, would they?

Then he waited. He sat on a plastic chair in a dank corridor. He was alone. The light above him buzzed and flickered periodically.

"Mr. Ambassador?" It was the President's personal secretary, and Sir Galloway was led to the President's office.

"Madame President," Sir Galloway said. He removed his hat and bowed.

"Sir Galloway, it's a pleasure."

President Belle led the British Ambassador to a sofa. She sat across from him, her legs crossed.

"Madam President," he began, "my government has asked me to meet with you personally."

"As America's oldest and most trusted ally, we feel we enjoy such a close relationship that the two of us—our two countries—can be candid with each other. Particularly when a situation may be difficult to view objectively.

"The British Empire—and the French—found ourselves in a very uncomfortable situation during the Suez Crisis of 1956, a crisis of our own making. It was the United States that came to us with clear eyes and blunt language, insisting that we must withdraw from Egypt.

"Emotions were running high. Egos were rubbed raw. But, in the end, we recognized that a true friend has a responsibility to be honest.

"America brought us back from the precipice of a very dark place.

"Madame President, the United States *must* step back from the brink. With the introduction of nuclear weapons—"

"We didn't do that," Cynthia snapped. "My Generals *assure* me, we did not employ nuclear weapons."

Galloway paused.

"That might very well be true," Galloway said—

"You don't *believe* us?"

"It's just that, we're all in a very difficult place," Galloway said. "Iran says they did not attack your aircraft carrier—"

"Oh, *please,*" Cynthia spat. "How can you say that with a straight face?"

"Madame President, please, if you could just see—"

"Et *tu*, Brutus?" Cynthia said, her arms folded against her chest.

Galloway blinked. "I don't mean to—"

"Get out," snapped the President.

Her words were like a slap to the face.

Cynthia walked to the office door with her back ramrod straight, and opened it.

"Good *day,* Mr. *Ambassador,"* she spat.

"Madame President, *please* …"

"Don't make me summon the Secret Service."

Galloway stood and tugged at his suit jacket.

"Very well," he said, and exited the room.

CHAPTER NINE

News of the Russian and Chinese ultimatum had broken, and a phone buzzed on Daddy's desk in the Compass Room. It was his backdoor phone.

"Longlegs," he barked.

Baltzer found it weird that the Vice President called himself by his nickname. *But whatever.*

Oberkirsch reported the British ambassador's visit.

"You're kidding."

"No, sir."

Daddy hung up and tossed his phone on his desk. *Goddammit!*

On the wall, China's CCTV reported that China was mobilizing its entire fleet, including all five of its Type 4 aircraft carriers.

China was also calling all reserve units to active duty. President Chiang Li had declared a national emergency.

Li vowed to prevent an American expeditionary fleet from traversing the Pacific to stage amphibious landings on the Arabian Peninsula. He claimed that Russian President Aleksandr Perchenko stood with China.

Daddy snatched his phone again.

"Mr. Vice President." Daddy could almost *hear* the plastic smile on the

British Ambassador's face. "How very nice to hear from you."

Daddy seethed.

"You stabbed us in the back, you *asshole*. You and your government."

Silence on the other end. It started to stretch. *Uncomfortable? Good, you piece of shit.*

"Hear me out, George, if you will,—"

"Fuck you, asshole," Longlegs interjected. "Don't think for a *minute* that I will ever forget this."

Daddy Longlegs hung up.

~ ~ ~

It wasn't just the UK. It was all of them. France, Italy, and—hardest for Daddy to swallow—Germany.

Our allies have abandoned us. They've abandoned ME.

It was a *fait accompli.*

No wonder they won't take my calls.

Daddy leaned back in his chair in his den—the Compass Room—and took a sip of wine. On the wall monitor, talking heads were yammering about the horrors of nuking an advancing Iranian armored division.

"A horrific day for America," one bespectacled commentator spoke— with performative indignation, of course. "President Belle denies that this was an American attack, but let's get real …"

So.

They don't believe that the Iranians sank the *Bush.*

And they don't believe that we didn't nuke the Iranians.

Typical.

"Geopolitics, please," Daddy said out loud with a sigh. His television scrolled automatically through a carousel of streaming channels.

A few cable segments, some podcasts, the usual Beltway bunk. Daddy closed his eyes and rocked in his chair.

Nothing.

"… Markets are in free fall. The US President was evacuated live on CNN. A nuke went off outside Dubai. And folks still think the real danger is pronouns."

Daddy opened one eye.

A guy in a studio.

No—more like a shack.

A shaggy-haired surfer dude with boards propped up behind him with sun-faded posters, and a lava lamp.

"From Biarritz, France: this is *The Big Picture with Breaker Bob*, and I'm your barefoot host with the salt-crusted soul…"

The TV continued to scroll.

"Go back," Daddy said.

The television complied.

"It's been a weird twenty-four hours. Let's get our bearings.

"At 4:17 p.m. Gulf Standard Time, a mushroom cloud rose over the sands outside Dubai. An Iranian armored division—*poof. Vaporized.*

"Now, the White House says it wasn't them. Israel is as mum as a corpse. Saudi Arabia hasn't said anything either—because, *guess what?* The King is dead, and—as of yesterday—*Saudi* Arabia doesn't exist anymore.

"Oh, and global markets are in free fall.

"All in a day's surf sesh."

Daddy Longlegs blinked. "What the hell is *this?*"

"But one thing we know," Breaker Bob continued, "those sand monster mushroom clouds didn't just rise on their own.

"But don't worry. From where I sit—here in Biarritz, on France's Atlantic Coast—the sea is glassy, the vibe is chill, and the croissants are warm and crispy.

"We are still very far away from the end of the world, folks."

"But you can see it from here," said a young woman's voice.

Breaker Bob snorted.

"Leave it to my wahine to spoil the fun."

Daddy took another sip of wine and smiled.

"Finally," he muttered. "Someone talking sense."

~ ~ ~

Zayne met Haidar at the thrift store and pawn shop warehouse.

Zayne was surprised to find Haidar already there.

Haidar was amped up. He was pulling boxes down from shelves. Several young men—Zayne counted ten—did likewise. These were some of Zayne's employees, but they were all Haidar's men.

"What's going on?" Zayne asked.

"You saw the message," Haidar responded.

"Yeah, but—what are you doing?"

"Letting the waters flow," Haidar said. He handed off a box. Sweat gleamed on his brow. He turned to Zayne and grinned. "Under the light of the moon."

Zayne blinked. "I don't even know what that means."

"Don't be sly, brother," Haidar said. "You know the time has come."

Ilyaas appeared, stepping into view. Haidar handed him a box like he was one of the crew. The boy took it and carried it away. He didn't even acknowledge that Zayne was standing there.

"What is *he* doing here?" Zayne demanded. "We agreed. This life is not for him."

Haidar's eyes went vacant, like that day in the cafè. "He's a soldier," Haidar said.

Zayne felt a chill.

Ahmed Farooq, the burly bushy-bearded delivery man, stepped up and Haidar passed him a box. Farooq was a simpleton. A zealot.

"Brother," Zayne said, grabbing Haidar's arm—but Haidar interrupted him.

"He who wavers in the hour of trial opens the door to Satan," Haidar said, stepping forward.

Zayne took a step back. A thought popped into his head, a thought that had crossed his mind many times before.

My brother sees no shades. Only what is sacred and what must be destroyed.

"But, *Ilyaas* …," Zayne managed. It was a whisper.

"What about him?"

Zayne stared at his brother. "He's a boy."

"He's a believer," Haidar said.

Zayne's mouth opened, then closed again. He felt his pulse behind his eyes.

"He could have a life here," he said, finally.

Haidar's face twisted into pure hatred. "As a *kafir!*" he spat.

Zayne recoiled. He turned and walked out.

Haidar stared after him. After a moment, he returned to taking boxes down from the shelf.

~ ~ ~

It rained. Traffic signals and lights dazzled and bled on the streets. The G-Wagon purred. Khaled's classic *Aïcha* poured from the speakers. Zayne drove. The Eiffel Tower filled his side mirror—gold and twinkling. It dazzled, too.

Zayne caught a glimpse of himself in the rear-view mirror. Only then did he realize he was crying. He didn't care.

Comme si je n'existais pas …

He wiped his face on his sleeve. A moment later, he was in the 17th arrondissement.

He spotted a gate guard kiosk and slammed his breaks. *Aïcha* still blared from the speakers.

Je n'ai que des mots …

The kiosk. Zayne wiped his face and looked at the building beyond it.

His windshield wipers swept back and forth.

I was here …

It was two years before. They had grilled him over Haidar's Cafè. Over the pawn shop. Over the thrift store.

Over everything.

They had nothing.

He reached over and opened the glove box, his eyes glued on the building before him. He glanced over. The .38 revolver gleamed under the dome light.

Zayne gripped it and held it for a long time. He put the Mercedes in park. Traffic maneuvered past. Slowly, in the rain.

Like the Mighty Mississippi, his tears had breached flood stage. They flowed without obstruction.

He placed the barrel of the gun under his chin.

"Aïcha, Aïcha, réponds-moi…"

Zayne took three quick breaths and closed his eyes tightly.

He squeezed the trigger.

But it didn't budge.

He forgot to unlock the safety.

~ ~ ~

Two uniformed officers in the gate guard kiosk knew instinctively that something was off when the Mercedes G-Wagon screeched to a halt not far from them.

The G-Wagon sat there in the rain, its headlights glowing, its engine running. Muffled music meant that it must be blaring inside the vehicle.

"Is he drunk?" asked the younger of the two. The older one grunted and reached to the wall. He pressed the Big Red Button. Tire spikes popped out of the ground in the driveway, and steel tube barriers rose swiftly into place.

The older one then keyed the radio on his vest. "We have a situation at the parking lot entrance. Silver Mercedes G-Wagon stopped in the middle of the road, facing us."

Several officers exited the building and cautiously flanked the G-Wagon, hands on their holsters.

An agent circled around the G-Wagon and approached, hand on holster.

Music blaring. A man … what was he doing?

The agent stepped closer—then stopped cold.

"He has a gun," he said into his radio, and withdrew his pistol.

Another officer pulled up beside him. "Let's do it."

He stepped up and smashed the driver side window. The first officer stepped up and shouted …

"Put the gun down!"

… his gun just inches from the driver's head. He reached in, and opened the door. The second officer pulled the startled driver out and threw him to the ground in one graceful motion, and then whipped his gun-holding hand in a wrist-and-elbow lock, the gun sliding away on the wet pavement.

"Ahhhh hahh hahhh … " the man bellowed.

He was bawling uncontrollably.

CHAPTER TEN

Night had come like sleep.

No sirens interrupted.

Like sleep, the night faltered and faded.

Daddy Longlegs awoke with the sunlight.

Shit. He rubbed his face. *Much to do.*

He was hoping to have woken up earlier, but at least he was up in time for the morning intelligence brief. On the large screen in his Compass Room were President Belle and all of her national security principals, most of whom were still with her at Raven Rock.

They looked like hell. Crumpled suits, bloodshot eyes, and half-lit bunkers behind them. Shaved and with a mug of black tea in hand, Daddy looked and felt downright refreshed in comparison.

"We had a peaceful night," announced Admiral Sorenson. "No missile strikes anywhere. Not here, and not in the Middle East."

"Thank God," sighed the President.

Daddy let that one marinate a moment.

Thank God? What would you have done if Iran hadn't paused? Offer 'em a coupon for peace talks?

But he said nothing. Sometimes silence said more.

Sorenson ran through overnight developments. On an adjacent screen, CNN's Bernice Hamdawana reported from Dubai. Her scarf whipped in the desert wind. Convoys of Iranian soldiers rolled behind her—transport trucks, fuel trucks, armored vehicles, and the like. Some soldiers smiled and flashed the V sign for victory as they went by.

That report was already several hours old.

CNN then cut to Bernice *live*. She was at Al Maktoum International Airport. It was utter chaos. Hundreds of thousands of people had descended on the airport seeking a flight out of the country. She reported that a similar scene was unfolding at the Sharjah airport, some forty miles to the north.

The main terminal at Al Maktoum is the largest in the world. Yet it was crowded far beyond its capacity. People were packed wall to wall. Bernice was continuously jostled and bumped as she reported. Most of the people appeared to be South Asian, whether Indian, Pakistani, or Bangladeshi. The majority of the UAE's population were foreign workers, and most came from South Asia.

The white faces of Westerners, though few and far between, were mixed in as well.

Bernice had to shout into her microphone.

"It is hard to separate fact from rumor," Bernice shouted. "But we've received reports that Iranian agents have arrived here at the airport, and are issuing orders—for example, refusing entry of American and Western airlines. CNN has not independently confirmed that as yet. There are some 50,000 American civilians working here in the United Arab Emirates. Any refusal of American or Western airlines would be of obvious concern."

"... 38,000 ... An additional 167,000 civilians—"

"Hang on," Daddy interrupted. He was confused. He was busy paying attention to Bernice on CNN. "Can you run that again?"

"Yes, sir," answered Lynn Benjamin. "There are 38,000 US military personnel on bases in the Iranian-occupied Gulf states. The Pentagon has been able to contact each of the bases. Iranians are allowing personnel to remain in the barracks and continue working, more or less. In addition to the military personnel, an additional 167,000 private American citizens work in the Gulf States."

There was a short pause as everyone contemplated the numbers.

Then Daddy spoke.

"Well, hell. We're talking over 200,000 American *hostages*, then, aren't we?"

~ ~ ~

Kyle had expected panicked constituents to bombard the office with phone calls and emails. But no. The calls and emails he *did* get were oblivious local yokels complaining about missed trash pickup or some other banal issue.

He was relieved when he got the call from the Senate Whip, California Senator Buck Arnold. The House and Senate leadership were jointly summoning Congress back into session.

After another dawn-patrol surf session—naturally—it was an easy commute. US Route 50 took him the entire 140 miles from Ocean City to the District of Columbia. A couple of turns later, and he would be at his DC home off Lincoln Park, which itself was just one mile east of the Capitol Building.

OC to DC: just two and a half hours overall. *Living on the Eastern Shore. What a bargain.*

This trip was anything but a bargain. At least, not at first. Kyle stopped at the Wawa convenience store and gasoline station just outside his neighborhood in Ocean City. It was his routine. But gas was $9.99 a gallon. *That* wasn't routine. It was triple the price from two days earlier.

No doubt the OC phone will be ringing off the hook today. Kyle looked at this phone. *Starting in about an hour's time.*

He paid at the pump. His Senate Official Personnel and Office Expense Account (SOPOEA) would cover it, but Congress would most certainly have to vote on boosting the SOPOEA program to cover this sudden hike in gas prices. *Now there's a bill that will have bipartisan support.*

Kyle went inside to fill his thermometer mug with fresh coffee.

"Ten bucks, huh?" he smirked to the cashier. Sally was obese, with bad knees and hips, and she moved in slow motion when patrons asked for cigarettes, vapes, or other things kept behind the counter. Kyle always knew when Sally was on duty by how long the line was. But she was always cheerfully pleasant.

Kyle hated her. Well, at first, anyway. He just wanted to be in and out with his coffee, and not wait all day on Sally.

I am a horrible man.

But her pleasantness had eventually worn him down. They were on a first name basis now. And she had seven grandchildren. Kyle had learned that tidbit at some point.

Sally gave him a look. "You know I'm going to catch it good today."

Kyle chuckled and tilted his head as he pocketed his change. "Yes, you will," he grinned.

On a monitor perched over her shoulder, the news showed recent footage of Iranian speedboats in the Persian Gulf, and oil refineries in the Houston area on fire. A ticker showed Dow Jones futures in free fall.

He nodded to the monitor. "There's the reason for the season."

"Be safe, Mr. Kyle," he heard as he walked out the door.

~ ~ ~

There was hardly any traffic between Ocean City and Washington. Twenty-four hours had passed since the first reports of a nuclear attack in the United Arab Emirates, and Americans were spooked.

Kyle turned on the radio. He had it tuned to Washington's BBC affiliate, and was immediately greeted with a commercial for Potassium Iodide pill supplementals—in case of nuclear war, you see, for protection against radiation. It was followed by a BBC report on how Americans were faring after two nights of ICBM strikes.

In short, they weren't faring very well at all. Americans were, in fact, quite panicked. From coast to coast, grocery stores shelves were stripped bare. Gas prices had more than doubled, and people were running out of fuel.

Naturally—this was America, after all—guns were flying off the shelves at Walmarts and sporting goods stores. Everything from handguns to AR-15 semi-automatic rifles.

Local news stations reported on the whereabouts of dusty Cold War-era nuclear fallout shelters. *Find one near you!*

Then there were the calls for blood. Americans were *angry*. How *dare* a foreign country bomb American cities after the USA had bombed *theirs*.

It wasn't supposed to work that way. And for nearly a century and a half, it *hadn't* worked that way.

Kyle reached the Chesapeake Bay Bridge. Still not a single car besides his own pickup truck. He sped across the four-mile steel bridge, rated as one of America's scariest because of its length, height, narrow lanes, and lack of shoulders.

It was even spookier without any traffic on it.

The Bay was glassy. Wispy fog clung to its surface.

~ ~ ~

"What's your name?"

The officer waited.

"Zayne Awada," he said, finally. His voice was barely audible.

"What was your intention?"

The officer waited again. After a long stretch of silence, he asked again.

"What was your intention?"

Zayne squirmed in his chair. "You need to listen to me," he said. "*You need to listen right now!*"

The officer yawned.

"What was your intention?"

"It's my brother Haidar," he said. "He's, he's—*there's going to be an attack.*"

"What kind of attack?"

~ ~ ~

Nearly twelve hours before Kyle Cropper was bantering with a cashier at a Wawa in Ocean City, Special Agent Eugene Claude of the Diplomatic Security Service scrambled to get dressed and check in with the Marines on the roof of one of the compound's maintenance buildings.

It was still dark. Another hour before the first evidence of sunrise.

Given the events of the past few days, and *especially* of the day before, Gene expected the worst. This posting required a seasoned veteran. It was *Baghdad,* for Pete's sake, and this wasn't Gene's first rodeo.

He didn't know exactly what to expect, but he was experienced enough to expect *something.*

The *worst,* even, whatever *that* meant.

Wrapped in body armor, helmet bobbling on his head, and the latest M4 carbine variant in his grasp, Gene jogged the quarter mile from his barracks to a facilities maintenance building near the northeast corner of the Embassy Compound.

The Embassy Compound took up a significant footprint of what had been the headquarters of America's occupation of Iraq some thirty (*30!*) years ago. Back then, it was dubbed the Green Zone.

The Embassy sat on the north bank of a left hook in the Tigris River. Just a mile to the east, the river turned northwest. Sadr City was an eleven-mile wedge that sprawled from the northeast bank to the west bank of the *Euphrates* River. Sadr City was the heart of Baghdad's Shia Muslim community, which made up half of Baghdad's population.

Iran, of course, is the hearth of Shia Islam. With news of the nuclear attack on Iranian troops—nearly all of them Shia Muslims—Gene expected trouble.

With a swipe of his identification card, Gene entered the maintenance building. He clamored up the stairs to the roof.

Before opening the door and stepping out, Gene paused for a moment to catch his breath. The moment turned into two. Then three. *Jesus! I'm too old for this shit. When did that happen?*

Gene stumbled through the door and was immediately thrown to the ground, rifle barrels at his head. A flashlight blinded him. "Jesus, man," somebody growled. "Wake up the whole neighborhood, why don't you?"

It was the Marines' Gunny Sergeant Alfredo Lopez.

Gene only grunted. He was helped to his feet. The Gunny Sergeant was the one he was looking for.

"How'd it go, Gunny?"

"It's been a quiet night."

"How quiet?"

Now Lopez grunted. Gene's question confirmed his own, silent, assessment. "Maybe *too* quiet."

Gene had slept only lightly. He had expected to be awakened at any time because of unrest or attack. The entire Embassy was on high alert.

"We've got movement, Gunny," a young Marine reported. He had a tablet in his hands.

"Show me," Lopez growled. He and Gene hovered over the tablet. On it was a live video feed from one of multiple drones the Marines were operating.

"That's in Sadr City," the young Marine reported. "About four klicks over there," he added, nodding beyond the northeast corner of the compound. Four klicks, or kilometers, was roughly two-and-a-half miles.

A fast growing rabble of men was gathering in the courtyard of what Gene thought to be the Al Khilani Mosque. They were arriving in cars, taxis, vans, three-wheel tuk-tuks, mopeds, and on foot.

And they were armed.

It wasn't like they were concealed. It was all right in the open. AK-47s were slung over every shoulder. Some clutched rocket-propelled grenade launchers. Almost everyone wore belts of ammunition.

Another group of fighters gathered at Amar Bin Yasir Park, just across the Tigris from the southern perimeter of the Embassy Compound. They were being watched by a second drone.

Gene looked to the east. There was a familiar sou—*"Incoming!"*

It was only a few seconds before a hollow whistle and a large *BANG!* produced a geyser of water in the middle of the Tigris River.

It was a mortar round. Whoever fired it overshot the Embassy Compound. It only takes a moment to adjust.

In the meantime, Gene used his phone to key in a code. Alarms all over the compound began to sound. A recorded voice came on loudspeakers: *Incoming. Incoming. Incoming. IDF Impact. Shelter in Place. Don IBA.*

The message repeated several times. Unlike most embassies, the US Embassy in Baghdad contained the Ambassador's residence, apartments for American staff, and barracks for its contingent of Marines and Diplomatic Security Agents. Most of the staff—including the Ambassador—were still asleep before the alarm went off.

Now, lights were coming on all over the Embassy's residential quarters, even as a young Marine yelled out once again.

"Incoming!"

Part Two

RAGE

CHAPTER ELEVEN

It was raining bombs. *Literally.*

Mortars rained down on the Embassy Compound.

It's a "bombstorm." Gene smirked to himself. *Store that one away.*

Strange what goes through your mind in such moments.

A memory flashed behind his eyes. His little girl giggling at a big swirl lollipop. He didn't remember when or where that was. She might have been three or four years old then.

She was almost thirty now. *I'm so goddamn proud of her—*

He bit his lip to keep himself from bursting into tears.

Get a grip, man!

Gene gripped his phone. He looked to the Ambassador. Baghdad was not a post for billionaire backers of Presidential campaigns. No, this guy was an astute and dedicated student of Islam and the Middle East. A man who believed in making the world a better place. A man who wanted to contribute in some way, however small, toward the betterment of, well, *Earth.*

Right now, the Ambassador crouched in a corner. He stared wide-eyed at the ceiling as the *"bombstorm"* rained Hell onto precious Earth above.

This is it. We're all gonna die today. The whole freaking Embassy staff. From the wide-eyed Ambassador to the visa-processing bureaucrats to the Marines to little 'ole me.

We're all gonna die today.

Gene pressed the call button.

~ ~ ~

"Longlegs," a man barked on the other end.

He sounded very annoyed.

Holy shit. It's the Man himself. Just like that SEAL guy promised.

"Who is this?" the gruff voice demanded.

"Sir, this is Special Agent Gene Claude."

Gene couldn't help but talk fast. *I hope he doesn't hang up on me.*

He had to yell into the phone over the bombs above.

"Sir, I'm with the Diplomatic Security Service in Baghdad. Our Embassy is under attack. I got your number from Admiral Oberkirsch. We're all going to die if somebody doesn't do something fast. This is a Hail Mary phone call."

There was silence on the other end.

"Sir?"

"Baghdad, you say?"

~ ~ ~

Yahya Arouri slipped his hands under the barrel and gripped the rim. "One, two, *three.*" He lifted from his legs and shuffled backwards.

"Easy!" he commanded as a younger hand struggled with the other end.

Yahya's muscles bulged, sweat broke out on his brow, and he grunted with almost every backward shuffle down the incline. As he reached the trawler, other young men rushed to his aid. They kept him from falling backwards and from losing his grip on the barrel.

They stood up the barrel and maneuvered it into the last open space among the other barrels on the boat's open deck.

Yahya pulled on the handkerchief that dangled from his back pocket and wiped his face.

He looked up.

A slender young man was squatting on the dock, looking down on the trawler. A predawn sunrise of dark blue and light pink behind him shrouded the young man in silhouette. His clothes billowed in the morning breeze.

"Last one?" Nizar al-Zahar asked.

Yahya was still breathing hard. He nodded.

~ ~ ~

"What's going on in Baghdad, Lynn?" Daddy was hot. "Are you aware that our embassy is *under attack* as we speak? *They're being goddamned overrun!"*

"I'm *aware!"* It was the first time the Secretary of State had raised her voice to Daddy.

Good. She understands the gravity of the situation.

"I won't have a Benghazi on my conscious!" Daddy said. "What is the State Department doing?"

"We're trying to work with Baghdad, but ..."

The line went silent for a moment.

"But *what*, Lynn?" Daddy was calmer now. There was concern in his voice.

"They're not answering their goddamn phones!"

Lynn was exasperated. How could she not be?

Daddy paced in his study as he thought. The line grew silent again.

Daddy's eyes fell on a large map of the Middle East that took up a whole wall of his Compass Room. He had stared at that map for hours, nay *days*, as he prepped for a war against Iran.

That thought brought a slew of *what ifs*. He shook his head.

"Are you there, Daddy? I really have to get back—"

"Give me a moment, for Chrissake, I'm *thinking!"*

He stared at Baghdad. It was far from the Indian Ocean where the

Obama and *Doris Miller* steamed. He did some back-of-the-envelope math.

We're talking 1,500 miles or more. Air and missile strikes will take roughly two-and-a-half to three hours. The Marines have to last at least that long.

"The President must order air strikes from the carrier strike groups," Daddy offered.

But it isn't enough.

Lynn didn't answer. She was barking commands in the background.

Daddy waited.

He heard Lynn breathe into the phone. She was back.

"The President …" Lynn's voice drifted off. "I don't know, Daddy. She's not in a good place."

"Goddamn it, lives are at stake!" Daddy exploded.

"She's reaching out to Beijing," Lynn said. She practically whispered it.

Daddy grew dizzy. He reached for his desk and steadied himself with one hand, clutching his chest with the other.

Oh Lord, don't do this to me now!

He forced himself to take deep, slow, deliberate breaths.

There's no way on God's Green Earth that Chiang Li or Perchenko would agree to such a thing.

"Are you okay, Daddy?" Lynn could hear him struggle to breathe normally.

"Daddy?"

Daddy's eyes darted back to the map. They traced northward from Baghdad, and his breathing slowed.

"Tell the Marines to *fight,* goddamn it," Daddy growled. "I'll get them their support."

~ ~ ~

"I just need to get from *here* to *there,*" Daddy said. He held a tablet in his hand with Google Maps on it, showing it to Melvin Bauer.

"Here" was One Observatory Circle. "There" was the Turkish Embassy, a half-mile away on the other side of Rock Creek.

"If George Washington could cross the *goddamn Delaware*, we can manage to cross *Rock fucking Creek.*"

The problem, of course, was protesters. He was the only Vice President in history, it seemed, that attracted as many protesters as the President. Even *more*, maybe.

They were camped out on Embassy Row, waving flags and cardboard signs, chanting:

Whose war? Daddy's War! Whose bomb? Daddy's Bomb! Daddy did this! Daddy did this!

The crowd had grown so dense along Massachusetts Avenue, including the front of the Turkish Embassy, that there was no way Daddy could simply drive the half mile and knock on the front door.

Melvin grunted. His mustache twitched.

Then … "Fancy a run?"

~ ~ ~

George Badal, Ambassador of Guyana to the United States, was normally out and about in the middle of the day. Meeting with Guyanese businessmen. Meeting with US AID officials. Meeting with Guyanese-American associations.

Or shopping.

But the missile attacks a few days ago brought the city to a standstill. And now there were protesters swarming into DC.

Truth be told, George was getting cabin sickness. *Mrs*. Badal was driving him nuts.

Or was it the other way around? Sure, sure, fair enough.

There was an incessant knocking on the front door. Guyana couldn't afford security guards or servants. The handful of Embassy staff lived in apartments of their own, and the Embassy wasn't open for business.

Not until things settled down.

"Are you going to get the door?" he shouted from his office.

He heard the door open and his wife gasp.

"George!"

George sighed. He heard his wife laugh nervously. "George?"

What's this about?

George stopped cold when came out of his office. He immediately recognized the tall, lanky man hovering in the foyer. But he had never met him before.

What in the world?

George smiled broadly. "Mr. *Vice President*," he said. He couldn't mask his surprise. "For what do I owe the honor?"

"Mr. Ambassador," Daddy said, shaking his hand. "Do you have a ladder?"

~ ~ ~

The fact that Daddy Longlegs was wearing cargo pants, a sweatshirt, and an Ohio State baseball cap, should have been a giveaway. Along with the smudge of dirt on his knees.

This wasn't a normal house call.

"Mr. Ambassador," Daddy barked. He wasn't speaking to George. He was on his phone. "I need to see you." There was a pause as the other Ambassador spoke. "Yes, if you please. Right now."

"Meet me out back," he said before disconnecting.

George held the ladder. Daddy paused before climbing. From a block away, he could hear drums and the echo of that damn chant again—

Who's War? Daddy's War! Who's Bomb? Daddy's Bomb!

He looked to George. "Thank you, Mr. Ambassador. Thank you for your help. I never forget help in a moment of need."

Daddy climbed. He reached the top of the backyard wall. It was only a few rungs high. He placed his rear on the plaster wall and swung his legs over. He roll over and lowered himself to the other side.

He dangled from his fingertips. Looking down, his feet dangled only about a foot in the air.

He let go and dropped to his feet. He brushed his hands together and turned around.

The back door of the Turkish Embassy opened. Tayfun Ulusoy stepped out.

"Mr. Vice President," he said. He shook his head in astonishment. He lit a cigarette, took a deep drag, and exhaled.

"Welcome to Türkiye."

CHAPTER TWELVE

The boats appeared to be barely seaworthy. It was a running joke among the crew. The trawlers were rust buckets, for sure, and had seen better days, but they were built sturdy. They would do the job.

It was the engines Yahya worried about, but that was Nizar's domain. It was why he was here. He would accompany Yahya on the command boat, and would be ready to do necessary repairs along the way, if it came to it. He was only twenty-three, but he had a reputation as one of the best car mechanics in Benghazi.

He also worked on boats.

The barrels were Yahya's responsibility, as were the electronics attached to the fuses. He was also responsible for rigging the navigation systems for remote control. Three of the four trawlers were, essentially, sea drones.

Yahya couldn't rely on volunteer martyrs. He wouldn't know where to find them, and he also wouldn't be able to trust them. *Suicide bombers? They are either ferocious religious zealots or ideologues, or mentally unstable, probably both.*

He had a job to do, and he needed some help doing it, but everyone needed to be clear-headed for it to work.

~ ~ ~

It was a chaotic day at Fort Neuf de Vincennes, the DGSE's state-of-the-art headquarters on the historic grounds of the Château de Vincennes in eastern Paris. The *Direction Générale de la Sécurité Extérieure*—France's equivalent of the CIA—was overwhelmed.

A chaotic *week* was more accurate. Hell, a wild *month*.

Signals Intelligence was drowning in electronic chatter. Director Philippe Karcher had never seen so much communication filling the ether. Chatter was high *before* the American aircraft carrier blew up. That was the reason it was deployed to the region in the first place. But after the sinking of the *George W. Bush,* and then the Iranian missile strikes on America, it went to a whole other level.

Most of it was social media posts expressing everything from disbelief to jubilation at Iran's shocking military success in the Persian Gulf and its strike on America.

The nuclear attack in the deserts of the UAE just hours ago sent the chatter off the charts. Everyone presumed it was the Americans. Or the Israelis. Or both.

The chatter turned chilling. There were calls for murdering Americans and Jews in the streets wherever they are found. The chatter was blatant and in the open. *Civilians* calling for blood on social media.

Most chilling of all, at least in Philippe's mind, was where so much of the chatter was coming from.

Europe.

"I think you might want to see this."

Karcher looked up. It was Luc Morel, his senior signals analyst.

"It's from Jerusalem to the Israeli Embassy here in Paris. Mostly routine stuff—visa applications, consular scheduling, that sort of thing. But the message ends with this."

He pointed to the final lines:

"Come, my people—enter your chambers and bar your doors; hide yourselves for a little moment, until the indignation is past. Yet if your heart cries, 'Oh that I had wings like a dove, to fly away and be at rest,' then at the place of wings a chariot awaits."

— A reflection shared to strengthen our people in these uncertain times.

— Shared by Ari Benjamin

Philippe read it once, then again. Slowly. Clearly it was a code.

Batten down the hatches, is what Karcher read. *They're expecting trouble.*

But that second part. *'Oh that I had wings like a dove …'*

What did it mean?

~ ~ ~

Philippe stepped onto the high-ceilinged main floor of Fort Neuf.

It was a sea of cubicles, and it buzzed with activity. Supervisors shouted questions, analysts shouted back answers and questions of their own.

It was like the floor of the New York Stock Exchange.

Pierre Cresson, Philippe's Deputy Director, caught up to him.

"We have roughly 30,000 French nationals working in the UAE," Pierre reported. "I emailed a list of the biggest companies they work for to the Foreign Ministry."

"Very good," Philippe said. "What about the others? Kuwait, Bahrain, and Qatar?"

"About 2,000 more total, split among them. The main problem is the UAE."

"The Air Force is readying A400s to help evacuate our people from Dubai," he continued. "But so far, there has been no response from Tehran."

It wasn't surprising. America's CNN was reporting that the Iranian military was denying all Western flights into the UAE.

"What about their embassy? Their ambassador?"

"Their ambassador says he has received no guidance from Tehran."

Philippe's mind drifted back to the Israeli intercept. *Ari Benjamin.* He was the Agency Executive of Aman, Israel's Military Intelligence Directive. *That means something.*

"Okay," Philippe nodded. His phone buzzed.

It was his counterpart, Michel Renard, at the DGSI—France's *internal* security agency. DGSI was about eight miles northwest of Fort Neuf in the Levallois-Perret district of Paris, on the right bank of the Seine.

"Michel," he answered. "How bad is it there?"

Huge parts of Paris—entire *arrondissements*—had erupted into mass celebrations the past two nights after Iranian missiles struck the United States. The celebrations were *mostly* peaceful. But cars were flipped over and set on fire. Shops were looted. Thankfully, there were no reports of anyone getting killed. *Yet.*

"It is quiet here," Michel answered. "*Too* quiet. The streets are empty all across Paris. There is a foreboding in the air. You can slice it with a knife."

Oh, that I had wings like a dove! I would fly away and be at rest.

"She is going to erupt," Michel continued. "We asked the President to mobilize the Army in addition to the Gendarme, but he isn't convinced."

Philippe was about to respond when Michel added, almost as an afterthought:

"Oh—and one other thing. We have someone in custody. Brought himself in, actually. Bit of a scene in front of our building. Gun to his chin, crying. His name is Zayne Awada. Owns Haidar's Cafè with his brother, as well as a thrift store in Saint Denis. His brother's on our radar."

That made Philippe sit up straighter.

"Wait," he said. "Haidar's Cafè?" He snapped his fingers, then cupped his phone and called out to the cubicles.

"*Luc!*"

"Where is he now?" Philippe asked Michel.

"In a holding cell. Honestly, he's a mess. But lucid enough. He says something is coming, and that we've all got it wrong."

"Sir?" It was Luc.

"What's the name of that cafè with the review by The Commander?"

"Haidar's Cafè."

"Did you just say The Commander?" Now it was Michel on the phone.

"Yes," Philippe said.

"He mentioned something about a commander as well."

Yeah, baby.

"Don't let anyone talk to him. Not until I get there."

Philippe stood in the middle of the sea of cubicles with Luc at his side. He said nothing for a moment. The moment stretched.

"Sir?"

Philippe grunted. "Walk with me."

~ ~ ~

Philippe walked slowly with Luc at his side.

"Israel is expecting trouble," said Philippe. "They must know something we don't."

"That's not the half of it," Luc said.

"What do you mean?"

Luc handed him a new printout. "This has gone out to all synagogues in France," he said. "And it's being read on Jewish radio stations."

Philippe read the printout.

"The fear we always carry is upon us once again.

If your heart trembles, we are already beside you. Come as you are, come quietly. A chariot awaits at the place of wings: in Paris, Marseille, Lyon, Strasbourg. Those who seek refuge will find it in the land of promise."

Luc followed Philippe into his office, and Philippe sat heavily in his chair. He rested his elbows on his desk and stared at the message.

"What do you think it means?" Philippe asked.

"It's pretty cryptic," Luc answered. "We ran it through Voltaire."

"Voltaire?" Philippe raised an eyebrow. "Is that what we're calling the

AI now?"

Luc nodded and handed him another printout.

Voltaire: "The message appears to be a poetic or religious call for solidarity and faith. For coming together as a community. References to fear, chariots, and wings likely signal spiritual protection or community gathering in the face of unrest.

Interpretation: symbolic reassurance, possibly urging recipients to gather at synagogues or local Jewish centers. Confidence: 87%."

Philippe stroked his chin.

"Okay," he said. "Get this to every district with a synagogue. We need to boost security in ways that are *visible*. I want *deterrence.*"

~ ~ ~

Marines were falling back.

That meant only one thing.

Gene's radio squawked.

"Indians have breached the fort!"

The Marines had conceded the northeast quadrant of the Embassy Compound just moments ago. Now the "Indians" were pouring in.

Gene's radio squawked again.

"You know you can't say that," a voice said. It was a young voice, probably another Marine.

Gene looked up. Everyone looked at each other with some confusion.

Another squawk. "You can't say 'Indians.'"

The whole room burst into laughter.

Gene smiled ear to ear. It felt good to smile. A weight was lifted.

Then the whole building shook.

"Jesus, what the hell was that?" someone shouted.

The building shook again. It literally moved laterally, back and forth, as though in an earthquake. Dust fell from the ceiling.

Gene stepped into the daylight, and another explosion sent him to his knees. An angry cloud of dust rose over the Embassy Compound from a block away.

Gene coughed. Then he heard it. The sound of jets.

It wasn't the "Indians." It was *Daddy Longlegs*.

Gene allowed himself to smile again.

We might live through this yet.

~ ~ ~

Click. "*Un*-follow."

Click. "*Un*-follow."

Click. "*Un*-follow."

Karen sighed. "What are you doing *now?*"

"I'm unfollowing everyone who's a fascist."

"Aren't they your friends?"

"Not anymore," Harv said, laughing.

Click. "*Un*-follow."

Click. "*Un*-follow."

Click. "*Ban.*"

Karen rolled her eyes.

CHAPTER THIRTEEN

Philippe left Fort Neuf in his beat-up Renault. It was nearly 7:00 a.m., and Paris was waking up.

He wanted to get a feel of the city. It was a go-to of his since the time he'd gone undercover as a bus driver.

He learned so much about people this way. He listened to conversations. He learned to identify people who stood apart from the crowd by poking their heads up, looking around, and making brief eye contact. People who were situationally aware. People who were predators or simply knew how to handle themselves.

He had also learned the physical layout of the city in detail.

He crossed the Seine and looped west around the Eiffel Tower.

The morning was light blue, orange, and pink. The Eiffel Tower was gloriously golden in the morning sun.

A cool mist hugged the river.

Philippe crossed the Seine again and passed the Élysée Palace. He slowed alongside the large and public Tuileries Garden. The car behind him blew its horn. Philippe stuck his arm out the window and waived the driver to pass, but it only blew its horn again.

"*Merde,*" Philippe cursed under his breath. He stared intently into the public garden, and slowed to a crawl. People were gathering there. It was still so early, and it wasn't the usual place for protests.

At the crosswalks on the side of the road, clusters of pedestrians gathered. Multiple flags of Palestine fluttered in the morning breeze above the crowd. They were ubiquitous, it seemed, in almost any protest in France.

He rolled past the Louvre, where he spotted a placard depicting the American President and Vice President with Hitler mustaches and Nazi armbands.

Philippe slammed his breaks. A large crowd carrying Iranian and Palestinian flags, and various placards—one image of Daddy Longlegs had *War Criminal!* written over his face—was crossing the street without regard for traffic signals.

Philippe waited. He spied as many individuals as he could while trying not to make eye contact. He got plenty of cold, hard stares, regardless.

And the crowd just kept coming.

Philippe phoned Luc.

"I'm at the Louvre. Things are beginning to kick off."

"It's only 7:00!," Luc said.

"Exactly."

~ ~ ~

As a young doctoral student in Electrical Engineering at the University of British Columbia in Canada's Pacific West, Yahya had watched with despair as Israel destroyed all of Gaza following Hamas' heroic surprise attack in October 2023.

It was then that Yahya's eyes had truly opened for the first time in his life. And he wasn't alone. Millions of protesters took to the streets of Vancouver and across the world, including the United States and Europe, against the savage Zionist entity. And it wasn't just the Palestinian diaspora of which he was part, and people of color, but white Canadians, Americans, and Europeans. Indeed, people across the West demonstrated in the streets and occupied university campuses to show their solidarity with Palestinians.

Yahya joined them. Reluctantly, at first. He wanted to return to Gaza, but his parents begged him to stay in Canada. *Finish your studies. Live your life.* His father had even berated him. *We sacrificed everything for you.*

His brothers, he learned, had joined Hamas.

Soon after, Gaza became impossible to reach, and he lost touch with his parents. Yahya could only follow events through the Internet, and the news grew worse by the day.

The protests were festive, but Yahya was lost. He imagined that his parents were dead, along with his entire extended family. Cousins. Uncles. Aunts. His brothers, too. They were all likely killed in the war.

Yahya was desperate to join his family in Gaza, or wherever they might be. He wanted to join his brothers in Hamas.

But he couldn't dishonor his parents. So he stayed.

But instead of coursework, it wasn't long before his days were filled with protests. They were exhilarating.

They flew Palestinian flags at daily protests, wore keffiyehs, disrupted traffic, and occupied university buildings. Day after day. He became close friends with other Palestinian, Arab, and Muslim students–even faculty–across the UBC campus.

They threw red paint on the walls and sidewalks of a particular synagogue one week, and another the next. Over months of protests, not a single Jewish synagogue was spared. Anti-capitalists, anti-fascists, and pro-LGBTQIA+ protesters all came out in support of Palestine and against Israel and Jews.

They were amusing.

Yahya was part of the global jihad—in Vancouver, Canada, of all places. And he even had arrests to show for it. Three, to be exact. And each time, he was released without charge. He simply couldn't be identified in any videos or photos of protesters harassing Zionists or damaging their property.

When the Engineering department scheduled his comprehensive examinations, he wasn't ready. He was busy protesting against the genocide of his people, after all.

So Yahya protested, and hundreds of fellow protesters came to his aid and occupied the department. They shouted and chanted, and splashed the walls red like the synagogues to symbolize the blood of Palestinian children. *"Professors, Professors, you can't hide. UBC supports genocide!"*

The Department acquiesced. *Yahya* would schedule the Ph.D. comprehensive exams when he was good and ready, not the Department. And surely they knew to give him a pass when the time came.

But one day, as he was walking to the bus stop, plainclothes policemen tackled him to the ground.

They were Canadian Border Services officers. They had a letter from Immigration, Refugees and Citizenship Canada: Yahya's study permit had been revoked.

A new conservative government had been elected, and they had run on the platform of stopping mass immigration, ending the protests, and deporting foreign agitators.

But Yahya was a student, not an immigrant, and besides, the majority of the protesters were Canadians.

Yahya was incredulous. He was treated like a criminal.

Protest organizers had taught him to remain silent, and he smiled as the officers bombarded him with questions. He had also memorized a crowd-sourced legal defense phone number, so once he was transported to jail, he told the officers that he wanted his lawyer.

One officer, a large white woman, smirked and held up the warrant. "This is a National Security warrant," she said, "and you are not a citizen."

After almost two weeks in jail, he and other prisoners were shackled and driven to the airport. He was being deported.

Just weeks away from earning my PhD!

Animals! Dogs! Zionists!

He had landed in Egypt, but he was lost along the way. A feeling of emptiness. And, truth be told, a mix of loneliness and fear. He had very little money and nowhere to go. He *did* have skills, though. He was an electrical engineer, after all. Surely he could find work *somewhere*.

That's what he pinned his hopes on. A new chapter of his life awaited him … somewhere.

He was surprised to find an old man waiting for him outside the airline terminal. The man was holding a sign with his name on it. Yahya looked around for a moment before stepping up.

Who could this possibly be?

"*I* am Yahya," he said.

~ ~ ~

"They say it's going to get hairy today, Bof."

Jean-Charles "JC" Lemaitre was a couple of years younger than Bof—his closest friend on the force.

Brigadier-chef Bruno "Bof" Castaing grunted. He fished out a stick of gum and shoved it into his mouth. Then he leaned over, tapping his shield with JC's before offering his friend a piece of gum.

"No thanks, Bof."

"It ain't nothing we haven't done before," Bof said.

Helicopters circled above.

Bof looked to a female officer standing to the side of the riot line. In her hands, she held what looked like a game console. She was piloting a drone.

"What do you see, Reka?" he asked.

"People milling about. Looks like a big street festival, if you ask me."

"I *am* asking you."

Laughter broke out down the line.

"Lots of Palestinian flags," Reka said, peering at the screen. "Iranian flags too."

"Weapons?"

"Not that I can see. It's packed down there. I can't get a bead on any-one in the middle."

Some in the crowd had spotted the drone. Despite the cacophony of noise—shouting, chants, distant sirens—they heard the whine of its rotors. A few pointed. Others flipped it off or threw trash at it.

A water bottle tumbled end over end toward the tiny helicopter, but she managed to maneuver the drone away from it.

"Bring it, bitches," she muttered, smiling.

People were still arriving, swelling the size of the crowd in front of Bof and JC's line. Bof, JC, and Reka stood at the intersection of Rue Boissy d'Anglas and Avenue Gabriel. Behind them stood an army of riot-shielded cops. On Avenue Gabriel, another army—this one of Gendarmes—filled the street.

On the corner of Boissy d'Anglas and Gabriel was, of course, the leafy American Embassy compound in Paris. It, in turn, backed up against the Palais de l'Élysée—home of French President Jacques Michelet. And on the other side of the Élysée was the Israeli Embassy.

This was Ground Zero for nearly every protest or demonstration that involved either the United States or Israel. On any given day, it was the most heavily monitored and policed area in all of France.

Reka piloted the drone higher to get a more panoramic view. Protesters were streaming toward them from as far north as she could see.

She swung the drone around to face south. Bridges across the Seine were jammed pack. Some protesters streaming in from the south might be stuck on the other side of the river.

Good.

Bof could hear a tinny bullhorn, but he couldn't make out what it was saying. It was a call-and-response, though, so he figured it out with the crowd's synchronized response.

Wah-wah-wah-we-ca … *"Death to America!"*

Wah-wah-wah-we-wew … *"Death to the Jews!"*

He stifled a yawn.

The drone flew over the western end of Jardin Gardens, the Fontaines des Fleuves and des Mers, and Pavyllon Paris, all on the North bank of the Seine.

"I see a lot of keffiyehs," Reka reported. "Hold on." A particular cluster caught her attention. It was a group of bearded men with black hair and dark eyes, each dressed in black.

They looked dangerous.

They were pulling on black balaclavas.

"Bof?"

"What?"

~ ~ ~

On the corner of Boissy d'Anglas and Gabriel, it was pandemonium.

Burly men in all black from head to toe—"We're fighting *ninjas*, JC!" Bof shouted as burly men in black tore at the barricades between them and the shielded police beyond. Water cannons knocked people back, but more took their place. This appeared to be a well-synchronized operation by the ninjas.

Ninjas were also battling the Gendarme on Bof's right flank.

He saw a metallic Frisbee arc through the air and land among the first row of Gendarme.

There was a flash, white smoke, and a *BANG* so loud that Bof jumped and his ears popped.

"What the hell!" shouted JC, clasping his ears. "That was a *bomb!*"

Bof's eyes remained glued on the front row of the Gendarme. Bodies lay twisted among metal barricades and riot shields. He couldn't tell if they were alive or dead.

Other Gendarme clawed at them, trying to come to their aid.

Bof heard stomach-wrenching screaming. He realized it was coming from some of the Gendarme laying on the ground.

Ninjas, meanwhile, swarmed the barricades on both streets, pulling on them, yanking them, dragging them away.

It was going to be hand-to-hand combat.

Against ninjas. I don't like those odd—pressure cooker!

The screaming of Gendarme cut through the other noises.

"It was a pressure cooker bomb!" Bof shouted—not just for JC's and Reka's sake, but for everyone's.

Right on cue, Bof watched as another pressure cooker twirled in the air.

It was coming right at him and his colleagues, and they had nowhere to run.

"Incoming!" someone shouted. It was JC.

Bof barely had time to raise his shield before the bomb detonated in midair. A deafening crack tore through the street. Nails and shrapnel tinkled on the street after ricocheting off shields, helmets, and buildings.

A ringing in Bof's ears muffled everything else. But then, blood-curdling cries cut through the chaos. Animalistic screams. Officers staggered and struggled to stand while others lay motionless on the ground.

"Bof! Bof!"

Bof blinked. Blood droplets peppered his helmet mask.

"Are you hurt?"

It was Reka. Her brow was furrowed with concern.

"I don't think so," Bof said—but he didn't hear himself speak.

He squeezed his nose and blew. His ears popped, and suddenly everything was loud.

"Here they come again!" JC yelled. He was reaching for his sidearm.

Bof followed his gaze.

Through the smoke, two ninjas charged from the far side of the boulevard. One—the closer one—flung another Frisbee-like bomb to the trio's right. JC opened fire and the ninja went down.

The other one—slender and agile—threw his frisbee farther. It sailed over the trio's heads toward the center of the police column.

The earth shook. The air was acrid.

More screams.

The ninja turned to run, but Reka had him in her sights. She squeezed the trigger and he, too, went down against the metal rails, his body twisting unnaturally as he fell.

~ ~ ~

"Bloody hell!"

Philippe slammed his hand on his desk as he spoke on his phone. He forcefully rubbed his face with both hands.

His chief analyst stood in his office doorway.

"They've got *bombs*," Philippe said. "They're *bombing the police!*"

"The President isn't budging," said Héloïse, one of the President's advisors.

On a television monitor on his office wall, live news covered the unfolding nightmare in the center of Paris.

"The President is going to hold a presser," she said. "He wants you there."

"I'll be there," he sighed.

He looked to Luc.

"'You've got it all wrong,'" Luc said. "Those were Zayne Awad's words."

Philippe nodded. "We've got to do something."

~ ~ ~

"I implore all Parisians—indeed, all the people of our beloved France—to exercise calm and refrain from violence."

President Jacques Michelet stood at the podium in the lavish Salle des Fêtes, or Hall of Festivities. Crystal chandeliers hung from the room's golden and ornate Beaux-Arts ceiling.

He was flanked by members of his cabinet, including the Minister of the Interior, the head of the National Police, the Director of the DGSI, and the Director of the DGSE—Philippe Karcher.

"I know people are angry," President Jacques Michelet continued. "I am angry, too. The world mourns the atrocity of a nuclear attack in the United Arab Emirates. The world calls for justice. *France* demands it.

"Today I call for an independent, United Nations-led investigation into the origins of the attack. I respectfully request that the United Arab Emirates and Iran allow investigators to conduct their work."

"We will work with our allies to ensure justice. We cannot shy away from whatever evidence may arise, nor turn a blind eye if it is not to our liking.

"Today, France stands with the United Arab Emirates. Today, France stands with the Middle East.

"Thank you."

The press immediately interrupted with a cacophony of shouted questions.

"Mr. President—do you condemn the violence today?"

"Are reports of police casualties confirmed?"

Michelet raised a hand and nodded toward a reporter.

"Emilie Caron, *France Télévisions*, Monsieur le Président. Why not issue a curfew? Why not declare a state of emergency?"

The President maintained a smile, but his eyes twitched. "Because France is a republic. Protests and demonstrations are a necessary part of that."

He pointed to another reporter.

"Sir, will you call out the Army?"

"We are far away from that. The Research, Intervention, and Dissuasion unit of the National Police—RAID—are on the scene. Let's let them do their work. Thank you. That is all for now."

As he stepped away, Philippe pushed off the wall and followed him.

~ ~ ~

"Philippe! I understand you've got news for me."

The President was somehow jovial after the presser. *What the hell?*

"Yes, sir, it's about Israel. I believe you need to see this."

"Israel?" He looked confused. "Dear God, what have *they* done?"

Philippe handed him two intercepted messages.

The President frowned, squinting as he read.

"What am I looking at?" he asked.

"A coded message, sir," Philippe said.

"What does it mean?"

"We believe they are warning of a major event here in Paris. The language is … urgent. Coordinated. Our analysts believe they're preparing for something significant."

"What kind of something?"

"That's just it—we don't know yet. But we're seeing unusual traffic around synagogues and Jewish centers as well. Messaging on community radio. Whatever they're doing, it's not just the embassy."

The President stood and began to pace, still holding the printouts. "You're saying this is about Jews? Broadly?"

"Perhaps," Philippe said. "At the very least, it's clear the Israelis are acting on intelligence they've chosen not to share."

"And," Philippe continued, then hesitated.

Oh, that I had wings like a dove …

That message stuck in Philippe's head.

"And what?" The President demanded.

"I think they are warning Jews to leave Paris."

The President gave a short laugh. He shook his head and sat again, the paper fluttering to his lap. "Nonsense. This is *France*, not some Balkan backwater. Jews do not flee from *Paris*. With all due respect, I don't believe your interpretation is correct, Director."

Before Philippe could respond, the President continued.

"I know what you're going to ask next." He waived his hand in dismissal. "DGSI wants the Army. Well, the Gendarme also wants the Army. The *Army* wants the Army.

"No, no, no. We don't send in the Army every time someone takes to the streets, do we?"

"They had bombs, sir," Philippe reminded him.

"And the Gendarme are investigating," he sighed. "Look, no one doubts that this nuclear situation is explosive, but let's be clear-eyed. The Muslim minority is a significant component of my government's coalition. To send the Army into the streets would be seen as discriminatory and provocative.

"These things always pass. Let's give them space to voice their anger.

"Now," he said, looking at his watch. "If that's all, I've got other business to attend to."

CHAPTER FOURTEEN

It had hit the one-time Mr. Oliver Taylor—now Trinity Taylor (*Madame, bitch*)—like a bolt of lightning. She still remembered the moment it happened. Everyone was talking about *Iran, Iran, Iran. I ran this, and I ran that.*

One of her girlie-girlfriends—*hey there, gurl, I'm talking 'boutchya*—wore an old Queers for Palestine tee from back in the day. And *that's* when it came to her.

Trans for Iran.

She wasn't tech-savvy, but she found a free website builder with pre-made templates for small businesses. And wouldn't you know it—one of them was for a generic T-shirt shop.

She selected it and was able to build a "product" (*a duck, a duck*) that looked almost identical to the old Queers for Palestine t-shirt.

She set up payment through her checking account.

And *voilà.* The "business" was live.

She sold a few within minutes. She ordered a few for herself, even.

Not that *she* made the shirts. Some fulfillment company—probably shipping mass-produced blanks from China—printed the design and sent them out. She made two bucks a sale. Within a week, the company had sold *thousands.*

"It was *in-say-hayne*," she singsonged. "In*sanity* is my *vanity!*" she shouted.

"Fuck off, grandma," Trinity growled in her baritone. An older French woman had given her a look.

She wore her *Trans for Iran* shirt with pride. It had paid for her trip. And here in Paris—her dream city—she saw other people wearing them too.

Getting out of America was the best thing she ever did. *Those motherfuckers triggered me every day, every day, every way, didn't they, didn't they, didn't they.*

And when Iran fired missiles at America? Sales blew up.

Ba-boom, baddah bing.

Cha-ching-a-ling.

Half a million, by her estimate. That'd make her a millionaire.

"Money bunny!" she shouted, then giggled.

She started to hop along the sidewalk.

~ ~ ~

The man—clearly a chauffeur—nodded and held his hand out, directing Yahya to a luxury Cadillac SUV.

Yahya climbed in, and the man drove away in silence.

Yahya tried not to fall asleep, but after awhile, he succumbed to jet lag. He drifted off to sleep.

When he awoke, they were in the desert.

On a highway.

He drifted off again.

~ ~ ~

Zayne was lethargic. Spent.

Officers led him to a police van. God only knew where they were taking him. He didn't care.

After a short drive, he was led into a hospital, and through a maze of corridors, before reaching double doors.

Inside, a group of men stood waiting. They turned when he entered.

"Mr. Awad," a middle aged man said. Zayne said nothing. His eyes lingered on the man before latching on to what was behind him: Two bodies. Each under a sheet. Each on its own steel table.

One of them was Haidar. He was certain.

Philippe looked to the guards gripping Zayne's arms. "Unshackle him," he ordered.

Zayne stared at the bodies. His eyes watered as the guards uncuffed him.

"I'm sorry, Mr. Awad, but we have to do this. We must confirm the identity of these men."

Luc Morel gestured to the first. "This one was leading the charge at the Embassy. We think he was coordinating the assault."

"They threw pressure cooker bombs," Philippe added. "Killed several officers."

"I warned you." His voice broke even though it was a whisper.

Zayne shuffled forward, his eyes brimming with tears.

He stood over the body and, after a moment, gave a slight nod.

The attendant peeled back the sheet.

Zayne audibly exhaled. He hadn't realized that he was holding his breath.

It wasn't Haidar.

Zayne blinked. "That's Ahmed Farooq. One of Haidar's men." His voice was dry, cracked.

Luc nodded. "From the warehouse?"

Zayne nodded, then motioned weakly. "The other ... is that my brother?"

The attendant folded the second sheet back.

Zayne stepped closer.

The room was silent. Only the low hum of refrigeration.

Zayne stared.

It was *Ilyaas*. His eyes were still open. A smear of soot on his cheek.

Zayne's knees buckled.

"Oh, *no!*" he bellowed. *"No, no, no …"*

"He wasn't … he just packed boxes. I kept him away. I thought I kept him away."

Luc went to help him up, but Zayne shoved him off.

"This life wasn't for him," he said. "Haidar knew that. He *agreed.*"

Philippe nodded to the guards, but before they could reach him, Zayne lurched to his feet—and bolted through the doors.

~ ~ ~

Zayne burst out of the front entrance.

The morning air was crisp and damp. The smell of dew was life-affirming.

It punched him in the stomach.

Zayne looked around. The hospital was embedded in a neighborhood, amid apartment buildings and street-level shops.

He gained his bearings, pulled the hood of his sweatshirt over his head, and started walking fast—then jogging. He followed the heavier foot traffic toward Avenue de Saint-Ouen. Minutes later, he saw where he needed to go: Guy Môquet station.

He took the stairs down two at a time. He bypassed the ticket machine and jumped the turnstile. Nobody seemed to notice, or care.

He stood on the platform for only a minute before the train screeched into view. Line 13. Northbound.

Zayne took a seat and tugged his hoodie lower. Across from him, a tired man in a reflective vest snored against the glass. A woman in a hijab cradled a sleeping baby.

He rode in silence, station after station: Garibaldi, Saint-Ouen, Mairie de Saint-Ouen.

A pair of eyes watched him in the window's reflection. When the train stopped, the eyes faded into a play of light: A trashcan against a wall; the station sign, and a broken light; an advert with different colors. When the train started again, the eyes would reappear, but in a different window.

It was a death stare.

It was Ilyaas.

When the train pulled into Saint-Denis—Université, Zayne stood, exhaled slowly, and stepped onto the platform.

~ ~ ~

The café was closed. Zayne tried the door anyway.

It was unlocked.

The bell above the door gave the familiar ring.

Zayne stepped inside.

It was dark. Quiet.

It took a moment for Zayne's eyes to adjust.

He spotted Haidar sitting at his usual table in the corner. He hadn't looked up when Zayne entered, despite the ringing of the bell.

He was hunched forward, elbows on his knees. His face was buried in one hand. The other dangled, a cigarette burning between his fingers. His eyes were fixed on the floor, unmoving. The ashtray on the table was full.

Zayne stood in the doorway, watching. He had never seen Haidar like this before.

He had been crying.

"Ilyaas is dead," Zayne said.

Haidar didn't react.

"But you already knew that."

Zayne took a step forward. Then another.

"You put him on that crew. He had no training."

Haidar still didn't look up. But he took a deep drag on what was left of his cigarette.

"You killed him. You killed your own son. *Why?*"

Now Haidar looked up at Zayne. His eyes—they were full of self-doubt. But they hardened and his face darkened. His lips turned up in a snarl.

"I *saved* him," Haidar whispered. "That … *kafir,*" he spat. "He died a *martyr.*"

Now it was Zayne's face that darkened.

He lunged at Haidar, tackling him where he sat. Both went sprawling to the floor, the table toppling over.

Zayne scrambled on top of Haidar and punched him in the face, repeatedly.

Haidar's hand reached for the ashtray that had fallen to his right. He gripped it as he tried to fend off Zayne with his left arm.

He brought the ashtray up and made solid contact with Zayne's cheek and temple.

Now Haidar was atop Zayne. He brought the ashtray down on Zayne's face again and again. Blood splattered.

Zayne had gone limp but Haidar didn't stop. He continued smashing the ashtray against Zayne's face.

Haidar slipped off of Zayne's body and sat with his back against the counter. He buried his face into his hands and wept.

After a long moment, he staggered to his feet and stumbled to the door.

He looked back.

Zayne's head lay in a growing pool of blood. His eyes stared blankly at the far wall.

Haidar turned and slipped out the door.

~ ~ ~

The rain had turned to drizzle. Steam rose from the asphalt. Neon signs reflected in the wet, foggy streets. Trinity Taylor stood in the middle of the avenue, arms outstretched, her *Trans for Iran* shirt clinging to her with rain and sweat.

She walked backwards, a rambunctious crowd before her.

"Say it proud, say it loud, gurls!" she roared.

"Trans for Iran!" the crowd shouted back. They were about thirty strong—mostly young, and mostly foreign. A few selfie sticks poked skyward. Rainbow flags, along with the flags of Iran and Palestine, waved in the night breeze.

Multiple rainbow hijabs stood out among them. The majority, including Trinity, had glitter-painted cheeks. Dua Lipa blasted from a portable speaker.

A French drag queen spun in a circle on rollerblades. A guy in a latex Ayatollah mask threw confetti. *Trans for Iran* glowed in projection on the side of a closed post office.

"Revolution is couture!" Trinity shouted, laughing and strutting down the street like it was a runway. "This is our moment, bitches!"

Laughter and applause permeated the raucous crowd.

Trinity spun for another selfie, pouting her lips and holding up a peace sign.

She was streaming live.

In her camera, she caught a pair of headlights moving *fast*.

She snapped her head around, still in her camera's eye. *There's a sassy look.*

The headlights went straight where the road curved and came straight at her.

~ ~ ~

He sat in his Range Rover Vogue. It was drizzling, then raining.

He had lost track of time. It was getting dark now.

He pulled into traffic. A horn blew.

The city was alive, and the traffic was heavy. It moved a few feet at a time.

But whoever kills a believer intentionally …

Traffic eased up and Haidar gunned it. He weaved through traffic, speeding up.

My brother.

Haidar gripped the steering wheel with both hands, still stained with blood, his knuckles turning white. *Why …*

Why did you become kafir, brother?

He was angry again. *Enraged.*

But then it fled as quickly as it had come.

His face broke.

He couldn't get the image of Ilyaas out of his mind.

My son.

"I *saved* him," he whispered. "I saved him."

But whoever kills a believer intentionally … Allah has prepared for him a great punishment.

His eyes fell on a cluster of flags ahead, all waving briskly in the evening air: Palestinian, Iranian, and … Rainbow.

Protesters.

He *hated* them. They had *nothing* to do with Islam.

He gripped the wheel and aimed straight for them.

"Grrrrrrrr …."

He jumped the curve and was briefly airborne.

Then it was like driving through a cornfield.

A blur of bodies and flags. The windshield spider-webbed and turned red.

"Allahu Ak—"

The Vogue slammed into a tree and came to an instant halt.

~ ~ ~

The wreck hissed.

Steam and smoke rose from the crumpled hood, mixing with the rain and fog.

Haidar was slumped against the airbag, blood running down his face. His door was twisted ajar.

Blood and sweat stung his eyes. He blinked slowly.

A leafy tree branch poked through the splintered windshield.

He couldn't feel his legs.

He tasted metal.

A man stepped up to his door and peered in. Haidar didn't understand. The man was wearing lipstick, a skirt, and a *Trans for Iran* t-shirt, though it was soaked and torn. Mascara ran down the man's face. He leaned forward, rain dripping from his jawline. His eyes showed concern, but then hardened.

"*Why*, motherfucker?" he asked.

Haidar blinked.

"*My son,*" he whispered. "*My broth*—."

Blood bubbled and gurgled out of his mouth and his eyes clouded over.

Lipstick-and-mascara man stared at Haidar's face for a moment, then turned away. Police had arrived.

"Don't bother," he said as the police approached the crumpled SUV, weapons drawn. "That fucker's dead, Fred."

CHAPTER FIFTEEN

A man stepped out of the steady downpour and entered the Spice Delight Indian Restaurant. Isaac watched him as he shook his umbrella and removed his hat.

He wasn't a large man, but he was compact. Solid. Bearded.

So far, it had been mostly young people who entered. A couple of older gentlemen had also entered, and an older couple—current or former faculty, Isaac presumed.

The bearded man scanned the room. He wasn't dressed in the staid fashion of a Harvard faculty member, though he was certainly old enough. He was fit and trim, but his lack of hair suggested middle age. He wore a hoodie.

The man locked eyes with Isaac and a flicker of recognition flashed in them.

Isaac rose and waived his hand.

"Professor Isaac Pfitzenmeyer?" the man asked as he approached.

Isaac nodded and extended his hand. "You pronounced it flawlessly. And you must be Mr. Walmsley."

Walmsley nodded with a smile and shook Isaac's hand with a strong, firm grip. "Call me Mack."

Sixty, or close to it, Isaac surmised now that he saw the man up close.

"Thank you for meeting with me," Mack said, as he took his seat.

Isaac replied with a side look. "Free food."

"Ha!" Mack laughed. "Spoken like a one-time graduate student."

"A *lifetime* student," Isaac corrected.

Isaac leaned back. A bright-eyed young waitress handed a menu to both Mack and Isaac. "May I get you something to drink?"

"Diet Coke," Mack ordered. "And a glass of pinot noir."

Mack looked at Isaac and smiled. "Don't judge me. I've never liked beer, not even when I was in the Navy. But, please, order what you like."

Isaac didn't know much about Mr. Mack Walmsley. Only what was listed on his personal website, where his novels were available for purchase.

He wrote war books and political thrillers. He was successful, obviously, because he was having lunch with Isaac to talk about funding a research project.

God, please don't let him be another rich crackpot with some harebrained idea that he wants to fund.

Isaac hadn't read fiction in years. He ordered a kosher pale ale from the local Remnant Brewing Company in nearby Somerville.

I was going to order one whether you liked it or not, Mr. Writer.

Mack picked up his menu as the waitress walked away, and Isaac followed suit.

"I love Indian food," Mack said. "I have to be careful, though. Can't have it every day. But what the hell, it's been a while."

Mack had intelligent eyes and a light demeanor that Isaac couldn't describe.

The waitress returned and took their orders, then departed again. They had time to talk.

"I have an idea for a research project," Mack said.

Yep. Here we go.

Isaac smiled and took a swig from his mug. He raised his hand as the waiter walked nearby. "May I have another?" he asked. His mug was still half full, but what the hell.

Mack ignored the disruption and continued. "I remember in college when my physics professor attached a hose to a can—a quart of olive oil. It was an air pump, and it sucked the air out of the can.

"The can crumpled. He told us not to think of the air pump as sucking the sides of the can inwards. Rather, it created a vacuum, and the air pressure in the classroom crushed the can."

Yeah, basic physics.

"Later, nanotechnology became a thing. Of course, it has really come into its own over the years."

You don't say.

"Anyway," Mack continued, "I've been on the lookout for something like barometric energy, and I haven't seen it."

Mack outlined his vision: a large dome-like structure—like a golf ball with 300 or more sides. "If a vacuum could be produced inside of the dome, barometric pressure would squeeze the dome, forcefully turning *billions* of nanogenerators to produce electricity."

Mack took a sip of his beer and shrugged.

"Potentially."

He leaned back in his chair.

"Tell me I'm crazy, and I'll go away," Mack said.

Isaac sipped his beer and placed the mug down. He looked at Mack, then stared over and past Mack's right shoulder with his eyes squinted.

Mack sipped his red wine while Isaac thought.

The moment lingered.

Mack sipped again.

The silence was beginning to grow uncomfortable.

"It isn't crazy," Issac finally offered, still looking off in thought. "Not entirely."

His eyes snapped back to Mack. "Let me run it by some people. I can get back to you in a couple of weeks. I can't promise anything, though."

"I thought you might laugh me right out of town," Mack said. He nodded at Isaac. "Of course, take as long as you need."

Isaac shook his head. That was three years ago.

~ ~ ~

The man shook Yahya awake.

They were at a gas station in the desert.

Another man opened Yahya's door and motioned him to a nearby truck.

Yahya looked to the chauffeur. He nodded.

Yahya climbed out of the Cadillac and stretched. He looked around. All desert.

Am I going to Gaza?

He climbed into the truck cab. The other man climbed into the driver's seat.

He smiled, revealing missing front teeth, and turned the ignition.

But he didn't speak.

~ ~ ~

The airstrikes were relentless.

The Marines held their ground into the afternoon.

But the "Indians" kept up their attack, despite being pummeled from the air.

Gene's phone buzzed. It was an "unknown caller."

"Hello?"

"How are you holding up, son?"

It was Daddy Longlegs.

"Sir, I can't thank you enough—"

There was a commotion among the Marines. A couple were pointing skyward.

Gene dashed to the wall, stepped on a crate, and peered over the edge.

His voice caught.

"Oh my God," he breathed into the phone. *"Sir, there are—there are paratroopers to our north."*

He gripped the wall. *"The whole sky is full of them."*

"That would be the Turks, son. They're our allies. Sit tight. Reinforcements are on the way."

~ ~ ~

Gene was starting to think that the reinforcements—if they ever made it into the city—were already too late. There were no more walled segments of the compound left to fall back to.

This was it. *The last stand.*

Worse—*could it really be any worse?*—gunfire had erupted in all directions. The whole city was joining the fight.

Gene laughed out loud when an image flashed in his mind. It was his gravestone with the words "Here lies the Great Hopes of Daddy Longlegs" inscribed on it.

The things that go through your mind.

I can laugh, he thought, *but I should cry.*

Then, silence.

Small arms fire still cracked in the distance, but it was softer and farther away.

Gene gripped his M4. Marines around him did the same. Their eyes were wide and alert.

The silence stretched.

This is it, Gene thought. *This is the End.*

"What are they doing?" a young Marine whisper shouted.

"Yeah," said another. *"What are they waiting for?"*

 More silence.

"Eh … someone, he name Gene, he here?"

What the hell?

A faint, electronic voice echoed through the courtyard. It was almost apologetic.

"Someone, eh … he name Gene … eh, he here?"

It was a bullhorn.

Marines exchange baffled looks at one another.

Someone looked back at Gene with wide eyes.

"Gene, I think they mean you."

~ ~ ~

Ari Benjamin was well versed in operations like this one. He had trained for it, even though the mission was on a scale unlike anything Israel—or any other country—had ever done. But it was something they had prepared for, regardless. No other people but the Jews would understand the necessity of thinking of—let alone preparing for—an operation such as this one.

There are some 450,000 Jews in France, making France the third-largest Jewish country in the world behind Israel and the United States. They are primarily concentrated in cities like Paris, Marseilles, and Lyon, with a smattering in Strasbourg and along the Mediterranean Coast. The Embassy of Israel in Paris and its Consulates in Marseilles and Strasbourg, and the Ministry of Foreign Affairs in Jerusalem, worked the last two days identifying and contacting as many Jews and Jewish households in France as they could.

It was all automated to make it efficient. Whoever answered their phones or read their texts received the same cryptic message in Hebrew, French, and English:

"The fear we always carry is upon us once again.

If your heart trembles, we are already beside you. Come as you are, come quietly.

A chariot awaits at the place of wings: in Paris, Marseille, Lyon, Strasbourg. Those who seek refuge will find it in the land of promise."

Mossad and *Sayeret Matkal*, Ari's own unit, monitored the news coming out of France with trepidation. Massive protests against the presumed use of atomic weapons by the United States in the Arabian desert had kicked off as soon as the sun peeked over the horizon.

But their communique seemed to have gotten through without alerting the French government. El Al were already reporting a surge at their gates.

Then came the news of pressure cooker bombs near the American Embassy. The American Embassy was adjacent to the Palais de l'Élysée, and on the other side of *that* was the Embassy of Israel.

Ground Zero. It was exactly where they were headed.

Mossad had agents on the ground. A daytime operation was obviously out of the question, but that was never a consideration anyway. Still, a range of routes were monitored, and no one had seen fit to abort the mission.

Then came reports of an Islamist vehicle attack on a pro-Iran rally in the evening. Just minutes, in fact, before their drop-dead decision time.

Decision time had come … and gone.

Ari and his team waited on the aircraft, watching the minutes tick away.

Ari's phone buzzed with a text message. It was one word.

Go.

~ ~ ~

Marc-André Delmas checked his watch. It was approaching eight o'clock in the evening. His stomach growled.

A few more minutes.

It had been a long day. Charles de Gaulle International Airport was on high alert ever since the news of the nukes in the UAE. As expected, protests had erupted across France, and both the DGSI and DGSE had issued warnings of likely terrorist threats.

France was now under an Elevated Alert—meaning a plausible risk of a terrorist attack. That meant more armed guards patrolling the airport, random bag checks, identity checks, and increased security in terminals and baggage claims.

It was a lot to oversee.

Marc's phone rang.

"Marc, I'm afraid I have some burdensome news to report." It was Augustin de Romanet, CEO of Groupe ADP, the company that owned Charles de Gaulle International Airport. De Romanet was Marc's boss.

"We've been ordered to raise our security profile to Emergency Alert. Something is happening. We must ground all aircraft, beginning at 3:00 a.m., for an hour or two. Also, effective immediately, any aircraft using the callsign of 'Olive' will be given authorization for takeoff without delay."

Marc was taking notes. His heart had picked up. *Something is happening.*

"Do you understand, Marc?"

"Yes, sir, I do."

"Thank you, Marc." De Romanet audibly sighed on the phone. "Marc, I hate to ask, but can you spend the night? I will need someone of your stature on site through the night. I know it's a lot to ask."

"No problem, sir. I'm happy to stay."

"Good, good, thank you, Marc. I knew I could count on you. I will keep in touch."

Marc hung up and stared at his desk for a moment. There was a lot to do.

But something was off. Mr. De Romanet sounded … *genuine.* Like an actual human being. Normally he was curt and pompous. In fact, never was he *not.*

Except now. *Something is happening,* he said. He seemed genuinely concerned. *I knew I could count on you, Marc.* What a change.

Marc had some phone calls to make.

~ ~ ~

Halfway up the ninety-one-story Spiral Tower—Tel Aviv's first super-tall skyscraper—were several floors officially rented to Kaplan Communications.

The floors housed server rooms, a high-powered computer laboratory, a supercomputer array, rows of high-tech workstations, and several state-of-the-art broadcast studios. Gaining access required an eye scan, a facial scan, and a thumb print—*all three.*

Kaplan Communications was not your typical telecommunications company. In fact, it wasn't a telecommunications company at all. Rather, Kaplan Communications was an off-site operations center for a specialized signals intelligence unit in Mossad.

And it had the best views of Tel Aviv and the Mediterranean of any Mossad office in Israel.

In one room, a young woman sat before a high-end condenser microphone and several monitors. Behind her, Tel Aviv stretched to the sea.

The room was cool and corporate. On the wall, three monitors pulsed with waveforms. The largest was labeled:

AUGUSTIN LINE – ACTIVE

The woman leaned toward the mic but kept her posture straight. She spoke into the microphone with a neutral tone. Her voice was smooth and crisp. She read from a teleprompter in French:

"Marc, I'm afraid I have some burdensome news to report…"

As she spoke, a real-time voice modulation engine reshaped her voice—lowered it, aged it, and added the nasal cadence of a Parisian technocrat. There was a delay, but it was practically imperceptible to anyone not trained to detect it.

The resulting voice was indistinguishable from Augustin de Romanet, CEO of Groupe ADP.

A technician to her right monitored the waveform comparison. Perfect match.

Another technician traced the signal route: a secure uplink, layered encryption, satellite bounce, and no metadata leakage.

"We must raise our security profile to Emergency Alert," the woman spoke. The conversation continued at a natural pace.

"I knew I could count on you. I will keep in touch."

When she finished, the operator lifted her hands from the desk, removed her headset, and turned to the team behind the glass. She smiled.

"Clean signal," said a technician.

"Speech confidence: 99.3 percent."

~ ~ ~

It was a BBJ. A Boeing Business Jet, courtesy of Mack Walmsley, founder and CEO of Walmsley Energy. He was in Tel Aviv for the grand opening of Israel's first Walmsley Dome barometric power plant when the Israeli government asked if they could borrow his private plane.

They didn't tell him what for, and he didn't ask. "Try not to wreck it, if you can help it," was his only response.

Le Bourget Airport, just four miles from Charles de Gaulle International Airport, was the premier private airport serving Paris. It was the obvious choice for a billionaire energy tycoon.

The plane was full of passengers, but the manifest was fake. All of the passengers were members of *Sayeret Matkal,* Israel's equivalent of the British Special Air Service. They were all in civilian attire, of course. Mostly stylish sweatsuits. They were the Israeli National Baseball Team, if anyone inquired.

Football—or soccer, as Americans called it—was out of the question. Too many people followed the sport. Baseball, on the other hand—who in France even knew what that was?

Multiple commercial buses awaited them. Ari didn't know who organized the buses or how. That was Mossad's territory, and *man* were they good at what they did.

Same for their sports bags. They were full of weapons. Somehow they were unloaded from the aircraft and loaded straight onto the buses.

Mossad. They were the hallmark of efficiency and professionalism.

The line of buses turned onto the A1, a highway with bridges and tunnels, in order to avoid commercial and residential roadways that might be blocked by protesters. Several drones operated by *somebody*—Mossad again, most likely—kept watch over the route.

The buses snaked their way down to the *Périph,* the Boulevard Périphérique, a beltway around Paris that was, likewise, a limited-access, high-speed freeway with multiple lanes, bridges, tunnels, and no cross traffic.

But there was no avoiding the Avenue des Champs-Élysées. Ari guessed that protesters would *most definitely* converge on the Arc de Triomphe along the Champs-Élysées, which the buses would pass.

The Arc de Triomphe was arguably the most famous landmark of Paris alongside the Eiffel Tower. The fact that it was late—it was approaching three o'clock in the morning—meant that the massive crowds of the day before would have petered out long ago.

That seemed to be the case. Traffic was extremely light, and there were no protesters. In fact, he didn't see any evidence that there had been mass protests at all. Perhaps they weren't concentrated along the Avenue des Champs-Élysées, after all.

The buses snaked around the Arc and continued to FDR Circle. There, they followed the circle before turning northeast. They stopped at the next street, blocking the entrance to a side road that was only two blocks from the Palais de l'Élysée, the official home of the French Prime Minister.

This was a tricky moment. The side road was closed off and manned by three armed French National Police.

Only three. Even after the previous day's events. *This is why we are here.*

Ari relaxed a little when he saw a familiar Israeli *Shin Bet* officer chatting with the guards. The officer waived and somehow seemed very relaxed.

Probably to downplay what was going on.

Sayeret Matkal soldiers in sweatsuits, armed with M4 commando rifles, disembarked from one of the buses and streamed into the Israeli Embassy. Still the Shin Bet officer continued chatting with the French officers—he even yawned.

Ari approached.

"Good morning, Abraham," said Ari.

Abraham nodded. "I was just telling these officers about the exercise."

"Ah, yes," Ari said, and now he yawned, too. "The exercise."

The flare of a cigarette in the darkness across the street caught Ari's attention. He stared intently. He could make out a trim man in a civilian coat.

The man tossed his cigarette and walked away.

CHAPTER SIXTEEN

They were crossing a border.

The toothless man was all smiles as he presented his passport and other papers—and an envelope discreetly tucked among the papers.

The border guard flipped through the papers and right past the envelope without acknowledging it.

He peered inside, first at the toothless driver, and then at Yahya.

He stared at Yahya for a long minute before handing everything but the envelope—which disappeared quickly into his pocket—back to the driver.

He waived the driver through.

~ ~ ~

Philippe Karcher was confused. Young men with sports bags disembarked from the buses and went inside the Israeli Embassy.

Philippe took a drag on his cigarette.

A man stared intently in Philippe's direction. He'd been the first one off the bus.

The cigarette.

You fucking amateur, Philippe scolded himself.

He flicked the cigarette away and started walking. He stayed in the shadows as best as he could.

Young men with sports bags. Fit young men.

Philippe stopped.

Israeli special forces?

Philippe looked back. A pair of headlights was leaving the Embassy. They turned in his direction.

Philippe stepped backward into a doorway. The car rolled past the end of the street where he stood, hidden in shadow. With nary a look, the car turned north.

Philippe sprinted for his car.

~ ~ ~

It didn't take long for Philippe to catch up. Traffic was light at this hour, so he had to be extra careful not to be seen. He stayed back as far as he dared, keeping the black Audi's tail lights just within view.

Philippe keyed his radio.

"Luc? I'm following someone. I need eyes on the embassy."

"Copy that."

"Whoever you send—make sure they are discreet. The embassy buses haven't moved yet."

"Understood."

The *Stade de France* loomed ahead. Philippe couldn't help but take his eyes off the Audi and behold the stadium. The whole structure—with its iconic stayed cable roof ringed by towering masts—was lit in shifting bands of color. Blues, purples, and ambers glowed against the night, bleeding into soft, fuzzy hues in the fog.

It was quite a sight.

Philippe followed the Audi around the stadium and it hit him—where the car was going.

Street signs soon confirmed it.

Charles de Gaulle Airport.

~ ~ ~

Philippe followed the Audi into the airport.

The Audi pulled curbside in front of the El Al terminal, and Philippe did the same, several yards behind. He watched the driver walk into the terminal.

Philippe took a deep breath—*Here we go*—and stepped out of his car. He walked briskly to the terminal doors, but then stopped.

Something wasn't right.

Whole families were converging on the terminal. Parents and children. Even grandparents. One family after another. They were ... *harried.* Some wore fear on their faces.

Philippe looked at his watch. It was after three in the morning.

He stepped inside.

It was pandemonium.

The front counter of El Al—Israel's national carrier—was overwhelmed.

Black-clad security guards in ski masks, armed with machine guns, checked a few passports and waived whole groups of people—obvious families—through.

Smaller groups and individuals, however, received more scrutiny. Even then, they were let through after cursory glances at their passports.

The rifles.

Philippe took a closer look. They weren't HK416s, the standard issue for French armed forces. They were American M4s.

Philippe's eyes swept the crowd. There were prayer shawls and yarmulkes. Hebrew was whispered among worried parents and grandparents.

They're all Jewish.

A line from the second message popped into his head.

Come as you are, come quietly.

What is going on?

Philippe thought better of flashing his badge to the security guards. Instead, he walked from the crowded El Al counters in search of a *regular* airport security guard, or someone who was obviously an airport employee.

He found two bored-looking guards at an empty screening line.

There was no screening line back there, Philippe realized.

Philippe showed his credentials. "Good morning, gentlemen. Can you tell me what's going on down there?" He nodded to the El Al counter.

"Don't know," one said. "We were told to stay away."

"Who told you to stay away?"

He shrugged. Then, nodding over Philippe's shoulder, "*He* did."

Philippe followed the guard's gaze. A man in a suit chatted with a woman concierge.

"Who is he?"

"The Airport Manager."

Philippe jogged over, thrusting his credentials out.

"Are you the Airport Manager?"

"I am," said the man. He squinted at Philippe's identity card.

"*DGSE?* Oh, thank goodness. Maybe you tell me what's going on."

Philippe was taken aback.

"You know," the man said, "about the situation."

"What situation?"

"Isn't that why you're here?"

Philippe shook his head.

"Listen Mister …"

"Delmas. Marc Delmas."

"… Delmas. You need to tell me what's going on here." Philippe put a hand on Marc's shoulder and pointed to the chaos at the El Al counters across the way. "Specifically, what is happening *there.*"

Marc blinked. "We're doing what you told us to do."

Philippe grabbed both shoulders.

"What the *fuck* are you talking about?"

~ ~ ~

Philippe and Marc stood at the glass wall overlooking the tarmac.

Ten wide-body passenger jets stood at the gates, each boarding in near silence. There were no overhead calls, no boarding groups, no announcements.

Airline attendants organized the families and passengers into multiple lines at each gate.

Families and passengers filled the air bridges. Security personnel flanked the doors. Airline staff wore no insignia. It wasn't just El Al. Some aircraft had no markings at all.

As soon as the allotted number of passengers stepped aboard, a plane sealed its doors and was pushed back without delay—even as passengers still waited in the air bridge. The moment one airplane cleared, another aircraft rolled in to replace it, and the next group filed aboard.

At almost every gate, a plane was either being pushed out or rolled in. Philippe had never seen anything like it.

A chariot awaits at the place of wings.

His mouth went dry.

Dear God. It's an evacuation.

No—an exodus.

Philippe fumbled for his phone.

"Wake up, Luc."

~ ~ ~

Luc pounded on the door.

He then stepped back, so the camera could see his face, along with the credentials that he was holding up.

"DGSE," Luc said. He gave an exaggerated smile for the camera.

After a pause, he heard the door unlock. It peeked open.

Augustin de Romanet stood in the gap, wearing silk pajamas and a scowl.

"What is this all about?"

"I need to ask you some questions."

"At this hour?"

Luc shrugged. "I'm here, aren't I?"

CHAPTER SEVENTEEN

Philippe and Marc-André Delmas sat outside an airport café, drinking coffee, watching the boarding gates in silence.

Philippe's phone buzzed. A text message. *Embassy buses are on the move.*

Luc arrived, walking briskly.

"Well?" Philippe asked.

Luc nodded grimly. "I just left de Romanet's place." He looked to Marc. "He never called you."

Marc blinked. "I *swear* it was him!"

Luc held up his hand. "Our agents are in your office as we speak. It's true. Your phone's log shows his number. But *his* phone's log shows no outgoing calls at that time. Someone spoofed his number—and his voice."

Marc sank into his chair. "Is that possible? I swear, it sounded just like him. Except …"

"Except what?"

Marc was embarrassed. He lowered his head. "He was nice to me."

Luc looked to Philippe and smiled. "Yeah, dead giveaway," he quipped. "I just met the prick."

Marc looked toward the tarmac.

"Thank you, Mr. Delmas," said Philippe. "You should return to your office. We'll contact you when needed."

"Uh … How will I know it's you?" Marc asked.

Oh, right on. Good question.

"We'll use a password that only the three of us know," said Luc.

"Good idea," said Marc. "What's the password?"

Luc smiled broadly. "How about … *'he was nice to me.'*"

~ ~ ~

Marc walked away briskly, head straight. Just like when Philippe had first spotted him.

He never looked back.

Luc pulled out a chair and sat with Philippe. "Now," he said, "can you tell me what's really going on here?"

Philippe took Marc's coffee cup and emptied it in a trash can before emptying his own. He then pulled a flask from his breast pocket, and poured Cognac into both cups.

"What is happening," Philippe said—taking a swig of Cognac—"is the evacuation of Jews from France."

"You mean, like, *all Jews?*"

"Those who want to," Philippe said. "If you're heart trembles, come quickly, come quietly." He was quoting the intercepted message.

Luc watched as more families boarded aircraft.

"What do we do?" he asked. "Do we call anyone? Do we call *everyone?*"

"We call no one," Philippe said.

There was a commotion at the front of the terminal. The embassy buses had arrived.

A new group of people, more families, poured into the terminal.

A man in a dark coat and baseball cap checked each group as they exited the buses. He ushered families to the guards in ski masks, who silently waved them forward.

A new aircraft pulled to the gate and an air bridge extended to it.

Luc glanced at Philippe, then nodded to the man in the baseball cap.

"Is that him?"

Philippe nodded slowly. "That's the man I followed from the embassy."

Luc watched as the man approached another bus, helped an older woman with her bag, and kept moving. There was purpose in his step, but nothing hurried. He didn't bark orders.

"Who is he?"

Philippe took another sip of Cognac.

"No idea."

Luc took a sip, too. "Looks like he's in charge."

The final bus arrived and discharged its passengers. A tall, silver-haired man and a woman—presumably his wife—were the last to step off.

"*He* looks familiar," Luc said.

"The Ambassador," Philippe noted.

The Ambassador shook hands with the man in the baseball cap, and the three of them walked to the gate.

The Ambassador and his wife embraced before she entered the air bridge. The Ambassador and the man in the baseball cap watched her go.

Baseball Cap looked to the armed guards. He whistled and twirled a finger in the air. The universal sign for *let's go.*

The armed guards jogged to the air bridge. The Ambassador and Baseball Cap watched them enter it.

Philippe approached.

The Ambassador and the man in the baseball cap turned and stopped.

Ari and Philippe stared at each other.

Philippe didn't know what to say.

Ari looked past Philippe and saw Luc.

Intelligence agents. High-ranking.

DGSE.

The Ambassador looked from Ari to Philippe to Luc, then back to Ari.

"Go," he said. Ari's eyes lingered on Philippe and Luc before he turned around and entered the air bridge.

The aircraft rolled away.

The Ambassador turned and faced Philippe and Luc.

"Gentlemen." He gave a nod and walked on.

Philippe and Luc watched as the Ambassador exited the terminal.

~ ~ ~

"Where is he going?" asked Luc.

"Back to the Embassy."

"I thought they just evacuated the Embassy."

"No," Philippe said. "They evacuated dependents."

He looked at Luc. "I saw a whole bunch of fit young men with duffle bags get off those buses at the Embassy—special forces, no doubt. Then they whisked dependents out on those same buses."

~ ~ ~

With the addition of the dependents of embassy personnel, the final aircraft—the BBJ that Ari and the airport *Sayeret Matkal* soldiers had just boarded—was crammed.

The mood on the aircraft was almost jubilant. Ari didn't breathe easy yet, though. He wanted to be airborne.

With everyone in seats or on the floor, they seemed to be waiting.

Ari went to the cockpit and inquired.

"Just waiting our turn," the pilot reported.

There were still several El Al aircraft taxiing ahead of them. One by one, they reached the headway, turned, and roared down the runway, lifting off into the night sky.

Three more to go.

It felt so slow.

Ari took long deep breaths to calm himself.

Their time came. Finally. The BBJ turned into position, its engines rising in pitch.

Through the cockpit windows, Ari spotted police lights in the distance. A lot of them. *Were they coming to the airport?*

He thought of the two intelligence officers in the terminal.

Let's not find out.

"Get us out of here, Captain," he ordered. He slapped the pilot on the back. "What are they going to do, shoot us down?"

The pilot shrugged. "They *might.*"

~ ~ ~

It took an hour. And for Ari, it was the most intense hour of the mission thus far.

They had reached the Mediterranean. The final aircraft with a callsign of Olive.

The sky was still dark, but the sea shimmered under the moon.

The pilot kept an eye on the aircraft's GPS. After a few more minutes, he nodded silently.

Ari took a deep breath, then exhaled slowly. "May I?" he asked.

The pilot grinned. "By all means."

Ari keyed the mic.

"Jericho, Jericho, Olive Gallia 1. We are no longer among the nations."

The mic was patched to the cabin, Israeli air traffic control, and to all of the planes ahead of them bearing the Olive callsign.

The cabin erupted in applause.

Another transmission followed:

"Jericho, Jericho, Olive Belgica 1. We are no longer among the nations."

Then another:

"Jericho, Jericho, Olive Germania 1. We are no longer among the nations."

The cabin applause turned to subdued reflection.

There were others.

Then …

"To all Olive flights—Gallia, Belgica, Germania. This is Jericho. Though you were scattered, you are gathered again. *Baruchim ha-ba'im.*"

Passengers erupted with renewed joy.

The pilot scanned the sky from the cockpit window.

There they were—two sets of blinking lights swooping down from the blackness above. A moment later, two IAF F-35 Adir stealth fighters pulled alongside, wingtip to wingtip, like sentries. One to port, one to starboard. Sleek silhouettes keeping pace with the BBJ.

He had been told to expect them.

The pilot pointed out the fighters to Ari.

"We've got angels."

~ ~ ~

It was only a few minutes before they entered the first town on the other side of the border.

It was definitely not Gaza.

Yahya wasn't the best at geography, but he knew enough: desert, the time it took to get here, and the fact that they weren't in Gaza meant only one other place: *Libya.*

The driver pulled into a gas station.

He smiled his toothless grin at Yahya and motioned for him to stay.

Is everyone mute around here?

A boy climbed in, smoking a cigarette. He was maybe twenty, and slight of build.

"Dr. Yahya!" the boy exclaimed, excited.

The boy started the ignition and threw the truck into drive.

"Welcome to Libya! How was your trip?"

Libya. Like I thought.

"I am Nizar al-Zahar," he said. The kid extended a hand and drove with the other while a cigarette dangled from his lips.

Yahya reciprocated and the boy shook his hand emphatically—he even took his other hand off the wheel and shook Yahya's hand with both hands, a cloud of smoke enveloping his head.

The truck lurched into the other lane, forcing the kid to put his hands back on the wheel.

He laughed.

"I am your mechanic," he said.

The kid was an endless well of enthusiasm.

"I am your *Scotty,*" he said. "You know, *Star Trek!*"

Yahya's face was blank.

"You're Captain Kirk, and I'm the mechanic—*Scotty!*" the kid said.

The kid was exhausting. Yahya found himself yearning for the silence of his two previous drivers.

So. I'm the captain …

"Oh," Nizar said, "I almost forgot." He reached under his seat and drifted into the oncoming lane again before snapping back—and produced an envelope. He had barely avoided a head-on collision with another truck, which blew its horn as it passed.

The kid seemed oblivious to their almost fiery deaths. He handed the envelope to Yahya.

It was full of cash—American dollars and Egyptian pounds. A few Libyan dinars—and a passport.

Yahya opened the passport. It was Libyan and it had his photo. *How in the world?*

A card dropped out. Yahya picked it up.

It was a note:

"The sea awaits its engineer. Your work will echo in the capitals of the West. Welcome to the jihad." — The Commander

CHAPTER EIGHTEEN

Alain Bordeaux stood just inside *Synagogue de la Victoire*, the historic Grand Synagogue of Paris. He watched Claudia make her way down the aisle and settle on a bench in a center row near the front. She wiped her eyes. She opened her sister's Tehillim, her leather bound and worn Book of Psalms. It still carried her sister's scent.

She dabbed her eyes again and turned a page. She swayed gently and prayed silently.

Alain smiled. He still vividly remembered the sarcastic young woman who had stolen his heart and never given it back. That was sixty years ago, yet his heart—the real, anatomical one, still beating in his chest—sped up at the memory like it was yesterday.

A tear fell on the Tehillim. Claudia was the younger of the two, at 78. So her sister's passing wasn't entirely unexpected, but it was sudden all the same.

Alain removed his hat and pulled out a neatly folded kippah from his inside coat pocket. He looked at it before he slipped it on, and smiled. It was the very first gift from Claudia when they had first started dating all those years ago. She had knitted it herself. It was a little frayed now, but only a little. Alain had always taken good care of it.

Alain took a seat in the last row of chairs. Claudia might be awhile. He broke out his phone. He and Claudia did their best to keep up with technology; in fact, it was a point of pride on Alain's part. He was a long retired electrical engineer who'd been involved in developing the wireless software and hardware that would, in time, become the modern infrastructure undergirding the world's telecommunications technologies.

Alain and Claudia had taken the bus straight from the hospital to *La Victoire*. It was almost noon.

As they made their way to *La Victoire*, the bus had filled up quickly. They weren't regular commuters. It was too late in the morning for that. The other passengers were men and wome—no, they were *entirely* men—of North African descent.

There wasn't a woman in sight.

Some of the men were even dressed in traditional garb: djellabas, kufis, or thobes.

There wasn't much conversation on the bus, and the men, young and old, stole hard glances at the elderly couple. There was definitely a tension. Alain could feet it. Claudia, though, was in a daze. Her mind was entirely on her sister.

The bus reached their stop on Rue La Fayette. Getting off was slow-going because the street was packed with people streaming toward *Le quartier de l'Élysée*, the political center of France.

Alain understood now. The full bus, the packed street.

Something was cooking off.

They turned off the crowded boulevard and walked a quiet block to *La Victoire*. Alain kissed his fingers and brushed the mezuzah on the door post. He held the door open for Claudia. She, too, kissed her fingers and tapped the mezuzah before stepping inside.

As Claudia prayed, Alain checked the news. He hadn't checked his phone in over a day. When he saw the headlines, he bolted upright.

~ ~ ~

Once again, President Jacques Michelet stood beneath the warm lights of luxuriant chandeliers in the regal Salle des Fêtes.

The podium was flanked by the French tricolor and the EU flag. Cameras clicked. Reporters leaned forward.

The President of the Republic stepped to the microphone. Behind him stood Philippe Karcher, Luc Morel, and Michel Renard. All three stood motionless, offering an image of unity. None of them spoke.

"To the citizens of France and our friends abroad," the President began, "last night, French security services successfully disrupted a major terrorist network operating in Paris."

A ripple of flashes lit the room.

"Several associates of the known radicals Haidar and Zayne Awada have been taken into custody. Haidar Awada carried out last night's cowardly vehicular attack on a LGBTQ+ rally—" the President paused and looked down at his notes "—killing six."

He looked back to the cameras.

"This was a particularly heinous act, targeting an already vulnerable population. Haidar himself was killed in the attack. His brother Zayne was found dead as police closed in."

"Additional members of the Awada network were found in possession of explosives, automatic weapons, and encrypted communications referencing attacks on state institutions.

"They were responsible for the bomb attacks on our police yesterday morning.

"This is a victory," he said. "A victory for our security services, and for the rule of law."

President Michelet turned around and thanked, one by one, Philippe, Luc, and Michel. Members of his staff, standing off to the side, applauded, as he shook their hands.

He returned to the podium.

"Unfortunately, we must also speak of betrayal."

A pause.

"Last night, the State of Israel carried out a clandestine evacuation of a large number of French citizens of Jewish descent. Without coordination. Without notice. In violation of every diplomatic norm."

He let the words hang.

"Multiple aircraft—some commercial El Al jets, others privately chartered—operated out of French airports overnight. These flights were not coordinated with our government. They did not seek clearance. This was a unilateral extraction—executed without our knowledge, and certainly without our consent."

The flashes intensified.

"This was a unilateral act of fear. An abandonment of dialogue. And it sends a false and dangerous signal: that Jews are no longer safe in France."

"And this was not limited to France. Similar unauthorized evacuations of Israeli diplomatic personnel and Jewish citizens occurred last night in Belgium and Germany. Aircraft departed in silence, under the radar, from European capitals."

He looked to the cameras now.

"This was coordinated. This was deliberate. And it sends a message— one that we reject: that Europe is no longer a safe home for its Jewish citizens."

He straightened at the podium.

"In France, we are not defined by our differences. We are united by the Republic. That is the meaning of *laïcité*. We do not sort our citizens into tribes. We do not negotiate with fear. And we do not accept the idea that any group must flee our soil to be safe."

Behind him, Luc remained still. Philippe looked down. Michel Renard blinked once, slowly.

The President ended with a practiced softness:

"France is not broken. France is not divided. France endures."

~ ~ ~

Two hours had passed by the time Claudia said her final prayer and stood.

Alain stood and grunted. He had grown stiff. He stretched his back slightly, then shook first his left leg, then the right, to loosen up.

He stuck out his elbow as Claudia approached, and she slipped her arm in. She smiled. He could see that she was at peace now. At least a little.

They walked slowly into the lobby. At the door, Claudia looked back and gazed at the Ark in the front of the synagogue. "Baruch Hashem," she said, softly. *Blessed is God.* Alain looked to the Ark and nodded.

They stepped through the synagogue doors and into the daylight. Alain paused. The street was quiet. He removed his kippah and donned his hat.

There was a low roar. It wasn't traffic. It was something else. The air was hazy and acrid with smoke.

Alain guided Claudia north this time. He did not want to go back the way they had come. Not with those crowds. Instead, he led Claudia toward Gare Saint-Lazare, one of Paris' main train stations. It was its first, in fact, and opened in 1837.

The station was several blocks away, but Alain hoped to snag a taxi.

Claudia gasped when they reached the next high street over. Alain gripped Claudia's arm tighter and pulled her close. Thousands—*tens* of thousands—filled the width of the street, stretching as far as the eye could see.

They were marching and chanting. Alain and Claudia were swept along.

"Death to America!"

"Death to the Jews!"

Claudia clutched her sister's Tehillim to her chest.

Alain had hoped that he and Claudia would be home before dark. But the dark, it seemed, had come early.

"Let's go inside," Alain whispered, searching for an open store, but Claudia couldn't hear him. And all of the shops were closed.

Then he saw it: the elaborately ornate belfry of the iconic *Église de la Sainte-Trinité*, rising high above the street. It loomed over the buildings.

It was only a block away.

We'll take shelter there. They will take us in.

Alain gripped Claudia's arm even tighter and carefully navigated them across the street.

But as they approached the church, another stream of marchers spilled in from the north, joining the swell along Châteaudun.

Now Alain and Claudia had to go against the flow, if only for a few yards.

They made it across, but not without drawing attention.

"Come, Claudia." Alain was breathless now. His heart pounded.

They climbed the stairs.

It was difficult. Alain's back ached. His knees were unsteady. Claudia took *his* arm now, and led him up the final few steps.

They reached the top. Alain rested his hands on his knees to catch his breath. He looked back.

The church had captured some of the crowd's attention.

A group of bearded men stood at the base of the steps, watching. Then they started up.

Alain stood and grabbed the church door handle.

It didn't budge. The door was locked. There would be no refuge here.

"Oh," Claudia muttered.

Alain turned around. He pulled Claudia behind him to shield her from the men coming up the steps.

The men were nearly upon them. One, a burly man with a bushy black beard, gripped something long and shiny in his right hand. With a sweep of his arm, he slashed Alain from hip to shoulder.

For Claudia, time stood still.

"Alain!" Claudia cried. Alain looked to the sky. He hadn't felt anything, but then he felt everything all at once.

His body stiffened and he stood ramrod straight. He swayed for a moment, then tipped over forward—slowly, like a tree—and fell long and hard onto the concrete steps.

Cheers erupted. *"Allahu akbar!"* they cried. *"Allahu akbar!"*

Claudia stared at Alain's prone body. A river of blood flowed from beneath Alain's head and body down the church steps. He didn't move. He was most certainly dead, she knew.

"Oh," she moaned, and crumbled to her knees.

The burly man stepped forward and cast a shadow over her.

Claudia looked up. The man sneered at her.

A calmness came over her. "I pray for you," she said. Claudia kissed her sister's Tehillim and brought it to her chest. She closed her eyes and whispered a prayer. "Into your hands I entrust my spirit." She swayed slightly as she prayed.

The man raised his machete high over his head and began hacking.

~ ~ ~

"I thought the terrorist cells were broken up," JC shouted.

Bof shrugged. "Did you forget about the nukes?"

"Yeah, yeah," JC said. "Guess everyone's still a tad pissed about that."

"Yeah, but *we* didn't have anything to do with it," Reka said.

Bof's unit was repositioned to Saint-Denis, in District 93. Protesters had nearly overrun the main precinct the day before. In fact, the National Police abandoned one of their smaller precincts, and it was set on fire.

Helicopters hovered overhead. Reka operated her drone, which buzzed at rooftop level.

It was early afternoon, and full-fledged unrest was underway again: chanting, sirens, cars flipped over, buses on fire. Firecrackers popped at odd intervals like distant gunshots.

Riot police—CRS and BAC units—were positioned at key intersections and squares. They were ready this time.

At least they *thought* they were.

Water cannons kept the rioters, wielding rocks and bottles, at a distance.

"Whoa, what was that?" Reka shouted. As she turned the drone, a shockwave washed over them with a *BANG*. At the same time, an armored car erupted in a ball of fire.

Bof and JC had no idea what had just happened. It was two blocks away.

"What the hell, Reka! What was that?" JC shouted.

Reka looked up from the controls. "I … I think it was an RPG."

~ ~ ~

Bof tilted his head. He hadn't heard *that* before. That is, not since his stint in the Army thirty years ago.

That's … automatic gunfire.

He looked to JC. JC's eyes were large.

"Reka," Bof demanded, *"where is that coming from?"*

Reka pointed.

JC was already pulling Bof by the sleeve. "We need to *move*. That's just up from the old precinct."

But it was too late.

The next burst came louder. It was sustained. It echoed through the hemmed-in street. Return fire followed, but it was much shorter.

Handguns.

Entirely outmatched.

Reka's drone banked over the rooftops. "Oh no," she whispered.

"What?" Bof barked.

"They're storming the station. I see at least a dozen—body armor, AKs, RPGs. They've got heavy gear, Bof."

There was another explosion, this one much closer than the first. A squad car flipped in the air and crashed back to the ground upside down, smoke curling like a ribbon into the sky.

"Bof," Reka pleaded. "There's an armory in there, in the station."

"Merde," JC shouted. *"We're not equipped for this!"*

Reka and JC started running. They ditched their riot shields and gripped their Glocks. Bof hesitated for a beat, then followed.

Bof looked back. Behind them, automatic fire ripped through the street. A National Police line had been there minutes ago. Now it was gone. A CRS unit fell back in disorder, dragging a bleeding officer with them.

~ ~ ~

Bof's lungs burned.

JC cursed every few steps. Reka said nothing, clutching her tablet to her chest like a sacred relic.

Only when they reached a quiet, elevated side street overlooking the square did they stop. Bof collapsed behind a stone planter. JC stood hunched over, hands on his knees, taking deep breaths. He was still cursing, between breaths.

Reka knelt and flicked the drone control back to manual.

She pushed it higher, past a rooftop clothesline, and swooped it over the smoking police station.

The drone feed stabilized. She hovered over the main courtyard of the precinct, which she could barely see through the smoke. She maneuvered to a better view point.

"There," she whispered.

Militants cheered. So many of them were dressed in black.

Ninjas. That's what Bof called them yesterday.

Bof and JC hovered over Reka's screen.

Ninjas fired rifles in the air. A couple of seconds later, their sound—a distant, sustained popping—reached them.

A few men appeared on the roof of the precinct. They held their rifles up in celebration. One held a black fabric in his hand.

"What is that?" Reka asked.

He hoisted it high and anchored it into the antenna.

It was a flag, they realized.

A moment later, a black flag with a five-pointed white star in the center, snapped in the wind above the police station.

"They have the District," Bof whispered.

Reka exhaled—but only for a moment.

One of the militants on the roof saw the drone. He pointed and shouted down to the street.

The crowd cheered and flashed the V sign to the drone. Some held up a middle finger.

The crowd began to part. Authoritative men with beards came out of the station, pushing people away, creating an opening in the square.

Behind them, two more men emerged. They dragged a bloodied officer by the collar. His uniform was torn. One arm hung limp.

JC groaned. "Oh, no…"

A burly man with a bushy black beard stepped forward. He looked up to the drone and smiled.

"Is that …?" JC asked, but his voice trailed off. He didn't need to complete his thought. All three had seen the video from the day before.

It's the same man that murdered that elderly Jewish couple yesterday, isn't it?

The man forced the officer to kneel, shouted something to the crowd, and drew a long blade.

"Reka," Bof said. "Cut the feed."

But she didn't.

The drone held steady as the man lifted the officer's head by the hair and raised the blade for all of France to see.

And then—

Reka dropped the tablet.

JC turned away. Bof closed his eyes.

It happened so fast.

A moment passed, and Reka whispered: "They wanted us to see it."

CHAPTER NINETEEN

"They ran," he said.

President Michelet paced.

"First their embassy. Then their—" he threw his hands up, searching for the word—"*exodus*. They even faked my civil aviation chief's voice to reroute Air France security. Mossad, Shin Bet—whoever they were."

Silence.

Michelet continued. "And by running, Israel confirmed every dark fantasy of the Salafists. It gave them their *justification*."

General de Bois shifted uncomfortably. "With respect, sir—"

"I will not send tanks into Saint-Denis," Michelet snapped. "There will be no Gaza in Paris."

"But sir," said his interior minister, "if this spreads further—"

"It already has," interrupted Philippe. "Reports just in from Brussels—whole sectors of Molenbeek and Schaerbeek have fallen. Antwerp is teetering."

Michelet waived his hand. "Let Belgium take care of Belgium."

"They're asking for NATO assistance," Philippe added.

The president exhaled heavily and sat. "This is all quite absurd, you know." He looked around the table. "These men in black with their Kalashnikovs and slogans? They're two-bit gangsters who got lucky.

The RPGs came from some depot in the Balkans or Libya—Philippe, *that's* where your focus should lie. Not … *Belgium,"* he snorted.

General de Bois started to protest, but Michelet held up a hand.

"I'm not underestimating them," the President said. "But they cannot hold what they've taken. Not for long."

He leaned forward.

"We lay siege. Like in the old days. Cut off the roads, the electricity, the signal towers. Let them stew in their own righteousness as they starve. And we wait them out."

A pause.

"Sir—" it was Philippe again—"every minute this *Caliphate* holds out, it is a symbol of defiance. It will serve as some twisted inspiration. And it is coordinated. It's happening in Belgium, Ger—"

"Enough with Belgium!" the President exploded.

"Sir—" it was General du Bois' turn, but Michelet held up his hand.

"Stop it. There will be no Army. This is a police matter."

The General bristled. The room grew awkwardly quiet.

"We smashed the Awadis, didn't we?" the President said. "And we'll smash these clown gangsters."

A young aide entered the room and placed a red folder marked "CON-FIDENTIEL" in front of the President. He opened it.

His face reddened.

"What do you think it is?" whispered Philippe. Michel Renard, his counterpart at DGSI, was standing next to him. He had been silent the whole time.

Michel leaned back toward Philippe's ear and whispered.

"A third arrondissement in Marseille has fallen."

~ ~ ~

It was worse than that. When Michel Renard returned to DGSI's headquarters at the 84, reports were coming in by the minute. A synagogue in Lyon was set ablaze. A Jewish cemetery in Strasbourg was defaced. As the day wore on, multiple synagogues across France were defaced or vandalized. Several kosher markets in Paris and Marseille were targeted by angry crowds and pelted with rocks. At least one was set on fire.

Philippe Karcher fielded similar reports at Fort Neuf, but these were from across Europe: Mainly Belgium, Germany, and the United Kingdom. In London, crowds pelted a Jewish school. The British Prime Minister declared a Tier 3 State of Emergency, deployed thousands of police, and placed its armed forces on alert.

In Germany, American stores and fast-food restaurants were also targeted: McDonald's and Starbucks pelted with rocks, and stores like Apple looted. The hardest hit cities with attacks on Jewish and American cultural centers and businesses were Frankfurt, Cologne, and Hamburg.

~ ~ ~

"Mr. Vice President," French President Jean Michelet spoke. "It is always a pleasure to hear from you."

Of all the times I have to field a phone call from the American Vice President.

A pause.

"Ah, Mr. President, same here—whatever the circumstances."

Circumstances? Here we go.

"I imagine you are referring to the protests in Paris and Marseilles, Mr. Vice President."

"Yes, it's true. I must say, the news we are receiving on this side of the pond is quite disturbing. And we saw your address. My President has asked me to reach out to you and offer any assistance you require."

"I thank you, Mr. Vice President—and please pass along my gratitude to President Belle. But rest assured that everything is under control. As you know, protests and demonstrations—even those that become a little turbulent are … how do you say? … a 'national pastime' in France."

"Oh, I don't know, Mr. President. We're seeing Jews slaughtered on the steps of a church in the middle of the day. A kosher market has been burned to the ground. I've lost count of how many synagogues have been burned or vandalized. You've got a goddamn *Kristallnacht* on your hands! And a whole district of Paris has been taken over by Islamists calling themselves the Islamic Caliphate of Europe. No wonder Israel is evacuating any Jew who wants to leave. Can you blame them? *Turbulent* is an understatement, don't you think?"

Michelet seethed.

"Our police and special investigators are working diligently to maintain order in Paris and beyond."

There was an unmistakable edge to his voice.

"Well, like I said," Daddy said. He spoke softer now. "We are ready to stand with our longstanding ally. Please don't hesitate to call us."

"Yes, yes, of course—thank you so much for your call."

The line went dead. Daddy put the receiver down in his Compass Room and ran a hand through his hair.

Fucking idiot.

In the Élysée in Paris, President Michelet shook his head. His face was red with anger.

Fucking idiot.

Daddy took out his satellite phone and looked for a contact. *There.* He hit call.

"Commander, it's Daddy Longlegs. Do you have any contacts in the French military?"

~ ~ ~

General Pierre du Bois sat in his office reading the latest reports from the DGSI and the DGSE.

If he was going to be exiled to the Hexagone Balard—France's equivalent of America's Pentagon—he was going to be as well informed as he could manage.

His encrypted cell buzzed. No number.

"General du Bois," he answered, his voice gruff.

"General," a strangely familiar voice spoke. "George Wartmann here—Vice President of the United States."

The General sat up.

He was too shocked to respond right away.

"Tell me, General, what the fuck is wrong with your President?"

Du Bois chuckled and leaned back in his chair.

"I imagine the same as what's ailing *your* President, Mr. Wartmann."

"Fair enough, General," Daddy said. "Fair enough. I'm working on that, though. But whatever *you* need to do to ensure the safety and security—and the *stability*—of France, of *Europe*—you've got the full backing of the government of the United States of America. Understand?

"And whatever it is you need to do, make it quick, will you? I can't have Europe unraveling while I'm still picking America up off the floor."

The line went dead.

The General made a quick phone call.

"Karcher. I need to see you. *Right now.*"

~ ~ ~

Three years, twenty publications, and several million dollars of funding after Mack Walmsley met Isaac Pfitzenmeyer at the Spice Delight in Cambridge, Isaac saw Lin Chen hovering near his office door.

Isaac sat with his feet on the desk of his laboratory office, reading glasses resting on the tip of his nose, as he underlined passages in an article in the latest *Advanced Materials* journal.

Lin Chen, a PhD student, was one of the team leaders of what they called "the Walmsley Project."

"What have you got, Lin?" Isaac asked.

"Sorry to interrupt. We think you should see."

Isaac looked at Lin over the bridge of his glasses. Lin had never before come to his office unsolicited.

Isaac was intrigued.

He grunted and swung his legs off the desk.

The team had built a thirty-two-sided dome, which took up a large portion of the warehouse space. Its sides were cartridges with a plastic outer shell and padding on the other side. Between the outer shell and the padding was a cushion of liquid filled with nanoturbines. The students manually operated an air pump by turning a crank. Once the air pressure inside the dome dipped below a certain threshold, the room's air pressure caused thousands of nanoturbines inside the cartridges to spin.

A chord led from the makeshift dome to a chandelier dangling from a stand.

The apparatus seemed promising, according to Lin, but they kept blowing out lightbulbs until they rigged a surge protector that could absorb or deflect enough power to keep the bulbs from blowing out.

The surge protector kept growing in capacity until it worked.

The team demonstrated the setup. One student cranked until the sound of popping was heard and, simultaneously, a red light came on, indicating that the determined psi was reached.

The chandelier lights burned bright.

Isaac had already seen this a few weeks earlier. But now there were *two* domes, and they appeared to *breathe*. One dome's cartridges, or panels, expanded outward while the other dome's panels sunk inward, and they would switch when they simultaneously reached their zeniths and troughs.

That was new.

Meanwhile, the lights continued to burn. Before, the lights went out when the single dome had fully collapsed inward. They would have to let air back into the cartridges and start over again. So the lights would burn only after the dome's cartridges were re-inflated.

Now, however, air bled from the sinking cartridges of one dome to the sunken cartridges of the other, re-inflating it. Then they'd switch again in a continuous loop.

The new setup produced enough relative energy that it required a hefty surge protector.

While I'll be damned.

Isaac walked around the contraption, examining it from all sides.

It works.

"Write it up," Isaac ordered. "ASAP. Show your work. I want to see *everything.* "

~ ~ ~

Harvey backed the truck up slowly. The crew began to unload the Amex ammonium nitrate mixture. Holes had been drilled a couple of days before, and now they were ready to blow a segment of the quarry's exposed bedrock.

The men went to work passing along the tube-shaped bags, and slipping them into the holes. It was a young man's job. Harvey chipped in when he could, but he was currently "on the IL"—as they say in baseball. His back hadn't recovered from the last time he chipped in.

He chatted while the men worked.

"I saw in the news that Israel was evacuating Jews from Europe. *Sheesh.* Can you believe that?"

The men continued passing bags and slipping them into the holes.

"I mean, who they are kidding? Right? They claim *victimhood* while massacring Palestinians. They've got Longlegs in their pocket, you know."

"*That* guy," Harv continued. He shook his head. "*War* criminal."

No one said a word. They just worked.

CHAPTER TWENTY

As the ship pulled out of Haifa, Gérard and Élise Valette watched the Israeli coast fade into the horizon.

Their feelings were mixed. They were enjoying a ten-day cruise that they had looked forward to for several years.

It was a celebration of their thirtieth Anniversary. They visited Barcelona, Mallorca, and Palermo. They were in Palermo when news broke of Iran's missile attacks on America.

But it was so far away. It barely registered in their minds.

Then came news of the nuclear bombs outside Dubai. *Now* things felt weird. The world burned while they cruised in opulence. They didn't want the cruise to end, but they were also eager to return home.

And now the news from France: the terrorist attacks, the unrest. The seizing of arrondissements by Islamists.

They weren't sure they wanted to go home.

~ ~ ~

Yahya looked to Nizar. The skinny kid had, indeed, proved to be an able mechanic.

And Nizar was more than a mechanic. He was Yahya's right hand. Whatever he needed, Nizar got it. Yahya needed laborers. *Reliable* laborers—not slackers and not zealots. Nizar found them.

And what had first appeared to be rusted fishing trawlers, boats that would likely sink the moment they entered open waters—now belched smoke and *growled* when he turned the ignition.

One by one, the boats hummed to life.

Nizar, watching from the dock, stepped aboard.

All of the barrels were in place and sturdy on each of the trawlers.

Everything was ready.

"Give the order," Yahya said. *"Ustadh Scotty,"* he added.

Nizar's head snapped up.

Ustadh. Master.

It was a title of respect.

And … *Scotty.* He remembered.

Nizar beamed and straightened. He pointed to the sea.

"Engage!" he shouted, smiling.

The four fishing trawlers filed out of Derna Harbor and into the open waters of the Mediterranean Sea.

~ ~ ~

The sea glowed copper. It was the last of the day's light. Night swirled.

Gérard Valette leaned against the promenade rail, his wine glass resting against the heel of his palm.

Three rust-streaked trawlers drifted just above the line of shimmer.

"Look at them," he said softly.

Élise sat in a lounge chair with a shawl wrapped around her shoulders, reading a novel on her ebook. She looked up.

"The boats," Gérard said, pointing. "Out there. They look like something out of a painting."

Élise put the book down and pulled up alongside him.

"Beautiful," she said. Then she closed her eyes and tilted her head, listening to the string quartet playing Fauré's *Pavane* nearby. The graceful melody floated across the deck like a breeze over still water.

"Ouch," she said, her eyes still closed.

"What?"

"One of the violinists played a sharp on the E."

Gérard smiled. "I don't think anyone noticed."

"*I* did." She opened her eyes and gave him a faux-stern look. "You always say I'm too generous with my students. I think you've grown soft."

"Just old," he replied, and kissed her forehead.

One of the trawlers lurched forward, passing in front of the cruise ship. Gérard lost sight of it and turned back to the other two.

After a moment, the two remaining trawlers also maneuvered past the bow before disappearing from view.

"They're charming," Élise said.

Gérard nodded. "It's peaceful."

He took a sip of his wine.

The sun met the sea.

A long, low metallic groan echoed beneath them. It wasn't loud, but it drew out like a bow too long on a string.

It was dissonant.

Élise flinched.

Gérard turned to her.

"That sound," she said, frowning. "Did you hear it?"

"What sound?"

The deck lurched, as if the ship had struck a submerged rock. Glasses slid off tables. Behind them, a waiter dropped a tray. Gasps rippled across the promenade.

"Ladies and gentlemen—" a voice crackled over the intercom. "We are experiencing a minor—"

Another lurch, this one sharper.

"Oh!" Élise gasped. She almost fell, but Gérard held her with one arm while gripping the railing with the other.

The ship's lights flickered twice and went out.

Then came the screaming as the deck buckled.

A third impact.

This one was heavier yet, and deeper.

People fell. Beverage glasses and dishes shattered all across the promenade.

The pool sloshed back and forth, spilling water onto the deck.

A plume of smoke burst upward from ahead and below, carried on the wind. The sharp scent of burning metal hit their noses—acrid and chemical, like scorched wiring and engine oil.

"It's a bomb!" someone shouted.

Élise coughed, waving smoke from her face. "What's happening?"

Gérard had no words. He just held her.

All around them, chaos reigned. Passengers stumbled over deck chairs. The string quartet instruments were abandoned. An older man lay motionless, bleeding from his scalp.

Another sharp pop sounded below deck—then the low whine of emergency alarms trying to start, failing, and restarting in bursts.

As the acrid smoke thickened. Élise clutched Gérard's sleeve, her voice rising.

"It's tipping."

"No," he began—but then he felt it.

Sun chairs toppled. The promenade lights, still dead, groaned under the strain as the metal beneath them warped and tilted.

They were listing. *Badly.* To starboard.

Children screamed. A woman shouted for her husband. Someone fell down the stairs. Dishes and trays clattered from the buffet behind them.

It was like watching an over-the-top Hollywood disaster film.

But it's real.

"It's the starboard side," Gérard whispered. "The breaches…"

Élise looked at him, her face pale. "We're going over?"

"No—no, there must be—" he stopped himself. *There should be counter flooding systems. Redundancies. But if they've lost power—*

Not only was the ship listing heavily, it was lower in the water.

A blast of static crackled over the emergency loudspeakers. "All stations … this is the bridge—" The voice cut in and out, clipped by static and feedback.

"…listing starboard—repeat—starboard. We have systems failure—multiple compartments breached—"

Another pause. A new voice—shouting in the background.

"—engine room is flooded! We've lost—"

"… lifeboats on port side … inoperable … instructing all remaining passengers to …"

The voice returned, lower now, almost calm.

"… abandon ship portside. Prioritize children … God help us…"

Élise and Gérard looked at each other.

~ ~ ~

"Stay close," Gérard commanded. He didn't have to.

"Someone said it was a bomb," Élise said.

"I don't know."

People filed out of the ship's dining area and onto the pool deck. Smoke poured from the lower decks. An orange glow danced below the starboard side.

The ship is burning.

Fires raged below decks.

All those rooms.

Gérard's mind raced.

Heat rises.

Élise's darted all about. She, too, went over a million plans.

Where do we go?

What do we do?

The deck pitched forward.

The whole ship tilted hard and fast, as if a great kraken had reached up with its tentacles and wrenched the ship sideways.

Élise screamed.

Gérard gripped the railing, but his footing gave way and he lost his grip. He and Élise went sliding across the deck from one side of the ship to the other, alongside tables, chairs, dinners, dishes, glasses, carts, and people—hundreds of people.

They tumbled toward the opposite railing, but the ship bumped and roiled, tossing hundreds of people *over* the railing—including Gérard and Élise—and into the darkness beyond.

Part Three

ZEÍTENWENDE

CHAPTER TWENTY-ONE

The ocean hit like a wall.

Élise floated limply atop the water.

She sucked in seawater as she breathed, causing her to thrash and gag.

She snagged a piece of debris floating next to her—a cushion from a lounge chair by the pool—and clung to it.

Her left arm didn't work. Nor did her legs.

She could barely breathe—her ribs were mashed.

"Gérard!" she gasped, but her voice was only a whisper. It pained her to breathe, let alone cry out his name.

She could barely keep her head above water.

"Gérard!" she whispered again. She slowly turned in the water, looking.

He was nowhere to be found.

More debris—and people—rained into the sea from above.

She heard a deep, rumbling groan, and looked up.

The *Chant du Soleil* loomed above her. It was an eighteen-story building tipping over, slowly.

Somehow, the ship had paused after hurling Gérard and Élise and hundreds of others into the sea.

The sounds it made—of flexing metal, twisting steel, bursting pipes, breaking walls—it was an ear-piercing symphony from hell.

The sounds of screeching metals reached a crescendo before the entire megaship—all 135,000 tons of her—rolled over and on top of Élise.

Moments later, the ship slipped beneath waves and was no more.

~ ~ ~

"Steady," Bof whispered.

Reka barely nodded, her thumbs twitching over the tablet. The drone hovered over Place du Caquet. Because it was after dark, the camera was in night mode, enhancing the ambient light of anything that emitted it: fires burning in oil drums, the light of cell phones, flashlights, headlights, lights reflecting in the wet streets. It was quite efficient. The picture was clear.

JC stood behind her, hands on hips, his face pale in the glow of the screen.

The black flag with a single white star snapped above the Saint-Denis police precinct. It was the flag of the newly proclaimed Islamic Caliphate of Europe—or ICE.

News of the *Chant du Soleil* disaster had spread fast. ICE had put out a statement within minutes of the attack, posting their cryptic message on social media around the world:

"And if We will, We could drown them; then no one responding to a cry would there be for them, nor would they be saved. Not even the Song of the Sun."

—The Commander

Once again, the District bustled with celebration. Young men and teenagers set off firecrackers and lit sparklers—more ambient light. Car horns blared. The flags of France, Israel, and the United States were stomped upon or set aflame.

Comparatively, however, the celebration of the *Chant du Soleil* attack was subdued.

It didn't appear to be spontaneous.

Rows of men dressed in black—*ninjas,* as Bof called them—their faces wrapped and rifles in their arms, stood atop burned-out police vans, leading chants of *Allahu Akbar.* People returned the chant. But to Bof, it seemed forced.

Bof's phone buzzed with a news alert. A statement from Élysée Palace:

"The President is closely monitoring the situation involving Le Chant du Soleil. A national security meeting has been scheduled for 10:00 a.m. tomorrow. No further comment at this time."

Well, that's good.

~ ~ ~

Maryland 7th Congressional District Representative Obo Ababio owned a row home across the street from Baltimore's scenic Patterson Park. The leadership of the Democratic Party gathered in Ababio's small backyard—including Ella Sanchez, the House Minority Leader, and Buck Arnold, the Senate Whip. Others included the Chair of the Democratic National Committee, and even a Baltimore-based television producer most noted for the gritty series *Alter Road,* set in Detroit.

They gathered for light fare: small sandwiches, chips, and soda, catered by a neighborhood deli around the corner.

The issue they had gathered for was anything but light. They were here to strategize about the impeachment and conviction of President Cynthia Belle and Vice President George "Daddy Longlegs" Wartmann.

It was a divided government in Washington. Republicans had the White House, and they held a slight majority in the House of Representatives. The Democrats, meanwhile, held a slim majority in the Senate.

"We can't afford a single Democratic defection," Ella said, "in either the House or the Senate. And no horse trading, either. This is about the survival of our country—hell, our *planet!* President Belle is in *dangerously* over her head, and Daddy Longlegs is a loose cannon. May God help us survive the coming days and weeks."

"If we impeach and convict President Belle, then Daddy Longlegs becomes President," Buck said.

"I've discreetly reached out to Justice Fumio Tanaka," Sanchez said. "He consulted with his staff and constitutional scholars at Harvard and Chicago. The consensus is that we cannot try both the President and Vice President together. We'd have to hold separate Senate trials."

"However, we can do one impeachment resolution," Ella continued, "with articles aimed at each. We wouldn't need to apply two separate articles. For example."

"The consensus was that we start with the President. To begin with the Vice President completely undermines the argument that the circumstances are dire and the President needs to be removed."

Heads nodded.

"I hate to be the party crasher," said Ababio, "but we're not the ruling party in the House. How are we going to get the articles through the House Judiciary Committee? How will we even get them on the agenda?"

All eyes turned to Ella.

"We can introduce Articles of Impeachment directly on the House floor via a privileged resolution. Assuming we have every Democrat, then we have 210 votes. We need eight from the Republican side for a simple majority that lets the House proceed."

"Eight, eh?" chuckled Buck.

"We need to go after both moderates and hardliners," Ella said. "See if we can peel off two or three here and there."

"Hardliners?" asked Ababio. "Aren't they the least likely to defect?"

"No one said this would be easy."

~ ~ ~

Sunlight spilled across the sheets in lazy rectangles. Jacques Michelet lay tangled in silk and laughter, one arm wrapped around the young woman beside him. She traced lines along his ribs, smiling with sleepy affection.

He didn't want to look, but he couldn't help it. He eyed the clock on the bed stand.

Oh thank God.

He still had a couple of hours.

He rested his chin on her head and sniffed her hair.

"You bring me back to where I belong, my English biscuit," he purred.

"Oh? And where's that?"

"To the world before the trials," he murmured with a grin.

"What trials?"

Suddenly animated, he flung off the sheets and stood on the bed.

"The *trials!*" he declared, arms raised like a stage actor. And in a high, ridiculous voice, he parodied the old Queen of Hearts:

"Off with their heads!"

He giggled.

There was a knock at the outer door.

Then another. It was firm.

Jacques' whole demeanor changed. His shoulders sagged. He sighed and sat on the end of the bed, putting on a shirt in silence.

The woman stirred. "Where are you going?"

He pulled on his pants and tucked his shirt, the smile on his face replaced with a heaviness.

"Back to the world above, my Tudor Rose."

He leaned over and gave her a kiss, and walked to the door.

"Off with their heads!" she screeched, and tossed a pillow at him. She giggled.

Jacques smiled. It was a faint, weak smile. He lingered for just a moment.

He turned and walked out.

~ ~ ~

Jacques Michelet stood at the window, stirring sugar into a delicate porcelain cup. The breeze from the open pane fluttered the edge of a crimson curtain. Below, the gardens were pristine. The chirping of birdsong was magical. Jacques closed his eyes and tilted his head. He listened and smiled.

He felt good. Tired, but good.

The door opened.

General Pierre du Bois entered first, flanked by two other senior military officers in uniform. Their medals caught the morning light and reflected in the window.

They entered like a storm.

Jacques didn't turn around right away. He saw their reflections.

Off with their heads!

"You're early," he said, sipping his coffee.

Behind the military officers was Philippe Karcher, Director of the DGSE.

Jacques tapped the remaining sugar off the spoon and dropped it into the cup.

Du Bois stepped forward, his boots heavy on the hardwood. "Forgive us, Mr. President. Time is not on our side."

"What now? Another ship lost? A new arrondissement fallen?"

Jacques turned around and faced the officers, coffee mug in hand.

"An asteroid?"

Karcher placed a single sheet of paper on the desk. It bore the presidential seal.

"Mr. President," Karcher said. He was calm, almost quiet. "Last night, at approximately 11:17 p.m., you signed this proclamation invoking an *état de siège*, thereby transferring operational command and emergency powers to the military."

Jacques blinked.

A moment stretched as he looked from Karcher to De Bois.

"I did no such thing," he said softly.

Du Bois stepped forward. "With respect, sir—you did. In writing. Witnessed and signed." His finger tapped the document.

Jacques walked to the desk. He put his coffee cup down and picked up the document.

The signature was perfect. It was *his* all right, down to the crooked serif on the "J."

Du Bois added, gently, "The Republic is in peril, Mr. President. District 93 has fallen. Police withdrew from Val-d'Oise—District 94—last night. Marseilles is slipping. The people need order. The world needs clarity."

Jacques's hands shook, a little. He set the paper down, as though it were aflame.

"And what do I do? Smile for the cameras and pretend I mean it?"

Du Bois stepped closer, his voice low.

"There will be no cameras. No speeches. You are *relieved*, Mr. President."

Jacques looked at each man in the room.

"And if I object?"

"You've already signed," Philippe said, almost kindly.

Jacques gave a soft laugh. It was not bitter. It was a … *resigned* laugh.

"To the trials, then," he sighed.

~ ~ ~

The room was abuzz as principals and their aides greeted each other. They spoke in hushed tones about their latest intel on the *Chant du Soleil* disaster.

As the clock inched toward ten o'clock, people began to take their seats.

Generals. Ministers. Directors. Aides.

General Pierre du Bois entered last. It was ten o'clock on the dot. He wore his full dress uniform. Without hesitation, he walked to the seat at the head of the conference table and sat.

The President's seat.

The room was silent.

Du Bois opened a leather document binder and held it up for the room to see.

"Gentlemen. Ladies. The President has invoked an *état de siège*."

Heads turned. Officers, ministers, and aides looked at each other. A few eyes narrowed. There was a quiet murmur.

Philippe Karcher sat with his arms folded. He didn't react. He eyed each person in the room to gauge *their* reactions.

Du Bois continued. He spoke with authority: "As of 11:17 p.m. last night, by presidential proclamation, all emergency powers are transferred to the military. Parliament is suspended until further notice. The Republic is under threat. We act accordingly."

The murmurs grew louder.

Du Bois laid the document flat before him. "Effective immediately, I am assuming operational command. Mobilization of the 1st and 3rd Armored Brigades is underway. A national curfew will be issued by tonight. Reinforcements will be deployed to Marseilles and the Seine-Saint-Denis perimeter within twelve hours."

He turned a page. "Call-ups will begin at once. Gendarme reservists are being notified. Airspace control will shift to military oversight. The Ministry of the Interior will coordinate checkpoints in all high-risk arrondissements."

Khadija Belkacem spoke up. "And the President?"

"He has done his duty."

Karcher unfolded his hands. He spoke to take the focus off Belkacem. "The international press will ask questions."

"They always do," Du Bois said. He glanced at Karcher. "What matters is that France endures."

Karcher almost choked on his tea. Those were the same words that

Michelet had used in his last presser.

Du Bois looked around the room, his tone hardening.

"We will not lose another arrondissement. We will not lose another ship. We will not lose this Republic. Not to chaos. Not to zealots. Not to ICE."

No one objected, and the meeting continued.

"What do we know?" General du Bois asked.

Philippe Karcher spoke. "Sir, *Le Chant du Soleil* is the single worst terrorist attack in history. Over 4,000 dead."

A collective gasp filled the room.

Live coverage of the disaster by BFMTV filled the monitors in the room. *515 survivants confirmés* glowed in red on a ticker beneath the live coverage. But no one had done the math. There were nearly 5,000 passengers and crew on board *Le Chant du Soleil.*

"It's worse than 9/11. French victims alone are an order of magnitude worse than the 2015 Paris attacks," Philippe reported.

"It is the second-worst peacetime disaster at sea on record."

Rain now tapped against the windows of the Élysée's secure conference room.

"Are we sure that it was an attack?" Belkacem asked. She was moving past the shock of the *état de siège.* She was doing her job.

Good.

"Cruise ships don't just blow up," General du Bois noted.

"The Greek Coast Guard is reporting a few survivor accounts," Phillipe spoke. "They say a fishing trawler—maybe two or more—rammed straight into the side of *Le Chant du Soleil.*"

"Could it have been an accident?"

"Not likely. Given the amount of damage involved, the trawlers had to be packed with explosives. A freak collision with an oil tanker couldn't have done this much. This was deliberate—this was planned.

"And within minutes of the attack, newsrooms around the world received a communiqué—all from *The Commander*. ICE is claiming responsibility."

"Okay, folks," the General said. "You have your assignments. Let's get to work. *Vive la France.*"

CHAPTER TWENTY-TWO

The mouth-watering smell hit first—smoke, vinegar, cayenne, and oak char. Smokey's Rib House was tucked into the Fairmount Heights neighborhood of Prince George's County, Maryland.

Inside was small and dim, lit mostly by neon beer signs and the flickering screen of an ancient box television bolted to the wall. Gospel music drifted from a kitchen radio. A portrait of Black Jesus hung near the register, the Savior mid-stride across turbulent water, hand outstretched.

The patio out back was a little more spacious, but not by much.

Senator Hank Willoughby, a Republican representative from Texas, walked in and nodded to the man behind the counter.

"Usual," he said. The man nodded back.

"I'm expecting some folks," Willoughby said. "You'll know 'em when you see 'em. Just send them on back." The man nodded.

Willa Denton arrived next, glancing around the place with polite curiosity. The man behind the counter jerked a thumb toward the back door.

"This is where you bring reporters when you want to scare 'em?" she said, stepping onto the patio.

Willoughby chuckled. "Only the ones who need humbling."

Moments later, Blake Holloway strode in, freshly pressed and per-fumed, as though he were headed to a fundraiser, not a hole-in-the-wall barbecue shack. He followed the thumb to the patio out back.

"I had to triple-check the address," he said. "Didn't know this part of town had soul food left."

"That's 'cause you spend too much time at cocktail parties and steak-houses," Willoughby said. "Sit down, son. You're about to get an edu-cation."

The waitress, a woman with gold hoop earrings and an apron dusted in flour, dropped off three cold mugs and a mountain-sized platter of pulled pork—smoky and tender, and still steaming—alongside corn-bread, slaw, and green beans. A bottle of North Carolina hot sauce sweated beside it.

And a pitcher of beer.

"This," Willoughby said, gesturing to the feast, "is why God created swine."

They dug in—Willoughby led the way. Holloway forked a lump of stringy pork. The pork *melted* in his mouth. Smokey, tangy flavors erupted on his tongue.

"Oh my God," he blurted. "This is *so good.*"

Denton grunted. Repeatedly. She took a swig of beer.

"So," she said, and smiled.

"So," Willoughby agreed, and nodded.

"So?" asked Holloway.

"Sooo," Willoughby began, "I understand the Democrats are rustling up articles of impeachment—for both President Belle and Daddy Longlegs."

"Assuming all Democrats are on board, they need eight Republicans to reach a majority," Willa added.

The three eyed each other.

"I'm on board," Willa said before shoveling more pulled port. She grunted again and licked her fingers. "I'm voting yes."

Willoughby smiled and nodded.

"Count me in, too," said Holloway.

"*Really?*" asked Willoughby. "You're an up-and-coming studmeister. Might not suit you to go all maverick."

"The way I see it," Holloway said, "going maverick is how you shake things up. Besides, if Nate Shepherd becomes President—who's the Ways and Means guy?"

"Frank Marcher," Willa helped. "But you know that."

Holloway smiled. "Right. Marcher. Most likely, if—*when*—Nate Shepherd becomes President, Frank Marcher will be his VP."

"So?"

"*So*, that opens up Ways and Means. And whoever chairs Appropriations takes on Ways and Means. Whoever chairs Judiciary will take on Appropriations." Holloway smiled. "And so on."

"You hope to jump in on one of those," Willa said.

"Somebody's gotta do it," he said. He smiled as he chewed.

"Well, that's two right here," Willa said. "I assume you're voting yes," she added, speaking to Willoughby—but he's in the Senate.

He smiled. "It's gotta get through the House first."

"We need at least six more," Holloway said.

"*You* were the wild card," Willoughby said. "If you're on board, there'll be *ten* more votes."

Holloway pushed himself from the picnic table. "How do you figure?"

"Like I said. You're a hot hand, son. People are lining up to hitch their wagons to *your* star."

"So," said Holloway. "That's the *House*. What about the Senate?"

"It's closer. We have some work to do."

Holloway stopped eating. His demeanor changed. "I vote yes—but only if we have the votes in the *Senate.*"

"Hedging your bet," Willa said.

"Hell yeah."

"What happened to being the young buck maverick?"

Holloway snickered. "What about you two? Why do you want to impeach the President?"

"She's in way over her head," Willa said. "She has no previous experience in government whatsoever. And Daddy Longlegs has run roughshod over her."

"That doesn't excuse her," Willa continued. "Going along with Daddy all this time. Look where it's gotten her. Look where it's gotten the *country.*"

"As for *him*"—Willa was fired up—"He's a *dangerous* man. He has no bones about starting World War 3. But we have to go through *her* to get to *him.*"

~ ~ ~

Daddy finished his morning run in Rock Creek Park.

Despite the continuing protests near the Observatory—and Melvin Bauer's conniptions—his morning runs somehow remained an unknown.

Not that any protester would even be up that early.

After a shower, Daddy joined Care in Number One's cozy kitchen.

Daddy scrolled through news and blogs on his tablet. Care did the same, but she preferred actual newspapers and magazines.

"There's a nice spread about Maryland's junior Senator in *Maryland Magazine,*" Care said.

Daddy was deep into a blog post. The Democrats were busy drafting impeachment articles and rustling up votes—including *Republican* votes.

Good luck with that.

"Seems like a nice young man. I think he's someone you might be able to work with."

"Uh huh."

Care glared at Daddy.

"I *said* …"

Daddy looked up. His reading glasses were perched on the end of his nose.

"… that there's a nice article about that *junior Senator.*"

She stood up and left the kitchen, taking her breakfast with her.

Daddy turned in his chair and watched her stalk out.

What the hell?

After a moment, he turned back to his reading—but his eyes latched on to a magazine that Carrie had left on the table. *Maryland Magazine.*

Daddy picked it up.

Surfer Boy Goes to Washington

From Ocean City to Capitol Hill, Maryland's youngest senator rides a new wave of politics.

There was a photo of a handsome young man in a suit, holding a surf-board.

Daddy started reading.

"Surfing clarifies things," the kid was quoted as saying. *"It strips everything down. There's no noise out there—just you, the water, and the next wave. You can't fake it."*

Daddy finished the article. He sipped his coffee and stared out on the backyard garden.

~ ~ ~

Daddy Longlegs stood on the tarmac of Naval Air Station Oceana, just outside the NAS passenger terminal. Beside Longlegs was General Alexander Pitt, Commander of the US Special Forces Command based in Tampa, Florida.

There was no press here. It was dusk. Daddy looked to the western horizon. It was aflame with vibrant pink and orange amid darkening hues of purple. It was a long familiar sight that left him feeling nostalgic, melancholic. He had stood here—not exactly *here*, but in Norfolk—nearly forty years earlier as a young Navy ensign. He had never been to Norfolk before then, and he had found it uniquely magical. The flatness of the lush land of dark green pines, hollies, and persimmons. Swamps and water always nearby. The fiery sunsets.

Longlegs and Pitt stood between two young Navy linemen, each no older than 20, in yellow vests. They stood at attention some distance away.

Two jumbo gray four-engine C-17 Globemaster cargo planes turned from the taxiway, one after the other. Their engines were incredibly loud.

The first lineman held an LED traffic baton over his head as though raising his hand in school. The lead aircraft turned toward the young lineman. He waved both batons now, out and in, out and in, instructing the pilot to continue forward. He stuck his left arm straight out at a ninety-degree angle while continuing to wave the baton in his right arm. He was instructing the pilot to turn.

The aircraft turned rapidly to face the second lineman, who stood with one baton held straight over *his* head before waving both of them to and fro.

It was a professional, synchronized, well-choreographed operation.

The planes had ferried some 400 US Marines and Navy SEALs, along with assorted cargo, straight from Camp Lemonnier in Djibouti, via Ramstein Air Base in Germany. These were the men who had fought their way from Bahrain and Qatar all the way down the western coast of the Persian Gulf to the border of Oman. Once there, elite Omani troops—at the personal appeal of Daddy Longlegs to the Sultan of Oman—had escorted the Americans to the coast on the Gulf of Oman, where Navy ships awaited them.

It was less than seventy-two hours since they had boarded the American destroyers *Richard Lugar* and *Telesforo Trinidad* and escaped from the Arabian Peninsula.

Every soldier, sailor, Marine, and airman left behind was now a prisoner of war. Some 40,000 of them—plus another 165,000 American civilians stuck across the various capitals now under Iranian occupation.

Daddy could feel his temples flush with anger. *Calm down*, he told himself. *One thing at a time.*

Soldiers streamed out of the cargo ramps and into the bright sunlight. Many shielded their eyes, stretched and shook their legs. It was a long flight.

"Welcome home, son," Daddy said as the first young soldiers approached. He looked each one of them in the eye and shook their hand.

He immediately noticed how gaunt they appeared. Only a few carried rucksacks or other bags. Most had only their rifles and the ripped and dusty uniforms on their backs. Many sported bandages. Some hobbled on crutches.

They were a sad looking lot.

The line of soldiers had gone fast, and the last of them—a motley crew of shaggy-haired men, some bearded—lagged behind. They transported baggage to a truck and escorted a young man to an awaiting ambulance. The young man looked like a kid barely out of high school.

Rather than wait for them, Daddy Longlegs walked over, with General Pitt in tow.

The men were fierce looking as he approached. *SEALs*, he surmised.

A bearded Chief Petty Officer looked at him warily as he approached. Daddy could read the man's mind from the expression on his face: *Who the fuck is this guy?*

Then his face lit up. "Oh shit, you're Daddy Longlegs," said the Chief Petty Officer, snapping to attention and saluting before shaking Daddy's hand.

"In the flesh," Daddy said. "Welcome home, Chief."

"Thank you, Sir," the chief beamed.

The other SEALs gathered around and Daddy shook hands with each of them. These were the men who had refused to surrender to 50,000 Iranian soldiers as they swarmed into Bahrain.

These were the men who kept Central Command in Tampa—and Daddy Longlegs—abreast of what was happening while surviving multiple air and missile strikes, Iranian paratroopers, and nuclear bombs.

"Who's the kid?" Daddy asked, nodding to the ambulance.

"Bryson," said the Chief Petty Officer. "A supply specialist."

"We commandeered him and another kid to help move equipment. He was our forklift driver," another SEAL chipped in.

"What happened to him?" Daddy asked.

The SEALs looked at each other. "A lot," said one. "He got buried by sand in the nuke attack. Got sand in his lungs."

"I just got off the phone with his parents," General Pitt offered. "They're driving down from Ocean City as we speak."

"Maryland?" Daddy asked.

"Yes, sir."

Daddy looked up at the sky. It was as if the clouds had parted and a gift had descended from Heaven.

He smiled.

A remaining SEAL walked over from the ambulance. He was the only one wearing a cloverleaf rank insignia, and was relatively well-groomed in comparison with the other SEALs.

"Commander Nigel Wood," said General Pitt, as the man approached.

"Ah, yes, General Pitt, so pleased to meet you." Commander Wood spoke with a cheery English accent. They shook hands, and Wood did a slight doubletake as he looked to Daddy Longlegs.

"Welcome home, Commander," Longlegs said, extending his hand.

"Mr. Vice President," Wood said. He bowed slightly as he shook hands with Longlegs. "So very nice of you to come."

Despite the cheerfulness of the young English SEAL—*an English*

SEAL? How does that work?—Longlegs sensed a deep weariness.

"Pleasure's all mine," Longlegs said. "General Pitt kept me abreast of your movements. Get some rest, you and your men."

He led the commander by the arm for a couple of steps. "I'd love to hear all about it over a beer sometime," then offered his hand one more time.

"Yes, sir." They shook hands and the SEALs made their way to the terminal.

Longlegs stood ramrod straight, hands clasped behind his back, as he watched them depart. "Speaking of beer, I'm thirsty."

Daddy looked to Pitt.

"Where are we going?"

~ ~ ~

The Screech Owl Bar and Grille on Owl Creek was maybe two football fields southwest of the Virginia Aquarium and Marine Center, and a mile as the crow flies from the Atlantic Ocean. It wasn't uncommon for locals who lived in the area for years to have driven past without noticing it. The Screech Owl was a dive bar, for one, with a tin roof and shabby roadhouse appearance. Further, it was backed up against Owl Creek and was mostly hidden by mature pine trees.

A rusted sign featuring a wise-looking owl in a sailor's cap haphazardly perched on its head and the fading words Screech Owl Bar below was easy to miss. If one did see the sign but wasn't a patron, it was easy to believe the old bar had long since been abandoned.

But abandoned it was not. The dive bar and grille had a dedicated and persistent clientèle over the years: generations of Navy SEALs, active or veteran, and retirees. The active SEALs came from the nearby Dam Neck Naval Base, which housed the famous (or infamous) counter ter-rorism unit DevGru, better known as SEAL Team 6, and from the Little Creek Naval Amphibious Base farther afield and astride the southern terminus of the Chesapeake Bay Bridge-Tunnel. Aside from DevGru at Dam Neck, Little Creek housed roughly half of the US

Navy's SEAL teams. The other half were based on the West Coast, in Coronado, California. Veterans and retirees that patronized the Screech Owl came from all across Norfolk and Virginia Beach.

It was dark now and a steady stream of vehicles, one after the other, turned onto the unpaved path that served as the bar's entrance.

Daddy Longlegs stepped from his Department of Defense armored Chevy Suburban, dressed in chinos and a hoodie.

When he entered the bar, the bustling room quickly hushed into silence and everyone, patrons and staff, stood at attention. Longlegs was puzzled for a moment—*veterans or active duty, the whole lot of them*, he realized. Longlegs smiled. "Please, as you were," he ordered.

The patrons sat down and the staff went back to work. Daddy made his way towards the back patio, shaking hands with tattooed young men and their wives and girlfriends at each table along the way. The men here—everyone of them a Navy SEAL, whether active duty or veteran—could pass as a chapter of Hells Angels.

Melvin Bauer shadowed Daddy. He was stiff and alert, his head on a swivel. "Relax, Mel," Daddy said, and slapped him on the back. "This might be the safest place on Earth." Mel shot him a dubious look and grunted.

Daddy strode through the bar toward the outdoor patio deck in the back. Tiki torches and incense sticks were lined up along the deck's railings, keeping mosquitoes and insects at bay. Crickets, however, were loud and musical. Several picnic tables had been brought together to serve as one long table with benches. All the men, and a woman, gathered around the long table were standing, waiting for Daddy.

"Admiral Oberkirsch," Daddy said, shaking hands with the SEAL and Chief of Naval Operations. "Thank you for coming. This your idea?"

Baltzer nodded and winked.

Daddy looked down the table. All the principals of the multi-agency Sean Connery Fan Club were here, along with their trusted staff: Joy Chatterjee, Director of the CIA; Oscar Schwartz, the President's National Security Advisor; General Alexander Pitt, US Special Forces

Command; Rear Admiral Ryan Phelps, Naval Special Warfare Command; and more.

Missing was Raymond Cole, the young Undersecretary of Defense for Intelligence and Security. There was still no word on whether he was alive or dead in Kuwait.

Everyone wore casual civilian clothes, including blue jeans and T-shirts.

"Thank you, everyone, for coming," Daddy said. He looked to Oberkirsch. "Good choice, Admiral. Exactly my kind of place. Sure as hell beats a bunker at Raven Rock."

Daddy sat down and everyone followed suit.

Waiters took their orders, and Daddy set the tone: beer, burgers, and fries.

~ ~ ~

Daddy leaned forward and lowered his voice so only his table could hear him.

"Team, I need to go to Baghdad to visit our Embassy there. I was the one who called in Tayfun Ulusoy, the Turkish Ambassador, when that place was hanging by a thread. And he came through—in spades. He didn't just send help. He sent the Maroon Berets."

He got a few nods around the table.

"I got word he'll be in Baghdad the day after tomorrow. Ceremony for the boys who pulled it off. I think I can sell the trip to the President.

"But from there, I need to get to Kuwait. There are 40,000 POWs there, and I'm tired of waiting for someone in Tehran to answer the phone.

"Hell, I might sneak right into *Tehran,* if I have to. Knock on their front door and ask if they'd like to chat over a glass of Kentucky bourbon."

His eyes suddenly went distant.

As a matter of fact ...

He waved a hand and chuckled.

"I'll have to pretend it's tea, of course—just like they'll pretend they don't drink."

~ ~ ~

The bar was a low-lit bunker of wood-paneled walls, faded photos, and old challenge coins glued to the back of the counter. A few off-duty SEALs laughed in a back booth. Heavy metal played on the jukebox. The soft haze of cigar smoke wafted under the overhang atop the deck outback.

On the back deck, perched over Screech Owl Creek, Daddy Longlegs leaned back in his chair, cigar between two fingers. He laughed heartily at a story told by Joy Chatterjee. The smoke curled upward like incense, mingling with the scent of beer and grilled meat. General Pitt nursed a whiskey. Oscar Schwartz had his tie loosened.

Movement in the bar caught Daddy's attention.

Two of the SEALs he had welcomed on the tarmac at Oceana Naval Air Station walked in. Daddy remembered their names: Commander Nigel Wood, the English-accented SEAL, and Master Chief Hector Gonzalez.

Daddy stood.

"Commander Wood. Master Chief Gonzalez." His voice was a little raspy from the cigar. "Come and join us."

Wood smiled. "Evening, Mr. Vice President."

Daddy gestured to the empty seats around the table. "You're among friends. Come. Sit."

Gonzalez gave a respectful nod, then walked over and shook hands with General Pitt before he sat. Nigel took the seat nearest Daddy.

"Give the man a cigar," Daddy said. Each was handed a cigar, and someone passed a cutter and a flame.

"I want to hear all about your escape from Bahrain."

Wood leaned in, cigar lit and eyes sharp. "You might want to pour yourself another bourbon, then, sir."

Daddy grinned. "Way ahead of you."

"Well," Wood said, and exhaled. "Here's the short of it then, yeah?" And he began: A missile strike, then an air strike, then Iranians at the front gate, their escape across the bay to Qatar. From Qatar, they made their way down to the UAE and then the Omani coast. But not before another airstrike on their convoy, a nuclear strike—luckily, they were on the outer edge of *that*—and a firefight with Iranian paratroopers.

Everyone at the table was mesmerized by his story.

"Hell of a thing," Daddy said, exhaling. "That forklift kid you dragged along—I believe he's from up the road here, in Ocean City."

He looked to Oscar Schwartz. "Isn't one of Maryland's senators from there?"

Oscar nodded. "Kyle Cropper. He's the junior senator. He's a former mayor of Ocean City, if I'm not mistaken."

Daddy smirked. "I thought so. Maybe I'll invite him down to visit the kid. Could be a good moment for everyone."

~ ~ ~

A TV perched in the corner of the outdoor deck was tuned to CNN, but nobody was watching. However, the words "BREAKING NEWS" nevertheless had a way of cutting through the cigar smoke and beer.

The news reported the supposed establishment of the Kingdom of Hejaz along the Red Sea coast of Arabia. "... *Zahran tribal forces have seized the port cities of Jeddah, Yanbu, and Rabigh ... tribal elders have proclaimed their leader, Abdulaziz Al-Zahrani, as King of the Hejaz. State Department officials say that Al-Zahrani is a complete unknown.*"

The news caught the attention of Nigel Wood even as the banter continued.

"You know," he said, lightning another cigar, "I know that guy." He nodded to the television.

Daddy Longlegs looked over his should at the screen, then back to

Nigel.

"We trained with his unit in Bahrain. He's in the Special Navy Security Units of Saudi Arabia—or was. We did fast boarding, hostage recovery, underwater demolitions. He was their commanding officer."

Master Chief Hector Gonzalez chimed in. "That's *him?*"

Daddy took a long drag on his cigar and exhaled toward the creek.

"Think you can reach him?" asked Daddy.

Wood looked past Daddy in thought. "We might be able to," he said after a moment. "We had back channel lines—desert codes. It'd take a message or two."

"He seemed to like us," Gonzalez said. "That's gotta count for something, right?"

Daddy turned his cigar slowly in his fingers, watching the TV loop grainy drone footage of armed men raising a black, green, red and white flag over the port of Jeddah.

"Reach out," he said. "Let's see if the King of Hejaz still answers old friends."

CHAPTER TWENTY-THREE

Harlan Clark was at his desk. He had a small stack of forms requiring his signature. Budget requisitions, reimbursement forms, even—surprise, surprise—a bill proposal or two.

His office administrator knocked, then entered. Harlan didn't look up.

"Sir, you have an unscheduled visitor."

Harlan looked at his computer screen.

"It's Tuesday. I don't do walk-ins on Tuesdays."

Harlan stopped what he was doing and looked up.

"But you know that." He leaned back in his chair. "Who is it?"

"Representative Ella Sanchez. Of New York."

"No shit," he said, looking curious.

"Well, alright. Send her in."

A moment later, Ella walked in.

Harlan walked in front of his desk.

"Miss Sanchez," he said. "It's a pleasure to meet you in person."

They shook hands. Harlan led Ella to two high-backed chairs arranged around a small round table.

"How can I help the House Minority Leader?" he asked. He was curious. But he was also amused. It was all over Washington that she and the Democrats were putting together a series of impeachment articles.

"I think you know why I'm here," she said.

"I think I do," he smiled. "Still. If you could amuse me."

"If that's what you want."

Harlan nodded.

Ella crossed one leg over the other and brushed away lint on her pants.

"I'm leading an effort to impeach President Belle and Vice President Wartmann."

Well, there it is.

"I know all about it, Miss Sanchez." Harlan stood and walked to the window. He looked out on the Capitol Building across the street and the National Mall that stretched out before it. Another massive anti-war, anti-Belle, and anti-Longlegs protest was under way. People filled the mall as far as the eye could see.

Smoke and tear gas blended together, hovering in the air above, like fog.

A typical Tuesday.

"You know I'm an ally of Daddy Longlegs."

Ella nodded.

"I don't understand," he said. "You want me to vote to impeach a Republican President. What makes you think I would even consider such a thing?"

"Republicans are going to be *slaughtered* in the Midterms. Nationwide. You know it, and I know it. Besides, you're an ally of Daddy Longlegs, but not Belle. And if Belle is *convicted* in the Senate, Wartmann is President."

Harlan sat back in the tall chair across from Ella. "Right. So why push for impeachment?"

"I'm interested in getting it over the line. Once it's in the Senate's hands, it's an all new ballgame."

Harlan leaned forward, his forearms on this thighs. He rubbed his head.

"Hang on," he said. "You think you have enough votes to convict *Wartmann.*"

Ella didn't say anything.

Harlan snickered. He was incredulous.

"That's a pretty big gamble, Miss Sanchez."

He stood and walked around his chair.

"And if you're *successful,* Old Man Shepherd becomes President."

Harlan shook his head. "He's still a Republican."

"Yes," Ella said. "But Nate Shepherd is a deft House Speaker and an institution in Washington."

"I am trying to save the *country,* Mr. Clark," Ella continued. "And we both know that Nate Shepherd would keep the ship afloat."

"Until the next election," Harlan added.

"Wow," Harlan said. He was still incredulous. "That's a lot to think about."

Ella stood and smiled.

"Don't hurt yourself," she said, and walked out.

~ ~ ~

Not long after the unorthodox visit by Daddy Longlegs to the Turkish Embassy, Tayfun Ulusoy was summoned back to his home country.

In fact, it was the very next message from Ankara after Tayfun sent his communique with Longlegs' desperate request.

The next day, a Turkish government Gulfstream 600 was waiting for him at Reagan National Airport in Washington. From there, he flew to Etimesgut Air Base in Ankara, a mere two miles from *Cumhurbaşkanlığı Külliyesi,* the Presidential Complex of Türkiye. It was after midnight when he landed.

An armored SUV whisked him straight to the Presidential Complex, despite the hour.

President Mimar Gökalp himself awaited him as his car pulled into the Complex. He wore his trademark double-breasted suit. He emulated the late King Charles II of the United Kingdom, who was always immaculately dressed.

"Welcome home, Tayfun Ulosoy," the mustachioed President said, his back ramrod straight.

Tayfun nearly tripped as he stepped out of the SUV. The President pretended not to notice, though he looked amused. *Then again, he always has a look of amusement on his face.* Gökalp extended his hand.

"Thank you, Mr. President. You needn't have waited up for me."

"I counted the hours of your flight with impatience," the President said, his eyes smiling. "We have much work to do. Much to catch up on. We have not a moment to waste."

~ ~ ~

"We can't move forward with the Kurdish Question perpetually chained to our ankles like an *ayak bağı*. We need the Kurds on our side, once and for all."

And with that, President Mimar Gökalp finished his pitch. His warm eyes twinkled.

Tayfun yawned. He couldn't help it. He had gotten some sleep on the eleven-hour flight, but not enough. He had drunk nearly two liters of strong Turkish coffee as his old friend the President presented his Grand Plan.

President Gökalp had talked through the night next to the cozy fireplace—the President's Reading Room was straight out of a Swiss ski lodge—while servants regularly refilled his and Tayfun's coffees.

They called it a "spectrum" in America. Autism or Asperger's. *Something.* Whatever it was, he was on it.

The Asperger President waited for Tayfun to say something.

Tayfun was hesitant. He was too tired to think straight and didn't want to say something stupid.

"I don't see how." Tayfun yawned again. "They don't trust us. I don't see a path where the Kurdish parties acquiesce to our demands without at least some degree of coercion." Tayfun paused. "It's been the same story for more than a century." He was almost apologetic.

"The times we live in—and the times that are coming—demand something different," Mimar said. "Something to meet the moment."

"What do you have in mind, Your Excellency?"

The President turned and looked up at the grandiose painting of Reycip Erdowan, the former President of the Turkish Republic, looming above the fireplace.

"An idea whose time has come."

~ ~ ~

The fluorescent lights buzzed faintly overhead. Thew Bryson lay propped up in bed, shirtless beneath a light blanket, a nasal cannula feeding him oxygen. A heart monitor beeped steadily nearby.

He was embarrassed. His parents had driven down from Ocean City in sheer panic. They had both been crying. He was afraid his mom would have a heart attack. She was practically hysterical when she first came in.

The door opened.

Thank God.

A train of people walked in.

A lanky older man led the group. He nodded at Thew as if he knew him.

Behind the tall man came a sharply dressed younger guy in a suit. And two SEALs—Thew recognized them immediately.

"Commander Wood! Master chief!" The remaining SEALs filed in.

Thew's parents stood, and the tall man turned to them.

"Mr. and Mrs. Bryson," he said, shaking their hands. "You raised one tough sailor. I hope you know that."

They both nodded. Thew's father was beaming.

"I'm proud of him. And I'm proud of *you.*" He glanced back at Thew, then back to his parents. "I wonder if we might steal a few minutes with him," Daddy added, gently. "Just some Navy talk. Nothing heavy."

Mr. Bryson glanced at his wife, then back at Daddy. "Of course. We'll be just down the hall."

"Thank you," his wife said. She wiped tears from her eyes.

Daddy winked. "We'll take good care of him."

Daddy waited for the door to close behind them, then turned to Thew.

"So you're the forklift driver who outran a nuclear bomb."

Thew blinked. "Uh … yeah?"

"I'm Daddy Longlegs," the tall man said, offering a hand. "Vice President—*of the United States,* in case you're wondering. And this here's Senator Kyle Cropper of Maryland. Says he's your neighbor, more or less."

Kyle stepped forward and shook Bryson's hand. "Ocean City, right? I'm from there too."

"Oh, right," Thew said. "You're that surfer mayor guy!"

Kyle smiled. "You mean the statue? That's actually my kid brother Jack."

Daddy Longlegs raised an eyebrow. "Do you surf, Bryson?"

"I try. But I'm not sure you'd call it *surfing.*"

"We don't want to keep your parents," Daddy said. "I just wanted to visit a young American hero. The country thanks you for your service."

"That goes for each of you," Daddy said, turning now to the SEALs.

"Thank you, sir," said Nigel.

But Daddy wasn't finished.

"Thank you for fighting. Thank you for surviving. I know that many didn't. Like your teammate, Danny Liu."

Turning to Thew, he added, "and your friend and fellow Logistic Specialist, David Skaggs."

Thew's face darkened, as had the SEALs', and he looked down.

Daddy paused. He looked down, too.

"Senator Cropper will have each of your names entered into the Congressional Record in honor of your sacrifice."

"I'd like for your families to be there," added Senator Cropper. "We'll be in touch through your units. We want to do this right."

~ ~ ~

Daddy and the young Senator made their way down the corridor. They walked casually, but silently.

The floor was shiny.

Daddy spotted vending machines glowing in a corner. He reached into his pocket and fished out some change.

A paper cup filled with a brown liquid that maybe qualified as coffee.

"You're a brave man," Kyle said.

Daddy pulled out the coffee, blew on it, and took a sip. He grimaced.

"The visit?" Daddy asked, walking again.

"The coffee."

Daddy chuckled. "I've had motor oil that went down smoother."

Kyle smiled. "You always make house calls like that?"

"A *house* call?" Daddy said and shook his head. "Back in my Navy days, they called it showing up. It's the least we can do, especially for the kind of dumb luck heroes we don't deserve—like that kid."

Kyle nodded. He looked down the hallway where Thew's parents had disappeared.

"They were shook up."

"Wouldn't you be?"

Kyle nodded again, and sighed.

A moment passed.

"It was nice to meet you, Senator Cropper," Daddy said, extending a hand.

Kyle shook it.

"So," Daddy asked, "You surf, huh?"

"Not so much anymore," he said.

"Make time for it," Daddy said. "It clarifies things."

Daddy dumped the coffee in a water fountain. He crumpled the paper cup and tossed it perfectly into the bin. He laughed—it was an oddly mischievous laugh—and his eyes sparkled.

He entered an elevator and was gone.

~ ~ ~

President Cynthia Belle stood near the Resolute Desk, arms crossed, reading the typed brief again under a lamplight. Aides had been dismissed. The television was muted. The images on it was being filmed right outside the White House: tens of thousands of protesters calling for her and Daddy's impeachment—and their trials at the Hague.

Amid fireworks and tear gas.

Vice President George "Daddy Longlegs" Wartmann leaned against a side table, sipping coffee.

"*Desert Knight?* That's what you're calling it?" the President asked.

Daddy smiled. "Has a ring to it, don't it?"

"This isn't a rescue mission, George. This is a *military* deployment into a sovereign country. One that's still on fire, I might add."

"Saudi Arabia doesn't exist anymore. There's no king. Riyadh's a free-for-all. For the Jeddah component, Jeddah actually *does* have a king— Al-Zahrani—and he's actually in command there."

"You're suggesting we trust a self-proclaimed monarch no one's ever heard of?"

"Not no one," Daddy said. "Our own Navy SEALs know him. They've worked with him. They trained with his unit. We've reached out to him. He's agreed to close his airport to everyone but *us*. And Hejaz existed as a political entity long before its incorporation into Saudi Arabia. Whether as an Ottoman vilayet, or as a short-lived

Hashemite kingdom after World War I. Al-Zahrani has the support of the people there."

President Belle sighed.

"Look *outside*, Daddy. I can't afford to get entangled in a new row. We just signed a ceasefire. The world's watching."

"Well," Daddy said, gesturing toward the window, "why don't we ask *them* what we should do? *They're* not the President. We have an opportunity to do something here.

"Israel just pulled this off in France, an *actual* sovereign country. We can't let 40,000 Americans sit there until somebody decides to *keep* them. We can't get to the other 40,000 in the East, not without a fight with Iran, but Iran isn't in Riyadh."

The President rapped her fingers on the Resolute Desk.

"And if it goes bad?"

Daddy chuckled. "We're already at the bottom, in case you hadn't noticed. There's only up from here."

The President shook her head. "You're working me. 'Cause even *I* know that things can *always* get worse."

"Well," Daddy said. His eyes sparkled. "You can't hit the ball unless you swing."

President Belle stared at him for a long moment. She picked up the phone.

"Get me CENTCOM."

Then, to Daddy: "Let's make it clean."

Daddy grinned. "Yes, ma'am."

"And don't think I didn't notice that little rider you stapled to the end of the op."

She folded her arms. "Baghdad?"

Daddy raised his mug in salute. "Just paying a visit. Morale and all."

"You get one handshake with the Turks, and ten minutes with the press—*if* you're not shot at. That's it."

"Oh, I'll be back in time for the headlines—just not the ones they're expecting."

Daddy laughed.

That laugh.

She picked the phone up again. The line had been blinking.

"It's a 'go,' General Pitt."

She hung up and looked to Daddy.

"Don't make me regret this."

~ ~ ~

Tayfun Ulusoy had a new title. He was no longer Ambassador of Türkiye in America.

He was *Grand Vizier.*

It was a job straight out of the Ottoman Empire. He was no longer President Gökalp's representative to *America*. He was now President Gökalp's personal representative to the *world*.

Tayfun's first mission was to the city of Diyarbakır, or Amed in Kurdish. Diyarbakır sits astride the banks of the upper Tigris River in southeastern Turkey. It is the biggest city in all of Greater Kurdistan and the unofficial capital of Turkish Kurdistan.

Greater Kurdistan is a contiguous Kurdish-majority region that stretches from southeast Türkiye and northern Iraq, and along a wide swath of territory in the Zagros Mountains that straddles the border of Iraq and Iran.

After World War One, the British and French worked to partition the Ottoman Empire and plan a post-Ottoman future for the region. But sectarian violence erupted throughout Anatolia along ethnic and linguistic lines as various groups sought political independence.

Mustafa Kemal Atatürk, one of the most decorated of Ottoman's generals, had other plans. He was a Turkish nationalist, and led the Turkish National Movement in battle against Allied occupiers and separatists alike–primarily Armenians, Greeks, and Kurds.

When it was all over, the Republic of Türkiye was born, and Kurdistan was partitioned into Turkish Kurdistan, Iranian Kurdistan, Iraqi Kurdistan, and even a small part of northeastern Syria–Syrian Kurdistan.

In an effort to Turkify the Kurds and other minorities, and develop a unified Turkish state, Mustafa Kemal Ataturk banned Kurdish and other minority languages, banned the Kurdish flag, and otherwise attempted to stamp out Kurdish culture and promote Turkish culture across the Republic.

Neighboring states followed similar policies. Kurds, who have their own language, customs, and traditions that date back over two millennia, have sought autonomy and even independence ever since. But they face an uphill battle. They are a minority in each country, and must wage resistance against each of them.

The same Gulfstream 600 that had whisked Tayfun from Washington to Ankara awaited him on the tarmac. It was a much shorter flight this time, only an hour and a half.

Tayfun had never been to Diyarbakır before. He expected the predominantly Kurdish city to be a dusty and impoverished frontier town with an air of malice hanging over. But the commercial airline terminal was clean and modern. Better than any airport he'd seen in America.

Tayfun picked up a rental car—a Fiat sedan—at the airport's Budget lot. Twenty minutes later, he drove through one of the narrow archways in the ancient walls surrounding Sur, the old city. The walls are part of the Fortifications of Diyarbakır, and are the second widest and longest complete defensive walls in the entire world, second only to the Great Wall of China.

When he approached the archway in the wall, the roadway narrowed. On the other side of the wall, in Sur, the street remained narrow. Sur is the densely packed old city, with narrow, meandering streets hemmed in by buildings hundreds of years old. *Now* an air of malice fell over Tayfun.

With the narrow, meandering streets, and clogged traffic, Tayfun drove slowly, following the GPS directions on his smartphone. Within a few minutes, he found himself at the walls of the Fortifications of Diyarbakır again. He followed the directions of the GPS along the wall-side road until he came upon a break in the wall. It was his destination: the Selahaddin Eyyübi Bazaar.

The Selahaddin Eyyübi Bazaar was a large open square full of pedestrians, families, and tourists, and surrounded by apartment buildings with street-level shops and restaurants.

It took a few more minutes before Tayfun found a parking space. He walked into the square and spotted the metallic-frame clock tower—it wasn't very tall—at the square's center. He walked toward it.

One of the great things about his political career so far was his anonymity, though that was likely to change, given his new role as Grand Vizier.

As he walked to the clock tower, Tayfun watched an elderly man on a bench feed pigeons with the bread from a half-eaten sandwich.

The man spotted Tayfun and waved. He stood and tossed the remainder of the sandwich on the ground. Dozens of pigeons flocked to it.

Tayfun stopped and looked the man over. Could he be Jwan Nouri?

The man wiped his hands and mouth with a napkin, then let the napkin go and the wind took it.

The man walked toward Tayfun. He was tall. He looked to be in his sixties or even early seventies, but his gait was that of a much younger man. He appeared unusually fit for a man his age.

"Mr. Ulusoy," the man said as he approached. His voice was deep, rich. He held his hand out.

"Mr. Nouri," Tayfun responded, and shook his hand.

Türkiye's National Intelligence Organization, or, in its Turkish abbreviation, MİT, had set up the meeting. Jwan Nouri was the leader of the Kurdistan Workers Party. Its abbreviation, in Kurdish, is PKK.

The PKK was originally a Soviet-supported socialist revolutionary group that set off bombs and advocated for an independent socialist Kurdish republic. Türkiye deemed them terrorists. The PKK have since abandoned their socialist roots, but they still advocate for Kurdish independence.

"Are you hungry?" Jwan asked.

Tayfun didn't answer.

"How about some tea, then?" Jwan directed Tayfun to a small coffee shop with outdoor seating.

CHAPTER TWENTY-FOUR

Tayfun laid out President Gökalp's proposal in full. Jwan listened intently while occasionally sipping his tea.

Tayfun stopped talking. "That's it," he said, after a moment. "That's the proposal."

Tayfun remained quiet as Jwan considered the proposal. Tayfun couldn't read his mind, but he imagined the thoughts running through Jwan's head.

Why all of this? After everything? You've already won ten times over, and yet ... What is your agenda?

"Tell me," Jwan finally spoke. "Why now?"

Tayfun shrugged. "Times, they are a changing."

Jwan laughed heartily. "Do you even know where that saying comes from?"

An uneasy smile turned up Tayfun's lips, and he shrugged again.

Jwan shook his head and snickered. "I must take this to my people."

~ ~ ~

It didn't take long at all.

Jwan Nouri called the number Tayfun provided him. Jwan had met with his people—presumably, the PKK—not long after Tayfun's visit.

After a brief but heated debate, they reached an historic, unanimous decision.

Tayfun was quite stunned.

The historic, unanimous decision?

"Yes."

~ ~ ~

Democratic Congressional staffers and interns burned the midnight oil.

It was a three-day marathon.

Pizza boxes and Chinese carryout cartons littered the room, along with soda cans.

Ella was alone in her office reading the latest draft.

She buzzed the lead intern in, a tall slender redhead wearing a Harvard sweatshirt. She was bleary-eyed. She took the draft from Ella and sauntered to the doorway, flipping through the pages. She paused within reach of the door.

"There are no markups," she said.

"That's right," Ella said, and smiled. "I think we're there. Email me the file."

The intern jumped up and down, then opened the door.

"Guys ...!"

Ella heard the other room erupt in celebration.

She picked up her phone and texted. *I think we've got it.*

She hit the Send button. It was to all House Democrats and a selection of Senate Democrats. She turned to her computer. The latest version dropped in her email, just sent by the Harvard intern. She looked it over one last time, then dragged it to the cloud-sharing folder where every House Democrat could view it.

She opened her email and slid the document in. She addressed it to Harlan Clark.

She looked to the door where staffers and interns still celebrated on the other side. She tapped her fingers on her desk.

She hit send.

~ ~ ~

Harlan was at his desk in the Rayburn Congressional Office Building.

Outside, anti-Belle and anti-Wartmann protests raged on.

His email chimed.

It was from Ella Sanchez. There was no subject line or message.

Just an attachment.

He immediately suspected spam or a phishing attempt, but dismissed both. The email was sent through the secure Congressional intranet.

He opened the attachment and read.

He skipped the legalese and got to the heart of it:

Resolved, That Cynthia Robinson Belle, President of the United States, and George Heinrich Wartmann, Vice President of the United States, are impeached for high crimes and misdemeanors, and that the following article of impeachment be exhibited to the United States Senate:

Article I: Dereliction of Duty and Abuse of Executive Power

"The President and Vice President willfully bypassed lawful channels for the use of military force, manipulated intelligence to provoke hostilities, and endangered U.S. civilians and armed forces by initiating armed conflict without strategic contingency. Their actions directly contributed to catastrophic loss of life, destabilization of the international order, and a coerced ceasefire dictated by foreign adversaries— an outcome that gravely compromised U.S. sovereignty and global standing."

Harlan scratched his head.

Just one. One article.

And President Belle and Vice President Wartmann were both named in the impeachment. There would be no voting "yes" to impeach one, and voting "no" to avoid impeaching the other.

He remembered Ella's words: *You're going to get slaughtered in the Mid-*

terms. You know it, and I know it.

His coalition either votes "no" and loses in a landslide—which might very well happen anyway. Even his own reelection wasn't assured.

Or we vote "yes" and hope to stop the bleeding.

Harlan had some phone calls to make.

~ ~ ~

"You wanted to see me, Mr. Roberts?"

Gary Roberts was solidly-built from years of working in a quarry. His mind was as hardened as the callouses on his hands. Working with explosives did that. You either paid attention to the smallest details, or you died.

"Sit down, Harv."

"What's this about?" Harv asked. His stomach tightened. Gary never asked him to sit before.

Gary gave him a stern look.

"I warned you, Harv. I said no more politics in the quarry."

"I *don't* talk politics," Harv said. He squirmed in his chair. He knew he was being defensive, but what else could he say?

"Now you're gonna lie to me? Because there is nothing I despise more than a liar."

Liar?

Harvey's face flushed red.

"What?" Harv said. "You want me to pretend that nothing's going on and just—what, be a *drone* and do what I'm told? Never mind that we're on the brink of a nuclear *war?* Just move along, nothing to see here?"

"You're fired, Harvey. Get your stuff. Turn in your credentials at the guard shack."

"You can't fire me," Harvey said, standing now. His heart raced. *What do I tell Karen?* "I've got almost thirty years here!"

"You had fair warning. You've got a solid 401k by now. It's transferable. I wish you luck, Harvey."

Gary stood and looked to the trailer door. He waved someone to come in.

A burly man in a hardhat opened the door, standing halfway in and halfway out. His eyes bored into Harvey's. His hands rested on his tool belt.

"You know Jerry. He'll walk you out."

Harvey gripped the back of the chair he had sat on, and leaned on it. He couldn't just walk out right then and there. His legs were trembling.

~ ~ ~

Something to meet the moment, President Mimar Gökalp had said.

The PKK was practically defeated. They had, once again, gone to ground. There hadn't been a single incident associated with, or attributed to, the PKK in months.

Instead of burying them, Gökalp offers them the very keys to the Kingdom.

The agreement would elevate Turkish Kurdistan to co-equal status with the rest of Türkiye. Not only that, but Türkiye itself would be reduced to a rump state. Gökalp would agree to hand over Kurdish lands, which comprise nearly thirty percent of Türkiye's territory, to the newly established and Turkish-recognized Republic of Kurdistan.

But there was a catch. *A master stroke.*

The Kurds had to agree to enter into union with Türkiye. It would be a Union of two states, Türkiye and Kurdistan, with a new Union Parliament. It would be based in Ankara, but separate from the Grand National Assembly of Türkiye—which would remain Türkiye's national parliament. One city, two parliaments. Kurdistan would have a Grand National Assembly of its own in Diyarbakır.

The ceremony marking the agreement was a sight to behold. Turkish fighter planes roared overhead. In Diyarbakır and throughout what would become an independent Kurdistan, large high-definition screens were set up in town squares to watch the ceremony live. People danced and partied. Families came out to celebrate.

In Türkiye proper, the celebrations were more subdued. No one was thrilled with the idea of a rump Türkiye and the idea of a new Union—a supranational entity akin to the earliest iteration of the European Union. Of course, one would have to wait and see.

President Mimar Gökalp and PKK leader Jwan Nouri stood side by side, smiling and waving to the crowd. A row of Turkish and Kurdish flags fluttered behind them.

The moment of truth had arrived.

The crowds at Anıtkabir—the mausoleum of Mustafa Kemal Atatürk, the founder of modern Türkiye—grew quiet as Gökalp and Nouri stepped forward, hand in hand.

Not far away, in Kızılay Square, the crowds also grew quiet as they watched the ceremony. Traffic came to a standstill.

The Turkish and Kurdish flags fluttering in the wind was the only sound when President Gökalp bent over a table and signed a document.

It was Jwan Nouri's turn. Without hesitation, he, too, bent over and signed the document.

"Mr. President," Gökalp said—and with those two words, crowds in Diyarbakır and throughout Kurdistan erupted in celebration. Jwan Nouri was now President of the Republic of Kurdistan.

Gökalp handed Nouri his pen.

"Mr. President," Nouri said. He handed *his* pen to Gökalp.

Together, the two held up the binder containing the Treaty of Ankara.

They turned and faced the flag pole on which a super-sized flag of Türkiye waved gently in the wind.

The flag had stood solo since the opening of Anıtkabir some eighty years ago. But a second pole was erected next to it. A new, equally large, flag was attached, and slowly rose to take its place alongside Türkiye's.

The new flag was identical to the Turkish flag—red with a white crescent moon and star—but with one significant difference: A gold band adorned the flag's border at the top and bottom.

It was the national flag of a newly born country—The Treaty Union of Ankara.

~ ~ ~

Tayfun Ulusoy flew into Baghdad as his first foreign assignment as Grand Vizier. The international airport at Baghdad was captured by Türkiye's special forces, the *Bordo Bereliler*—the Maroon Berets—not long before they liberated the American Embassy there.

Windows throughout the airport were still blown out. The airport terminals were, consequently, wide open-air hallways. The daytime heat was stifling, and it was still only 9:00 a.m. Glass crunched beneath his shoes as he and his entourage of Maroon Berets toured the airport.

Official events and honors awaited him at the American Embassy that the Maroon Berets had liberated. Daddy Longlegs was there to personally thank him. Tayfun remembered finding Daddy in his embassy's backyard after he had climbed the wall separating Türkiye's embassy from Guyana's. He was trying to avoid protesters lined up on Massachusetts Avenue, the main road in front of Türkiye's embassy, and to keep his presence there discreet.

He appealed to Türkiye as a member of NATO. He pleaded for immediate assistance. The American Embassy was under a sustained assault, and the United States had no assets in the vicinity to protect or evacuate its personnel. He promised a Great Rapprochement between America and Türkiye after nearly three decades of diverging interests. This would be a brotherhood forged in blood.

But first things first.

Thirty minutes later his convoy avoided the American Embassy altogether, and crossed the Tigris River. They stopped at the *Amanat Baghdad,* the headquarters of the city's municipal government.

Like the airport, the Amanat Baghdad was in bad shape. Its windows were blown out, and gaping holes pockmarked the building. Unbeknownst to Tayfun, Amanat Baghdad stood astride the Al Khilani

Mosque, whose courtyard was the staging ground for the Iranian-backed Shia militants who had launched the attack on the American Embassy.

He presented his diplomatic credentials to the building's guards, but there really was no need. The guards stood aside the moment they saw the Maroon Berets.

Tayfun found his way to the office of the *Ameen Baghdad*—the Mayor of Baghdad.

There was no door to the office. It had apparently been blown off its hinges during the fighting.

A balding, mustachioed man sat behind a large wooden desk that was also damaged and chipped. He looked up when he heard glass and debris crunch under Tayfun's feet.

"Who are you?" he demanded. Maroon Berets filed in behind Tayfun, and the man pushed himself away from his desk. His demeanor changed in an instant.

"W-what may I d-do for you, gentlemen?" he asked.

"Your Excellency, your city has endured much. The Parliament of the Treaty Union of Ankara stands ready to act, pending only your signature."

Tayfun presented an ornate leather binder. It contained a document adorned with beautiful calligraphy.

The Ameen looked it over. It was titled *"Petition for Stabilization Assistance to the Parliament of the Treaty Union of Ankara, submitted by the Municipality of Baghdad."*

"I don't understand," the Ameen said. A sweat had broken out on his forehead. "Th-this should b-b-be—"

"Be what?"

"B-be from the P-p-president. I am only the Ameen."

"The president of what?" Tayfun asked.

The Ameen's eyes were large. He looked from Tayfun to the Maroon Berets and back to Tayfun.

He licked his lips.

"Iraq." His voice was a whisper.

"What is this Iraq you speak of?" Tayfun walked around the desk. "Where is it?"

"The Americans, for one, would surely like to know." Tayfun continued: "They appealed to this so-called Iraq to protect their embassy. There was no Iraq to be found."

"Now, *I* look around and I see *Turks*—" he swept his hand over the Maroon Berets—"providing security for the Americans." Tayfun was nearly nose-to-nose now with the Ameen.

"And for you."

Tayfun placed the document on the Ameen's desk. He reached into his pocket and retrieved a pen.

"You know, the Qur'an teaches that those who return with sincerity are to be welcomed, not punished. Baghdad is returned to the bosom—and we will shelter her."

Tayfun tapped the document with his finger.

"Now sign the fucking thing."

CHAPTER TWENTY-FIVE

By 0500, the attacks had stopped.

Captain Treviño stood near the embassy's front gate sipping the last of his bottled water. The air was still thick with tension. It was quiet now, but Treviño wasn't ready to let his guard down.

"They went to bed," muttered Sergeant Rivas, squinting east. "Militants get tired too."

Treviño didn't answer. He continued to scan the city with his night vision binoculars.

High above the city, invisible to radar and silent to the naked ear, a Navy MQ-45 Devil Ray drone loitered in the dark sky. Launched hours earlier from the USS *Barack Obama* in the Gulf, the Devil Ray was feeding real-time thermal and multi-spectral imagery directly to the 26th MEU's command node.

"Nothing within ten blocks," came the voice of Gunnery Sergeant White from the overwatch trailer aboard the USS *Wasp*. "We've got scattered heat signatures, but no groups larger than three. Looks like they've pulled back."

Treviño nodded. "Copy that. Any vehicles moving?"

"Negative," White replied. "Dusty streets and empty alleys. Let's get you out."

Three minutes later, the first MV-22 appeared low on the horizon, shimmering in Treviño's binoculars. Then a second. Then a third.

They had lifted off from Riyadh International Airport, where US Air Force special forces commandos—Combat Controllers and Special Tactics Teams—had secured a corner of the airport earlier in the evening.

The Ospreys came in low and fast, ducking under radar and drifting down behind the embassy compound wall. There, an extraction landing zone had been hastily carved out of a garden and two tennis courts.

The evacuees—embassy staff, their dependents, and cleared civilians—had already been lined up by 0400. They were bleary-eyed. Some carried sleeping children.

"Two minutes per bird," Treviño barked at the evacuees. "No extra bags. If you can't carry it while running, it stays."

"*Devil Ray* confirms clear corridor all the way to the ridge," White crackled in again.

By 0534, the last Osprey lifted off.

The embassy was empty, save for Treviño, Rivas, and six rear-guard Marines. One carried the folded Stars and Stripes.

A final thermal sweep came through.

"You're ghosted," said White. "Nothing but sand and scorpions."

"Then we're done," Treviño said, turning toward the idling tiltrotor—this one a sleek Valor.

The Valor rose into the dawn and banked south.

But the *Devil Ray* remained on station for another hour, circling silently above the capital—until the last in a long train of C-17s lifted off from Riyadh International Airport, ferrying the evacuees out of the country formerly known as Saudi Arabia.

Down below, Riyadh waited for the sun to rise and the chaos to begin anew.

But the Americans were gone.

Operation *Desert Knight* went off without hitch.

~ ~ ~

Harlan sat in the back of an armored Cadillac SUV as it sped across the tarmac of Joint Base Andrews.

The Cadillac rounded the tail of a hulking C-17 Globemaster.

There. Floodlights bathed a C-32 in pale gold. A stair truck idled beside it.

At the base of the stairs was the unmistakable form of Daddy Longlegs. He clutched a leather satchel, which dangled at his side. His coat snapped briskly in the wind.

He looked like some kind of super secret agent man.

Or villain.

Harlan Clark stepped out.

"You got word?" Daddy asked.

"Yes sir. Miss Sanchez will introduce the resolution tomorrow."

"Well," Daddy smiled. "I better get out of here before the President orders me back."

Daddy could read Harlan's face. He was conflicted. Even his shoulders sagged. He was in a political vice. The whole Republican Party was.

Daddy slapped him on the shoulder and offered a broad, toothy smile.

"Lighten up, buddy," he said. "It's not the end of the world. *That* doesn't happen unless I say so. "

Harlan smiled weakly. He straightened.

"We will fight," he said.

"You will do no such thing. I want you to vote 'yes.'"

Harlan blinked. "You want me to vote … to *impeach* you?"

"You bet," Daddy said. He laughed, but his eyes were predatory. "They're itching for a fight, and they don't have a clue who they're getting into the ring with. They should have been careful what they wished for."

Daddy's phone buzzed. He held it aloft. "I've been waiting for this. I have to take it.

"You're a good friend, Harlan. Now go on."

Daddy turned and looked up at the aircraft, the phone pressed to his ear.

Harlan looked, too.

The colors of the aircraft were … *pretty*. A baby blue bottom half, topped by white. And the words "UNITED STATES OF AMERICA" above the windows.

"… He needs to believe it's real," said Daddy into the phone. "Not eighty percent. Not passable. But *one hundred percent* real. I want that tarmac cleared like the Ayatollah believes he's come to welcome the return of the Mahdi himself—right there on the runway."

"You'll have it before you land."

"That's why I called *you*, Ari."

Daddy hung up and climbed the stairs without looking back.

~ ~ ~

Inside the aircraft, Daddy poked his head into the dimly lit cockpit.

"Gentlemen," he said, greeting the pilots. He shook hands and offered small talk.

"By the way," he added, "we'll be going dark as soon as we're aloft. It's a communications exercise. Trying out some new high-tech spoofing technology. At any point during the flight, we might be ordered to turn around and come back."

The pilots stared blankly at Daddy.

"But they'll need the right password," Daddy said.

"What is the password, sir?" the co-pilot asked.

Daddy grinned.

"Buckle up."

~ ~ ~

The walls were sandblasted and the windows blown out. The air held the scent of gunpowder and Turkish cigarettes.

But the flag was still there.

Vice President George "Daddy Longlegs" Wartmann stepped into the compound's main atrium. Broken glass and chipped concrete crunched under his feet.

Dozens of embassy staff stood in loose formation—some in rumpled suits, others in flak jackets or dusty polos. Behind them, Turkish Maroon Berets lined the wall. They were young and fit to a man, with rifles slung over their shoulders. Daddy was impressed.

But he went to the Americans first. He moved down the line, shaking hands, making small talk, and asking if they needed anything, especially food, water, and shelter.

Next, he stood among the Embassy Marines, who gathered around him in a circle.

"I am proud of you," he said. "You held."

Some nodded. Some had dust in their eyes.

Then came the Turks. Daddy made his way to the back where the Maroon Berets were lined up in columns.

Daddy didn't say anything. No politicking *here*. These were *soldiers'* soldiers. And foreign ones at that.

He simply walked slowly, making eye contact and nodding to each one. Tayfun Ulusoy walked beside him.

After nodding to the final man, Daddy turned to Tayfun.

"My friend, please join me for a private meeting." He turned to a Marine. "Take us to the Ambassador's office."

~ ~ ~

The commander of the Maroon Berets—a tall, clean-shaven, stone-faced colonel—followed a step behind Daddy and Tayfun.

Daddy paused and looked to the colonel, then to Ulusoy.

"I was hoping for a—"

"I prefer that he comes," Tayfun said. "He'll stay out of the way."

"Of course," Daddy said, and smiled.

The Ambassador's office, deep in the compound, was untouched by combat. From the oak tables and cabinets, to the posh chairs and sofa, to the cozy lamps, it was an island of cozy comfort.

Rather than sit at the Ambassador's desk, Daddy chose a working table against the wall so the two could sit across from each other.

As equals.

To placate the vibe emanating so strongly off Tayfun that I'd have to be comatose to miss it.

Daddy fished through the Ambassador's bar in the corner and fetched a couple of shot glasses. He brought them to the table and sat. He reached into his breast pocket and retrieved a golden flask.

He half-filled both of the tiny glasses and slid one to Tayfun.

"My personal favorite," Daddy said. "Kentucky bourbon. There's a distillery right across the river from Cincinnati."

Daddy raised his glass as a toast. Tayfun obliged.

Both downed a shot.

"You pulled our chestnuts out of the fire, Tayfun," Daddy said as he refilled the glasses.

"I wanted to thank you personally." Daddy extended his hand. Tayfun took it and smiled. He was already relaxing. It was strong bourbon.

"I still remember you climbing over the wall into my backyard in Washington," Tayfun said. He laughed. He and Daddy downed another shot.

"Imagine, Daddy Longlegs climbing walls like a thief in the night."

Daddy chuckled. "Barriers are made for climbing."

He tossed back the rest of his bourbon, then set the glass down with a soft *clink*.

A moment passed.

"You wouldn't happen to have a few extra eyes in the sky," he said, "that might be inclined to *not* see a particular bird ... say, at a particular time?"

Tayfun didn't answer right away. But after a moment, he leaned in and poured them each another shot.

"For you?" he said. "For you, George ... perhaps."

Tayfun looked around the Ambassador's office.

"Tell me, George, what is going to happen here—to all of this?"

Daddy was momentarily perplexed. "Well, I suppose—"

"I mean," Tayfun interrupted, "why would America maintain an embassy in Baghdad when the capital is in Ankara?"

Tayfun nodded to the Maroon Beret colonel, who stood by the door. He walked over and presented Daddy the leather document binder— the *Petition for Stabilization Assistance to the Parliament of the Treaty Union of Ankara.*

"Signed by the Mayor of Baghdad," Tayfun said. "And ratified by the council."

Daddy's smile faltered.

~ ~ ~

Daddy and Tayfun stood shoulder to shoulder on the tarmac at Baghdad's airport. A gray C-17 cargo plane with US Air Force markings loomed before them, its engines revved up.

"One more thing," Daddy shouted. "You never saw this on the tarmac."

Tayfun nodded.

"And what should I say you flew out on?"

Daddy grinned.

"Say I took a flying carpet."

He took a few steps toward the ramp, then paused and turned back.

"Oh—and if things go sideways in Kuwait ... there's a team with eyes on. If you could make sure they've got a clean lane to fish me out ..."

Tayfun gave a slow nod. "You always travel with insurance?"

Daddy winked. "I never leave home without it."

Tayfun watched Daddy board the aircraft. Then he turned and scoured the desert in the distance.

The hair on the back of his neck stood up. Quite suddenly, he felt like he was being watched by a thousand eyes.

CHAPTER TWENTY-SIX

Ari Benjamin stood behind the shoulder of a young tech in the Spiral Tower. A massive screen displayed a side-by-side dashboard: on the left, intercepted Iranian comms. On the right, the interface of a rapidly deployed deepfake network codenamed *Silkroad Echo*.

"We've spoofed their Foreign Ministry DNS completely," the tech said. "They think they're exchanging encrypted messages with Beijing."

"And we're inside their message thread?" Ari asked.

"Every thread," said another tech. "Our replies even mimic a diplomatic cipher they used with China last year. Metadata's been backdated to match."

Ari leaned in. "Have they mentioned the Supreme Leader?"

"Just now. Tehran's scrambling to verify a flight plan from Beijing to Tehran—callsign *Red Lantern 1*. Supposed to be the Chinese President himself."

A third analyst chimed in. "They're checking overflight rights with Azerbaijan. Landing path's now aligned—coming in low and slow over the Caspian."

Ari nodded. "Good. Keep feeding confirmations from our 'Chinese' back channel."

"What's the final message?" the first tech asked.

Ari walked slowly to the center of the room. He glanced up at the blinking red dot marked *Bourbon Force 2*, approaching from the north.

"Tell them this," he said. "'Our leader comes with deep respect and sincere regard for His Eminence. He wishes a quiet and private dialog—without ceremony or press. Out of deference, his aircraft will be forced to return if discretion cannot be guaranteed.'"

The room was silent, save for the beeping of computers. Then one of the techs said, "It's being passed to Imam Doran, the Supreme Leader's Chief of Staff."

Ari went to the window and looked out on the Mediterranean in the distance.

This has got to be the craziest stunt in history. If we pull this off, I'm buying you a drink, Daddy. Scratch that. You're buying me one, you crazy bastard.

~ ~ ~

The Grand Ayatollah Sayyid Ali al-Milani stood beneath a hastily erected canopy at the edge of the tarmac on Doshan Tappeh Air Base in eastern Tehran. He was flanked by Habibollah Nasirzadeh, Iran's highest-ranked military officer; Imam Jalil Doran, the Supreme Leader's Chief of Staff, and two members of his private guard.

There was no press, no flags, no cameras. Only the wind—just as President Li had requested.

It was his first time above ground since the war began.

The snow-capped peaks of the Elborz Mountains loomed above the skyline of Tehran.

Milani's eyes scanned the sky.

There.

Dipping out of the blue sky, and framed by the snow-capped mountains, a large gray aircraft—a Xi'an Y-20, China's premier strategic airlift cargo plane—descended against the darkening landscape.

The aircraft landed and immediately slowed as it traveled down the runway. It turned onto the taxiway and raced toward the tarmac.

It made a final turn, its engines ear-piercing, pulling up next to the canopy.

Only then did Al-Milani and his entourage see the US Air Force roundel and the words U.S. Air Force stenciled on the side of the aircraft.

Al-Milani smiled. *They are precise in their subterfuge, aren't they?*

The four engines spooled down in a long descending whine. The aircraft's rear ramp lowered.

A moment passed.

Then he appeared.

A tall, gaunt, broad-shouldered man in a tailored suit descended the ramp alone.

Not President Li.

Al-Milani squinted.

It was America's Vice President, George Wartmann.

Daddy Longlegs.

The man smiled broadly, as if in … *Surprise!*

Al-Milani didn't know whether to be infuriated … or be in awe.

It was awe that came naturally. He couldn't help but smile.

The audacity.

Al-Milani stepped forward.

He was immediately struck by how the tall the man was.

"Your Eminence," Daddy said, bowing his head just enough.

The Ayatollah's expression was unreadable. "Mr. Wartmann," he replied. "This is … unexpected."

Daddy's smiled widened. "History rarely knocks before it enters."

Al-Milani nodded. He wasn't sure what to do next.

Do I have him arrested?

He looked back to the aircraft. Armed men in black—even their faces were painted black—nonchalantly took up positions around the aircraft, kneeling and facing outwards.

"Oh, right," said Daddy, looking back, too.

"I'm almost intrigued about what the headlines would be if we were both cut down right here on the tarmac due to a—well, it would entirely be my fault, wouldn't it?" Daddy chuckled.

His laugh was genuine.

The man is as comfortable in his skin as a King on his throne.

The Supreme Leader didn't react. He turned and walked, slowly, hands clasped behind his back.

Daddy walked at his side.

"Why have you come, Mr. Wartmann?"

~ ~ ~

The sun had slipped behind the Alborz Mountains, casting a golden haze over Tehran's longest and most storied boulevard. Streetlights flickered on beneath the canopy of sycamores that stretched in both directions, snaking around turns, their branches whispering with the soft breeze. Along the eastern edge, a vibrant stream trickled beside the walkway, its waters catching glimmers of orange and violet from the fading sky.

This was the famous Valiasr Street, in northern Tehran.

Police had cordoned off a two-block stretch of the busy road, allowing two tall men to walk side by side beneath the trees, unmolested by crowds. One wore a simple black robe and soft leather shoes, hands folded neatly behind his back. The other wore a dusty suit, open at the collar.

For several minutes, neither spoke. Daddy took in the sounds of Tehran: heavy traffic just a block away in either direction, but far enough to be muffled; the percolation of water in the stream; chirping birds; the wind threading the branches above.

Weathered buildings stood just beyond the trees.

Tehran was far more cosmopolitan than Daddy had anticipated. It was a bustling, modern city, teeming with life.

I should have known better. This is the heart of the fabled Persian Empire.

They walked a few more paces. Ahead, there was a small café, lit by soft golden bulbs under an awning of climbing vines. A boy was stacking chairs. The Supreme Leader gestured subtly, and the boy froze.

"We will sit here," said Al-Milani. "Ice cream?"

Daddy looked surprised. "I never say no to pistachio."

Moments later, the two men sat in quiet dusk, each with a paper bowl of *bastani sonnati*—the saffron-pistachio kind, flecked with bits of frozen cream. They ate without speaking until …

"God*damn,*" Daddy spoke. "That's the best ice cream I've ever had, Padre."

Al-Milani took another spoonful and studied Daddy out of the corner of his eye.

He is so … vulgar. How did he become Vice President of the United States? How has he been such a force in Washington for so long?

Al-Milani smiled. *It's an act. If he were Iranian, he'd be IRGC all the way.*

"What do you want, Mr. Wartmann?"

Daddy looked up. "The release of 205,000 Americans from the lands you occupy." He continued with his ice cream.

Al-Milani was about to eat another spoonful, but stopped. He put his ice cream down.

"The Koran says—"

"*Save it,* Preacher."

Al-Milani blinked. His mouth hung open before he closed it. His face flushed briefly with anger.

Daddy put his ice cream down. "I'm sorry, Your Eminence, but I didn't come all this way for a sermon. I came for my countrymen. My time here is short."

Al-Milani said nothing. He glanced at his melting ice cream, then stood. Daddy followed.

The two began to walk again.

Al-Milani was taking too long to think, so Daddy broke the silence.

"You are holding over 200,000 Americans *hostage*," Daddy said. "You are responsible for the well-being of every single one of them."

"We are not in the business of holding hostages, Mr. Wartmann," the Imam said.

"I suppose I can put aside the 444-Day Iran Hostage Crisis. I guess it's been long enough. The statute of limitations might even apply on *that* ordeal."

Daddy chuckled.

"So, you agree to allow my citizens to leave, then."

"They're free to leave—just not on American or allied aircraft."

Al-Milani stopped and faced Daddy.

"Who knows what would show up in a fleet of American aircraft? An hour ago, I was waiting for the President of China. But look what turned up instead."

Daddy smirked. He tossed his empty bowl and spoon into a trash bin.

"Touché, Padre."

So, if not American or allied planes, then who?

Daddy thought back to an incident some thirty years before. An American P-3 spy plane had made an emergency landing on Hainan Island in China after colliding with a Chinese fighter plane over the South China Sea.

China did not allow America to send maintenance crews to repair the aircraft and fly it home. In fact, China wouldn't allow the aircraft to fly out at all. It had to be taken apart and flown out on a cargo plane—a *Russian* cargo plane.

"I have a proposal," Daddy said.

~ ~ ~

The House chamber was full. Every seat was occupied, and the aisles were crowded with aides. Every gallery was full, too, crammed with journalists, photographers, and TV cameras.

At exactly noon, Speaker Nate Shepherd stood at the rostrum, his face as solemn as any other day. He struck the gavel. "The House will be in order," he said in his signature bored, gravelly voice.

The din of conversation ebbed. The House Chaplain stepped to the podium. He glanced at Shepherd.

Keep it short, Shepherd had warned him. *Do your homina homina and get the fuck off the stage.*

The Chaplain cleared his throat. "Let us say the Lord's Prayer."

When it was over, Shepherd nodded his approval.

Next up was a young girl scout from some Congressperson's district in Nebraska. She enthusiastically led the House in the Pledge of Allegiance. Most congresspeople mumbled their way through it, hardly getting any of the words particularly right.

Shepherd returned to the podium.

"The Chair has examined the Journal of the last day's proceedings and announces to the House that it will stand approved unless there is objection."

Shepherd scanned the Chamber.

"Hearing no objection, the Journal stands approved."

He looked down at his notes, then spoke again.

"Under clause 2(a)(1) of Rule IX, the Chair recognizes the gentlewoman from New York for the purpose of presenting a privileged resolution."

Murmurs filled the Chamber once again as Representative Ellen Sanchez, Minority Leader from Brooklyn, stepped into the well of the House. She carried a black leather binder in her left hand, stamped in gold with the Seal of the House of Representatives.

"Mr. Speaker, pursuant to notice previously given to all members of this House, I rise today to introduce House Resolution 597—impeaching President Cynthia Belle and Vice President George Wartmann for high crimes and misdemeanors."

Although everyone knew what was coming, the Chamber nonetheless erupted into murmurs and whispers—even applause.

Shepherd struck the gavel again. "There will be order in the Chamber."

Ella continued, her voice small but clear:

"This resolution reflects a moment of national gravity. It does not come in anger. It comes in sorrow—and in duty. I submit the text of the resolution for immediate consideration as a privileged motion."

Speaker Shepherd nodded slowly. "The gentlewoman from New York has submitted a privileged resolution. Without objection, the resolution will be read and entered into the record."

Ella handed the binder to the reading clerk, who opened the binder. The clerk cleared her voice and began.

But it was Ella that remained at the center of the Chamber's attention. She stood rooted in place, listening and watching.

Reporters and photographers busily scribbled notes and snapped photos.

Members of Congress sat unusually raptured in their seats.

They were witnessing history.

~ ~ ~

On the second floor of the White House, President Belle was sprawled on a sofa in the residence Treaty Room.

The First Gentleman, Archie Meglowin, paced behind her, nursing a glass of Cabernet. He stayed quiet while the President's Chief of Staff, Martin Hartshorne, kept tabs on the vote.

"There are 210 Democrats in the House," Martin said. "Let's assume that all of them vote 'yes.' They would still need another eight votes."

"Eight?" asked Archie. "That's *all?*"

"That's a lot," Martin assured. "The second that *one* Republican goes rogue, they will be tarred and feathered—and they know it."

The voting had already begun. So far, it was split along partisan lines.

"Where's Daddy?" sighed the President.

"He landed in Baghdad," said Bernie Mentzel, her National Security Advisor. "We've been calling the flight crew nonstop, but they keep asking for a password."

"What password?"

Mentzel shrugged. "No one seems to know."

"You know that's *him*, right?" Belle said. She snickered and shook her head. She almost admired him. "Typical Longlegs."

Belle looked to Hartshorne. His eyes were glued to the television monitor. Belle followed his gaze. She had to squint to see it, but there it was. A list of names and their votes.

They were in the C's now. Every name with an "(R)" after it had a "Nay" beside it.

All but one, that is:

Harlan Clark (R)—Yea.

"Jesus Christ!" Belle exploded. *"Where the fuck is Daddy!"*

~ ~ ~

"Tell us about Harlan Clark," the First Gentleman asked.

"Well," said Hartshorne, "he's a diehard conservative. And a hawk. He was supportive of us going to war with Iran. But he's been highly critical of accepting the cease fire. He calls it a capitulation."

"Is he a problem?"

Hartshorne exhaled slowly. "He's a rabble-rouser. A leader in the Freedom Caucus. He's either just bucked his own bloc, or he's leading a rebellion."

A few minutes later, they got their answer.

Two more Republicans—so-called Blue Elephants, known for sometimes aligning with Democrats—had also voted *yea*. But it was another Freedom Caucus member who signaled the end: Bob Larson of North

Carolina. His district included Fort Bragg.

That made four Republican defections. Only four more were needed.

When the third Freedom Caucus Republican cast a *yea* vote, President Belle rose from the couch.

There was no longer any doubt about the outcome.

She turned off the monitor. Then she turned to Hartshorne and the First Gentleman.

"Our defense starts now. We need to assemble a team."

"I'll make some phone calls," Archie said. "Time to call in some favors."

Archie was the youngest son of the late British billionaire financier Alfred Meglowin. His eldest brother Earl currently ran the firm. Though based in London, the Meglowin Group was global.

Earl would be his first call.

"What are you waiting for?" Belle asked.

An aid entered, and leaned into Hartshorne's ear.

"Is it official?" Belle asked.

Hartshorne nodded. "They just reached 218 *yeas*."

President Belle and Vice President Wartmann were officially impeached.

CHAPTER TWENTY-SEVEN

The final tally was 220 *yeas*—including *ten* Republican defections.

"To 220!"

A loud cheer spilled into the night on 8th Street Southeast, just across the Southeast Freeway from Navy Yard.

The Black Shoe was a local favorite, a sports bar with a spacious rooftop deck overlooking 8th Street.

It sat directly across from Washington's iconic redbrick Marine Barracks. Within walking distance of both the Barracks and Navy Yard, it was one of the only true military bars in DC—owned and operated by a retired Navy Senior Chief Petty Officer.

Most of the staffers, and even a few of the politicians, were oblivious to its identity. If they noticed the naval décor, they assumed it was part of a touristy gimmick—if they gave it any thought at all.

But Ella was a military brat. Her father was a retired Navy Chief Petty Officer. She recognized The Black Shoe for what it was the moment she stepped inside. And when she did, the boisterous crowd erupted.

"The woman of the hour!"

"Woman of the year!"

Ella accepted a beer and held it aloft. "Thank you everyone for your hard work!"

The bar hushed as she spoke.

"But let's be honest: the hard work is only just beginning."

Ella glanced around the room. Each tap handle resembled a ship's wheel. The bar bell was a ship's bell. The restrooms were marked "The Head."

She caught the eye of the bar manager. He didn't look thrilled.

She pulled out a chair and started to climb up. A few aides offered hands, steadying her as she stood tall above the crowd.

"I propose a toast," she said, lifting her beer again.

"*A toast, a toast!*"

Ella looked back to the manager. *Or is he the owner?*

"To country, not party!"

~ ~ ~

The Impeachment Managers assembled at the base of the House chamber steps. There were seven in total, and each a woman. That fact—that the team wound up being all women—was neither deliberate, nor purposefully symbolic. To a person, they were selected for their reputation as thoughtful, hard workers and leaders in the House.

It helped that each was a former—and formidable—prosecutor or attorney general, with over a century of courtroom experience between them.

Ella Sanchez stood at their head, flanked by Congresswoman Willa Denton of Maine, the lone Republican in the delegation. As cameras clicked and aides cleared a path through the corridor, Ella caught a voice just behind the press line.

"*All women,*" someone snickered. "*Against the first woman president. That's a hell of a headline.*"

The speaker was a young, slick-haired, reporter. Her credentials swung around her neck as she angled her phone for video.

Ella walked right up to her. "You think this is about *gender?*"

The reporter blinked.

"This is about *leadership*. About *accountability*. And about *country*. Not party. And *certainly* not gender."

Ella pivoted back to her colleagues.

They began a solemn walk across the Capitol, trailed by aides and photographers. The Articles of Impeachment were carried in a hardbound folder by the Republican, Willa Denton.

Okay, *that* was symbolic.

They entered the Senate chamber through its ornate doors. The room quieted.

All of the senators rose.

The House Managers stepped forward. Willa Denton—the Republican—delivered the documents to the Senate Clerk, then spoke.

"The House has appointed Managers to conduct the trial, and now asks that the Senate proceed with all due form."

At the far end, the Senate Sergeant-at-Arms stepped forward and raised his voice with practiced formality.

"Madam President," he said, addressing the Senate's presiding officer. "The House of Representatives has appointed Managers to conduct the trial, and I present them, along with the Articles of Impeachment, to the United States Senate."

The Managers turned and exited the Chamber.

~ ~ ~

The lights were low in the comms suite, just the soft green glow of instruments and an occasional flicker from the encrypted display. Daddy Longlegs sat alone at the secure desk, a steaming mug of black tea cradled in one hand, the red folder marked EYES ONLY resting on the table in front of him.

A knock, then a voice through the cracked door.

"Sir? It's him."

Daddy nodded. "Patch him through."

The screen blinked once, then stabilized. There was no image, just a pulsing signal.

And then a voice. It was as clear as if the speaker were sitting across the table.

"Mr. Vice President," said President Chiang Li of the People's Republic of China.

"Mr. President," Daddy said. "Thank you for taking the time."

"Of course," he said. "I have spoken with Tehran. The Supreme Leader relayed your proposal."

Daddy waited. He took a slow sip of his tea.

"It is … quite unorthodox," Li said.

"It's not without precedent," Daddy countered. "It's a page out of Jiang Zemin's playbook, after all."

There was a pause. *They're scrambling to find out what I'm talking about.*

Daddy was patient. *They'll find it—the P-3 incident.*

"I *see,*" Li said, finally. He sounded genuinely intrigued. "A very constructive approach."

Another pause. The ball was still in Li's court.

"We welcome the opportunity to contribute to stability," Chiang continued. "Especially in a time of global flux. In Tehran, in Paris … and unfortunately, even in Washington."

Daddy didn't respond to that, and so another pause ensued.

"We will proceed," Chiang said. "You will hear from my defense ministry shortly. We will move quickly. It is in everyone's interest."

"Thank you, Mr. President."

Daddy thought for a moment.

So … how do I break it to the President?

He smiled.

Like ripping off a band aid, of course.

~ ~ ~

Air Force Two landed, jolting Daddy awake.

He rubbed his face and looked out the window. *Andrews.*

Moments later, the C-32A turned into the Presidential Ramp.

"Uh oh," the Pilot said. "Sir, you might want to look out your window," he called back to the Vice President.

Daddy leaned toward the glass—and almost laughed.

A fleet of black armored SUVs was waiting for him, some flashing blue and red lights. At the center stood President Cynthia Belle, arms folded in a tailored navy power suit. She was flanked by her national security team and what looked like half the Cabinet.

She did not look happy.

Well, he thought. *Guess it's time to pay the piper.*

Daddy put on his suit jacket, tugged its fit, and stepped out.

He saluted the two Marines at the bottom of the stairs.

He winked at them. "Even the VP has to face the music sometimes."

"Good luck, sir," one of the Marines whispered without moving his lips.

"Ha!" Daddy said. "Luck favors the prepared."

Daddy offered his famous mischievous smile.

"And I'm prepared."

~ ~ ~

"Where the hell have you *been … Wartmann?*"

Daddy was right. The President was not in the best of moods.

"You. Went. *Rogue.* I could have you arrested for *treason!*"

"Imagine the optics of *that,*" Daddy offered. He was downright jovial.

"Don't get smart with me. *I'm* the fucking President. *Not* you. Do you even know that we've been *impeached? Both* of us! The trial starts *Monday!*"

"Hmmm," said Daddy. "So does the airlift. You'll have to approve it, of course."

Belle lowered her head, but still glared at Daddy.

"Okay," she said, "I'll bite. *What* airlift?"

~ ~ ~

The President and Vice President walked together, slowly, on the tarmac.

From a distance, it appeared that the two were having a friendly talk. Everyone knew better, though. Even the Marines standing by the stairs of Air Force Two, who were silently rooting for Daddy.

Daddy summarized his visit with the Grand Ayatollah in Tehran, the proposal, and the phone call from Chinese President Chiang Li.

The President stopped and glared at him some more.

"You just buried us," she said.

Us? Daddy thought. *There's no 'us' in 'you'.*

Two C-17s turned onto the Presidential Ramp.

"What is *this?*" the President demanded.

Daddy turned around, then looked back to President Belle.

"Oh, *that,*" he said. He smiled sheepishly.

The ramps lowered, and Americans began walking off the jets.

"Embassy personnel," Daddy said. "Yeah, about that Baghdad trip—"

"Oh dear God."

~ ~ ~

While the contraption was simple in concept, it was far from rudimentary.

The nanoturbines were biodegradable synthetic organisms designed for one purpose: to spin when pressed.

What began as a small team—Isaac and a handful of PhD students—had grown to include scientists across disciplines. Isaac brought in Dr. Linda Swope, a nanobiologist down the road at MIT, as co-PI.

It took two weeks for Lin and his team to write up their report, and another two weeks for Isaac and his co-PI to verify and doublecheck every detail. It was yet another two weeks before they had received feedback from select colleagues across the discipline.

Everyone agreed. The math was sound.

Built to scale, the contraption—they called it a Walmsley Dome, named after their project's sponsor—would generate as much power as the average coal-burning plant, around 500 megawatts.

With improved technology over time, its production capacity would surely grow.

It was time to make some phone calls.

But first things first. Isaac went into his email and found the contact he was looking for. He began to type.

Dear Mr. Walmsley …

CHAPTER TWENTY-EIGHT

Marine Two touched down in front of Number One Observatory Circle.

Daddy stepped out and looked up at the Queen Anne mansion.

Home.

Care awaited him in the foyer. She took his jacket and offered a kiss and a hug when he entered.

"Aren't *you* a sight for sore eyes," Daddy said. His voice was soft.

"Phone's been ringing off the hook since the moment you left," Care said, hanging up his jacket. "The White House."

She looked amused. Daddy smiled.

"Well, I don't think they'll be calling again anytime soon. I am officially *persona non grata* over there. The President informed me herself."

Care made Daddy a sandwich, and they sat in the kitchen. She drank tea while he ate.

He told her about his visit to Baghdad and Tehran, and also about the phone call from President Li.

"Are you sure you know what you're doing, Daddy?" she asked. Her eyes were bemused, and they sparkled.

"I know what I'm doing," he said, nodding—and smiling. "Whether it's *right* or not—well, I guess we'll see."

"You *are* a dreamer, Daddy Longlegs," Care said. "Most people wouldn't mean that as a compliment."

Daddy's smiled widened. "And that's why I married *you*, Miss Care."

An armored SUV pulled into the circular driveway. Oscar Schwartz, the President's National Security Advisor, stepped out.

He looked uncertain.

Care opened the front door. Daddy stood beside her.

"Come in, Oscar," she said.

Oscar sighed and shook Daddy's hand. Care took his jacket.

Oscar looked at the two of them, smiled, and shook his head. "You know, we can't even say your *name* in the White House now. We'll be marched right out the front door and off the grounds."

"I'll let you two talk," Care said, and made her exit.

"Come into my study," Daddy said. Oscar followed him into the small den off the living room.

Maps lined the wall. A high-definition monitor was perched in a corner. A desk full of papers and a large computer monitor. A leather sofa and chair.

"Welcome to my Compass Room," Daddy said.

"This is nice," Oscar said. He sat on the black leather sofa. "It's cozy."

"Want anything?" Daddy asked. "Water? Bourbon?"

"A bourbon would be nice."

Daddy poured Oscar and himself a glass of bourbon, leaving the bottle on the table within reach of both.

"Help yourself to more," Daddy offered. He leaned back in his black leather chair.

"What can I do for you, Oscar?"

Oscar looked at his drink.

"I'd like you to walk me through your thought process. I need to know what we're dealing with."

"What's there to understand? I'm bringing home 200,000 Americans from Iranian-occupied lands."

"But," Oscar hesitated, turning his drink in his hand, "there's the way you are doing it."

"There is no other way. We either bring them home, or we don't."

Oscar nodded, but he clearly wanted more.

"*And,*" Daddy leaned forward … "I'm clearing the board."

Oscar tilted his head.

"Clearing the board?"

"If we get our people back—it doesn't matter *how* we get them back—there are no hostages. No hostages means no leverage—for Iran or anyone else. Which means, we have freedom of movement."

Daddy smiled. "And I can do whatever the fuck I want."

Daddy's menace hung in the air like smoke.

Oscar took a breath.

"China?" he asked.

Daddy waved his hand in dismissal. "So they'll have their moment in the sun. It will pass. And when it does—when the smoke clears—the board is *mine.*"

~ ~ ~

Marine Two again.

This time it was a more spacious V-280 Valor.

Daddy and Care had met with a group of families first. They were special guests of the Vice President of the United States of America. Put up in nearby hotels the night before, they now gathered in the garden of Number One Observatory Circle.

Daddy and Care excelled at small talk, at putting people at ease—even now, when they could both sense the tension among their guests. President Belle's impeachment trial was starting that very day, after all.

Daddy learned long ago to just roll with it. Own it, if you have to, in intimate settings like this. Be gracious. Be humble. *Even if I'd rather stab them in the eye.*

Their guests included two spouses whose husbands were based in Kuwait; two sets of parents whose sons were based in Bahrain and Qatar; the teenage daughter of an officer in Kuwait; the sister of a young sailor in Bahrain; and the mother and daughter of an oil worker in Khobar, Saudi Arabia.

When everyone boarded the V-280, Daddy noted four empty seats. Members of two families had either canceled or refused to show up—undoubtedly because of the impeachments.

Figures.

It was a leisurely thirty-minute flight from Naval Observatory One to Dover Air Force Base in Delaware.

It was a cold, rainy, foggy day. It was May on the coast.

For their guests—whatever their politics—the ride in the tilt-rotor helicopter/aircraft was an absolute *thrill.*

After landing, a Marine held the door open for Daddy and Care.

Daddy stepped off, followed by the other passengers.

He saw the President and her staff. It appeared they had only just arrived as well. He looked at his watch. There was still some time before the first aircraft would arrive from Kuwait.

Daddy scanned the edge of the tarmac and spotted a familiar face among the uniformed personnel—Logistics Specialist Seaman Thew Bryson, clipboard in hand, standing beside a folding table marked "NAVY." He looked sharp in his dress whites.

Daddy crossed the tarmac toward him.

"Crackerjacks," he said with an approving nod, noting Thew's uniform. It sported a single purple ribbon on the left breast: the Purple Heart.

Thew stood at attention and saluted.

Daddy returned the salute.

"Looking sharp, sailor."

"Thank you, sir," Thew said.

There was a stir in the bleachers. Daddy tilted his head and listened.

There it was—the low whine of a jet engine, distant but closing, somewhere in the foggy sky.

It was time.

~ ~ ~

Senators filed into the chamber and took their seats. The public galleries were packed. As the clock on the dais chimed the hour, the gavel sounded, calling the Senate to order.

Chief Justice Graham McAllister rose from the bench, laid aside his robe, and spoke into the hush:

"The Senate will come to order. Pursuant to the Constitution and the Rules of the Senate, the Articles of Impeachment against President Cynthia Belle have been received, and the trial shall now commence."

A clerk read aloud the lone Article of Impeachment charging the President with "high crimes and misdemeanors" for "initiating armed conflict without strategic contingency." As the final words echoed off the chamber's carved oak, another clerk handed two leather-bound volumes to the Senate Clerk.

Chief Justice McAllister turned to the Senators.

"All Senators are now sworn. Please rise and raise your right hand."

A ripple of mumbling through the chamber. Every Senator—Republican and Democrat—swore the oath of impartial justice:

"I do solemnly swear that in all things appertaining to the trial of the impeachment of Cynthia Belle, President of the United States, now pending, I will do impartial justice according to the Constitution and laws, so help me God."

Once the Senators were seated again, the Chief Justice directed his attention to the House Managers, waiting at the dais to his right.

"Managers of the House, you will now be sworn."

Ella Sanchez stepped forward first, hand on the Bible, and intoned, "I do solemnly swear…" One by one, her colleagues followed.

The Chief Justice then invited opening statements:

"The Managers of the House of Representatives will now present their opening argument. Counsel for the President will have the opportunity to respond thereafter."

All eyes shifted to the lectern on the left, where President Belle's defense team—headed by former Solicitor General Marcus Flynn—rose to speak.

The trial of President Cynthia Belle was officially under way.

~ ~ ~

"Ladies and Gentlemen," a voice boomed over the loudspeakers. "Please take your seats."

The speaker sounded like a boxing emcee. *Are you ready to rum-bulllllll* …

"The first flight of *Operation Homebound* is arriving now. We have *ten* inbound flights, each aircraft carrying 300 passengers."

The crowd erupted in applause.

It had the feel of an air show.

And you're getting an air show, alright, Daddy thought, smiling inwardly.

The headlights appeared first as the plane dipped out of the clouds. The plane itself was a hulking gray mass amid the fog and mist. The lights seemed to dangle in midair for a moment before the plane grew larger and then lowered to the runway.

It sped past—leaving a trail of water vapor and mist in its wake—and out of view.

A moment later, the aircraft reappeared, taxiing the opposite way, at a steady, slower pace.

The crowd applauded again. Family members jumped up and down with anticipation.

The aircraft maneuvered a couple of turns, then headed straight for the audience, its engines *loud*.

A crewman stood in a forward hatch, holding a flag aloft outside the aircraft.

As the plane drew closer, murmurs rose from the audience. The plane turned away and then stopped parallel to the audience and VIPs.

Murmurs turned to gasps … and then silence.

The flag was unmistakable: It was a red banner with a yellow star in the upper left quadrant flanked by four smaller yellow stars—the flag of the People's Republic of China. And painted near the tail, bold against the dark gray of the fuselage: a red star with wings on either side, each with a yellow outline—the roundel of the People's Liberation Army Air Force (PLAAF).

The aircraft was a Chinese Xi'an Y-20 cargo plane.

~ ~ ~

Breaker Bob stood in the media tent with arms crossed, looking out toward the tarmac. He pinched his left bicep *hard*, trying not to burst out laughing.

He'd received an invitation only two days ago. There was no return address, no official seal, just an embossed card that read:

Your presence is requested at Dover Air Force Base. Operation Homebound. Media access.

Now here he was, shoulder to shoulder with stunned journalists, Pentagon officials, and congressional aides, watching what had to be the most surreal damn thing he'd ever seen.

A Chinese military aircraft landing on US soil. Delivering Americans. At Dover Air Force Base.

Breaker Bob let out a sharp bark of a laugh—he couldn't contain it—drawing a few sideways glances.

He broke out his phone, found his broadcast app, and *voila*, he was broadcasting live on *The Big Picture with Breaker Bob* across multiple media platforms.

"Breaker Nation, I am live back in the USA, at Dover Air Force Base in Delaware. I was invited as media to cover the return of Americans from the Middle East. They're calling it *Operation Homebound*, and …

Oh. My. God."

He turned his phone around to face the Y-20.

"I shit you not, but the first aircraft of Operation Homebound *is a Chinese airplane!* That's a red star on the tail, people! A *Red. Star!* Chiang Li just pulled off the Berlin Airlift in reverse.

"And here comes another one!"

A second Y-20 pulled up now as passengers were still disembarking from the first one.

"Breaker Nation, you are witnessing *history.* Not the kind they'll tell your grandkids about. The kind they'll try to *bury.* Like Jimmy Hoffa, but with chopsticks and trade deficits."

The camera trembled slightly in his grip as he laughed.

He caught Daddy Longlegs in the distance shaking hands with evacuees and posing for photos.

"Oh, he *planned* this, folks," he whispered. "This is Daddy's grand finale. And I gotta say—if the man's going down, he's doing it in *style.*"

He turned the camera phone back on himself.

"This ain't just geopolitics, folks. This is a rogue wave. You either drop in and ride it, or you wipe out hard—and don't expect your own country to come rescue you. Not when Beijing's the one bringing the boards."

He turned slightly, catching the red flag flapping from the cockpit window of the second Y-20 as it rolled to a stop.

"And Chiang Li don't surf!"

CHAPTER TWENTY-NINE

Each of the House Managers gave their closing statements, one by one.

Ella Sanchez stood. She was the last.

"We have presented the evidence—which we believe is clear and indisputable—documenting the actions of President Cynthia Belle and her Administration. These actions, we believe, rise to the level of high crimes and misdemeanors. We have heard testimony from high officials and dedicated civil servants. We have seen the destruction wrought on our cities. The lives of ordinary American citizens, destroyed.

It is not too late to restore balance. To restore faith in our democracy. To restore trust in our leadership. But we must *act*—and we must act now."

Ella paused and swept the room with her eyes.

She took a deep breath.

"On behalf of the United States House of Representatives, thank you for your attention—and your service."

~ ~ ~

The Senate had voted to reconvene after the House Managers made their closing arguments.

Buck Arnold, the Senate Whip, made his way down to the well of the Senate. The House Managers were collecting their things.

"Well done," Buck said to the seven women. He was all smiles.

Ella, in contrast, was subdued. "Well, it's in the Senate's hands now. Think you still have the votes?"

Buck looked around the Chamber. It had quickly emptied of Senators.

No one had peeled off into huddled clicks. Wherever two Senators appeared to be chatting, they were mostly jovial, even laughing— clearly they weren't discussing evidence or anything of import related to the trial of the President.

"Guess we'll find out."

He shook the Managers' hands and went for a stroll. As the Whip, he needed to know what everyone was up to.

Buck spoke with several Senators and staff as he followed the foot traffic to the Capitol Subway System. A few minutes later, he was in his inner office with the door closed.

He needed to decompress, if only for a few minutes. He even laid on his couch and closed his eyes. He went through the trial in his head, and counted the votes that he was more or less sure of. Then he started through the ones he wasn't sure about.

He had the Democrats' votes. *That* was a certainty. But he needed sixteen Republicans to jump ship. He was *pretty* sure he had seventeen— but you never can tell. There were a lot of backroom deals and promises that got him there, but anything could go wrong.

This is pointless. They'll vote how they'll vote.

Buck was restless. He got up. Twenty-five minutes had passed.

He walked down the narrow hallway of the Russell Senate Office Building. It was empty. The doors to the Senator's offices were all closed.

Nobody, it seemed, wanted to be seen.

Everyone's hiding.

The floor below was the same. Hardly anyone was around.

He phoned the Majority Leader.

"Call it," he said. "Let's reconvene in 20 minutes."

~ ~ ~

Nizar was back to work as an automobile mechanic. His reputation as *The Engineer's* protégé was well known.

But now he got to supervise, though he often pushed aside his "pupils" and did the work himself. To show how to do it *right*.

The title *Ustadh*—Master—had taken.

He had done just that, and was under a beat-up Toyota Corolla, turning a wrench in one hand and leveraging a vice grip with the other, when a commotion on the street caught the attention of his fellow mechanics.

"Ustadh, come see!" one of the young mechanics called.

Nizar came out from under the car, and stood. He dusted himself off and stepped out of the garage bay.

It was strange—but quite an honor—to be called *Ustadh* at 23. It would take some time to get used to it.

The bustling street had come to a standstill. Everyone was looking skyward, toward the desert.

Nizar followed their gaze.

The sky was filled with parachutes. They were striking against the clear blue sky.

It was quite a beautiful sight. They were so graceful, floating lazily in the sky. More parachutes blossomed above them as they streamed out the backs of large aircraft.

"Americans," a boy said, his eyes wide. He turned to Nizar. "They're coming for you."

"Ustadh!" One of the young mechanics was in a state. *"What do we do?"*

Nizar's four mechanics—each slightly younger than he—were the same ones he'd hired for Yahya, to help move the barrels onto the boats.

"The Engineer," Nizar muttered. *He'll know what to do.*

"*What is that?*" someone shouted. Nizar heard it, too.

A high-pitched whine. *Two* whines. Like bees.

"They're *drones!*"

"*Stay away from us!*" someone shouted, shoving one of the mechanics into Nizar, knocking both to the ground. The young man ran away.

Two drones hovered just above, one at each end of the street, corralling Nizar and his mechanics. Nizar propped himself up on his elbows and stared, slack-jawed, at the drones.

It's like Star Trek!

Both drones exploded where they hovered, shattering windows and pockmarking buildings with shrapnel. The street was shrouded in smoke.

The smoke slowly thinned.

Young men and boys came out of hiding.

Nizar and the young mechanics lay scattered about, their clothes shredded. One nineteen-year old was still alive, but he struggled to breathe. He gasped and gurgled, choking on blood. Then he was gone.

A boy approached Nizar. His skinny frame was shirtless. His jeans were reduced to rags. He twitched—once, twice—then was unnaturally still.

Nizar's eyes remained open. He stared at the sky where the first drone had hovered.

His face was frozen in awe.

~ ~ ~

There was no objection. No backlash. No attempt to delay.

The Senators were back in their seats.

The Chief Justice gaveled the chamber back into session. "The Senate will reconvene."

He looked to the Majority Leader.

"The Senate is back in session," the Majority Leader said. "The Clerk will call the roll for the vote on the Article of Impeachment."

And with that, the voting had begun.

~ ~ ~

"See?" asked the young warehouseman. The whole *corner* is gone. I swear it was there yesterday."

Gary stroked his chin. He knew who did it. He just couldn't believe it.

"That's a lot of explosives, you know?" the kid said. "Th-that's why I called you."

"You did the right thing," Gary said.

There are protocols for this, he thought. *I'm supposed to call the ATF, I think.*

Their Philadelphia branch phone number was somewhere in the safety manual.

CHAPTER THIRTY

It was the third day of *Operation Homebound.*

And every morning, before dawn, he returned.

Daddy Longlegs stood at the edge of the tarmac at Dover Air Force Base, just shy of the cargo ramp where the planes taxied in.

Same spot.

Same long coat waving in the breeze.

Same smile.

He never checked his watch. He never held anything in his hands.

His scanned the gray horizon until the hulking form of a Xi'an Y-20 appeared, like a mirage out of the morning Delaware fog.

Daddy knew the image he was projecting. Cameras were trained on him.

Democrats and Republicans alike scorned him for allowing *China* to ferry Americans home. The media trashed him.

Traitor. Sell out. Failure. Insurgent. Wannabe Dictator. The Devil Incarnate.

Daddy smiled to himself.

The worm always turns.

Daddy tilted his head. He heard the now familiar, distinctive whine of the Shenyang engines. He saw the charcoal gray aircraft moments later, its hulking mass descending.

With each flight, a crewman stood out of the hatch above the cockpit holding the flag of China aloft as the Y-20 pulled alongside the reception area.

The Chinese markings on the aircraft fuselage were also hard to miss.

But with each aircraft, the shock was less than the previous one.

What mattered most was the fact that Americans were coming home.

And Daddy was there for all of them.

~ ~ ~

Yahya's heart pounded in his chest.

I am why they are here.

Yahya stood on the roof of his apartment along with others, watching as paratroopers filled the sky over the desert.

And everyone knows it.

I must go. Right now.

He rushed inside, grabbed a duffel bag, and stepped into the street.

"Mr. Engineer!"

It was the voice of a young man, and Nizar turned around.

He was confused. A woman stood in the street in a full body niqab.

Did she just—

Pfft. Pfft.

Yahya pursed his lips. Blood squirted out of his mouth.

His legs disappeared beneath him, and now the sky lay in front of him.

What is happening …

The woman in the niqab filled his vision. It was a man's eyes behind the veil.

He made eye contact, but only in passing. The eyes were disinterested in *his* eyes. Instead, they peered down at his body.

Then the woman walked on, satisfied.

"Allahu Akbar," someone cried out. *"The Engineer's dead!"*

The shout was repeated and echoed through the street.

But he wasn't dead.

And then he was.

~ ~ ~

It was raining now. A steady downpour.

Daddy stood in his usual spot, waiting for the next plane. His long coat flapped in the occasional breeze. A Marine stood beside him, holding a large black umbrella overhead.

The Marine had to reach—his arm fully extended, and his posture stiff—like the Statue of Liberty holding her torch aloft.

There was a commotion among the press corps. They began snapping photos. Multiple flashes caught the periphery of Daddy's vision. He ignored them, but he smiled inwardly.

Marvin Bauer, chief of his Secret Service detail, approached. He leaned into Daddy's ear.

"Sir, the Senate has convicted former President Belle. You are now the President."

Other aides converged. The flashes were relentless now. The press erupted. Reporters shouted questions over each other.

"Let's do it here," he said. "We have the press. Go fetch the Chief Justice—and Miss Care."

He looked up at the gray sky, then around at the rain-slicked tarmac.

"It's not how I imagined it would be."

He nodded, mostly to himself.

"But it's perfect."

~ ~ ~

Thirty minutes later, the Chief Justice of the Supreme Court stood under a tent on the tarmac of Dover Air Force Base, Delaware.

Steady rain tapped the canvas overhead.

Daddy stood facing the Chief Justice, his right hand raised, his left placed on a Bible held by Care, who stood at his side.

Daddy repeated after the Chief Justice: "I do solemnly swear … that I will faithfully execute the Office of President of the United States … and will to the best of my Ability … preserve, protect and defend … the Constitution of the United States … so help me, God."

The Chief Justice of the Supreme Court extended his hand.

"Congratulations, Mr. President."

A Xi'an Y-20 cargo plane touched down behind Daddy. Moments later, it eased into the reception zone, a crewman holding the Chinese flag aloft above the cockpit.

Operation Homebound continued.

And Daddy welcomed the passengers home.

~ ~ ~

It took a lot longer for the first soldiers to arrive than the people of Derna had anticipated.

It wasn't until the next morning, in fact.

During the night, flashes of light lit up the southern horizon, and the rumble of thunder rolled in from the desert.

The Americans concentrated on taking the airport first, which lay some 14 miles from the town. Then supplies and reinforcements could be flown in.

In the morning, first it was drones. Not like the two small drones the day before that killed Nizar and his four young mechanics. These were large, industrial-grade military drones. Maybe a hundred of them.

Every square inch of the city was covered.

People stayed inside. Businesses remained closed.

With the exception of a few stray dogs, the streets were empty.

A column of sand-colored armored vehicles approached the town along the main road from the airport. It was the *only* road that connected the city with points East … in Egypt.

The column stopped before entering the city.

A drone had spotted six dead bodies lying in the road just outside town.

A tracked robot wheeled into action. It tugged at each of the bodies in search of booby traps. Above, two more drones observed every detail.

After an hour of probing, an armored vehicle approached. Two men in bomb suits got out and went to work.

The bodies belonged to six young men. One had been shot twice. The other five had been killed by shrapnel, it appeared—tiny pellets that shredded their clothes and bodies.

On each of their bare stomachs, a phrase was written: *Le Chant du Soleil.*

Well, thought the commander. Someone had beaten them to their primary mission: the capture—dead or alive—of the *Chant du Soleil* terrorists.

Their primary mission *on paper,* that is.

~ ~ ~

In the meantime, hundreds of soldiers quietly seized the bluffs that loomed over the city. Artillery pieces and snipers were at the ready.

The first armored vehicle snaked its way along the highway and emerged out of the bluffs.

It slowly rolled into town. It sported a large red banner with a white crescent moon and a single, five-pointed white star. Gold trim adorned the top and bottom of the flag.

It wasn't the Americans after all.

~ ~ ~

Daddy and Care sat on the living room sofa.

It was their first night together with Daddy as President. Care was snuggled against him, his arm wrapped around her.

On the wall monitor, the screen was split into six frames: CNN, BBC, France24, DW, RT, and China's English news channel.

Nearly all of the news celebrated Belle's ouster.

Then there was the fact that Daddy was President. *"Dear God, let us live to Monday,"* snarled a CNN pundit, practically begging for Daddy's conviction.

The sentiment was shared across networks. And before long, they each cut to the Dover ceremony: Daddy's lanky silhouette beneath the rain-swept tent, coat tails flicking in the wind as he vowed no new policies—and pledged to stay put at Number One Observatory Circle until his trial wrapped up.

He'd refused to be presumptuous.

Care shifted closer as the camera lingered on him while he waited for the next Y-20 to land. The media couldn't look away—his tall frame, his long coat, the steady poise against the storm.

The photograph was already iconic.

The next morning was déjà vu. It was a replay of the previous three days, sans a swearing-in, of course. The Senate paused for a day before the start of his trial. And once again, Daddy struck his pose on the tarmac at Dover Air Force Base.

All day long.

It was continuity.

And more time for the worm to turn.

CHAPTER THIRTY-ONE

It was like a Presidential signing in the Rose Garden.

There was the university counsel. Mack Walmsley's attorney. Harvard's president. Isaac and Linda, the co-PIs. Each member of Isaac's and Linda's teams. And, of course, Mack Walmsley.

Each had their own line to sign per page, sometimes two or three per page.

There were lots of pages.

Patents—the project produced quite a few—were legal documents, after all.

Same for investor contracts.

Harvard's president and the Harvard Management Company have a long reach. Harvard alumni, and investors from around the country and the world, were privately afforded the opportunity to invest in the nascent Walmsley Energy Company, pending patent approvals.

$250 million was pledged.

More was needed, but it was a start.

Besides links to investors, Harvard enjoyed political connections. *Everywhere.* Especially in its home state of Massachusetts.

It didn't take long for the Governor and the Legislature to get on board and clear whatever legal hurdles there were.

Ten weeks later, Mack, Isaac, Linda, the research teams, and the President of Harvard gathered behind the Governor of Massachusetts—everyone was wearing hardhats—as he thrust a shovel into a pile of dirt while cameras flashed.

It was the official groundbreaking on the District Energy site of Harvard University—of the world's first Walmsley Dome barometric power plant.

~ ~ ~

It was a shabby airport. It hadn't seen regular commercial traffic in years. And even *then*, it wasn't a very busy airport.

After almost two decades of war, the airport was a shambles.

In every way, it was worse than the airport in Baghdad. *That* one's damage was fresh. This one's was decades old. Time and neglect had done more damage than combat.

The Maroon Berets were able to get the main runway ready to accommodate even the largest of aircraft within a few hours.

A four-engine turboprop Airbus A400 Atlas, carrying the Grand Vizier of the Treaty Union of Ankara, was the first aircraft to land at the one-time Martuba Airbase and International Airport.

From there, Tayfun Ulusoy rode in a convoy of Otokar Cobra armored tactical vehicles.

Instead of snaking down the bluffs and into the city, the Cobras veered into a residential compound.

Tayfun stepped out.

The two-story house wasn't all that much by itself. But the view was *astonishing.*

Derna filled in the narrow plain between the cliffs upon which the compound was perched, and the Mediterranean Sea stretched to the horizon.

It had been more than a decade since Storm Daniel—an extremely rare Mediterranean tropical cyclone—slammed into Derna. It's torrential rains washed out Derna's two major dams that had been neglected during years of conflict.

A mountain of water burst through the ravines and washed out much of the city. Some 20,000 people were estimated to have been swept out to sea.

The scars of that disaster were still evident from here.

Tayfun gazed at the scenery. *I may have found my first investment as Grand Vizier.*

Maroon Berets produced the owner of the compound.

He was a chiseled, world-weary man with soulful eyes. The Maroon Berets kept a sharp eye on him—he looked like he knew how to handle himself.

"I am very sorry to intrude," Tayfun said. The man said nothing.

"I need the signature of the Mayor."

"I run a construction business," the man said. "I am not the Mayor."

It was true. There *was* no mayor. The one man who could have passed for a mayor was the local warlord. But he had fled in the direction of Benghazi at the first sight of Maroon Beret paratroopers.

Tayfun looked around at the compound. Again, there wasn't much to it, but it was the biggest in Derna. *And the views.*

"And a very successful business, I imagine," Tayfun said. "You will do."

He opened a binder and showed it to the compound's owner.

At the top, it read: *"Petition for Stabilization Assistance to the Parliament of the Treaty Union of Ankara, submitted by the Municipality of Derna."*

Tayfun smiled and produced a pen.

~ ~ ~

Kyle rocked in his chair in the Senate Chamber as the House Managers presented their case anew. Rather than rehash everything they had covered during President Belle's trial—all of which was entered as part of the record in the trial of George Wartmann—the Managers focused on two additional aspects: Daddy pressuring Belle into war with Iran, and Daddy's deal with China to bring Americans home on Chinese aircraft.

They had shown the footage of the Vice President, rain drenching his coat, welcoming families off the gray transports—and then cut to close-ups of the Chinese star on the aircraft's fuselage. They meant it as proof of betrayal.

But it was the families' faces that Kyle saw: the laughter of children reunited, the tears of parents and grandparents, the genuine relief in every hug. He remembered how the Managers had called those scenes "a spectacle of political theater," but in his gut he knew they'd gotten it wrong.

On Saturday, Kyle's knee bounced nonstop. It was Team Daddy's turn, and they pounced on the very point that Daddy brought Americans home. Their closing argument was almost elegant in its simplicity: *"Love him or hate him,"* the lead counsel had said, *"but he gets things done."* They'd reminded the chamber that without Wartmann's China deal, there would still be over 200,000 Americans trapped overseas with no way of getting home.

On Saturday night, Kyle could barely sleep. He kept coming back to that Thew kid. Along with a squad of Navy SEALs, who had dragged him along in their escape from Bahrain, he had survived multiple missile strikes, air strikes, firefights, and even a nuclear bomb—*two* nuclear bombs.

Daddy had met them on the tarmac, just like he was doing at Dover. He found out that Thew was from Maryland, Kyle's state, and invited Kyle—whom he had never met—to accompany him and visit Thew at the Naval Hospital in Norfolk.

It was the kind of thing that attracted Kyle to politics in the first place—the difference you can make in someone's life.

And the way Daddy interacted with the SEALs and young Thew— Daddy was genuine and real. At no point in his interactions with Thew, the SEALs, or Kyle, was he even close to the caricature of evil that the media—and his own party—promoted.

It would be so easy to just go along with the Party. Nearly everyone was senior to him, and more experienced. And if he didn't, *Lord knows there will be hell to pay.*

But he could hear the voice of his father as he finally, mercifully, drifted off to sleep: *"Croppers don't do easy. Croppers do what's right."*

~ ~ ~

Buck did a quick rundown on the numbers and sat back in his seat. He beamed from ear to ear. Try as he might, he simply could not hide the smile on his face. History had already been made with the conviction of President Cynthia Belle. But history was about to be made again with the conviction of the Vice President—now President, though it had only been for a few days—Daddy Longlegs.

Daddy Longlegs would be known as the US President with the shortest time in office, ever. The current record belonged to William Henry Harrison, who died after just thirty days in office in 1841. He had likely caught pneumonia after giving the longest inaugural speech in history on a cold and rainy day in Washington.

Daddy wouldn't make it to one hundred hours.

Voting had begun. Senators made their way down to the Senate Desk to record their vote with the Legislative Clerk as she called their names.

Buck tried to be discreet as he smiled and nodded at fellow Democrats. He looked over his shoulder to see how the Senate Majority Leader was handling things. He looked grim. He had lost twelve Republican Senators, after all, which led to the bipartisan conviction of President Belle.

Those same twelve Senators were also expected to convict Vice President Daddy Longlegs. Every single Democrat, of course, voted to convict Belle and likewise was expected to—

Something caught Buck's eye. Kyle Cropper, the junior Senator from Maryland, was making his way down to the Senate Desk. He was a handsome, youthful man. A potential party leader.

But something was off with the young Democratic Senator. He slouched as he walked. His eyes were cast downward. He looked as if he carried the weight of the world on his shoulders. Like he was about to—

Buck leapt to his feet and walked briskly. He cut across the Senate floor and intercepted the young Senator, placing a hand on his chest.

The young Senator stopped cold in his tracks. He was startled.

"What are you doing?" Buck asked.

A quizzical expression crossed the young Senator's face like a shadow.

"Voting," he answered. His voice was shaky.

"*How* are you voting?" Buck demanded.

The Senator straightened. The quizzical expression on his face vanished. It was replaced by something ... different.

Resolve.

"You're in my way," said Kyle. He gently brushed Buck aside and walked on.

Buck watched the Maryland Senator walk up to the Legislative Clerk. His heart raced.

Oh, shit.

~ ~ ~

Kyle stepped to the bottom of the dais and spoke to the Senate Clerk.

He turned around and walked back to his seat the way he had come down to the well: with his eyes cast downward, shoulders slumped, his lanky arms dangling, as the next Senator stepped up.

"Senator Cropper: Not guilty," the Senate Clerk reported.

Kyle didn't know what to expect. But so far, there was nothing. Senators were speaking with each other in low tones or checking their phones.

Kyle breathed a sigh of relief. It was done.

As he took his seat, a low-volume murmur rose in the Chamber.

It grew louder.

"*Traitor!*" someone shouted. It was a red-faced Democratic Senator from Oregon.

The Supreme Court Chief Justice struck his gavel. "There will be order in the Chamber!"

The murmur only grew louder.

The Chief Justice struck it again. "Order in the Chamber!"

Kyle ignored the sudden unrest. He kept his back straight and looked down on the well as other Senators cast their votes.

~ ~ ~

Buck's phone buzzed in his breast pocket.

It was incessant.

He ignored it for now. He walked back to his desk and broke out his notes. He did another round of inventory.

He had calculated that that he had 70 votes to convict Vice President—er, *President*—Wartmann, the same number that had convicted President Belle.

Conviction required 67 votes. He had just lost one—a *Democrat!* Buck felt his face flush with anger.

He was down to 69 now. *It isn't lost.*

He pulled out his phone. He had text messages from several Senators who had yet to cast their votes.

He scanned them.

Senator Blake Foley of Ohio: *WTF? Should I vote Guilty or what?*

Barry Sickles of Missouri: *U said u had the votes.*

Jackson Rogers of Pennsylvania: His was an emoji of a boy with his hands and shoulders raised in a shrug.

Buck texted back. His thumbs were a blur.

Hang in there! We got this!

Sickles: *How can you be sure?*

Nothing from Foley. Buck scanned the Chamber, looking for him.

Shit. There he was. He was next in line to cast his vote.

Foley cast his vote and turned away.

"Senator Foley, Not Guilty," reported the Senate Clerk.

Damn it!

Buck slapped a palm on his desk. The Chief Justice's head snapped in his direction.

68 now.

Buck couldn't help but squirm in his chair with each vote cast.

We got this, he told himself. *We got this.*

"Senator Jackson Rogers, Not Guilty."

67. Buck's heart was beating as though he were in a sprint.

Not long after: "Senator Sickles, Not Guilty."

And there it was. Just like that.

Murmurs once again swelled in the Chamber. And once again, the Chief Justice struck the gavel. "Order!"

The very last Senator lining up to vote was Maximilian Zaporowski, of Upstate New York. He was a new Republican Senator. New York Republicans have generally been more moderate than the national party, so Buck held out hope.

Come on, Max. Surprise us.

Buck admonished himself. *I should've gone after him harder.*

But Max was a retired four-star Army General. There's no threatening or cajoling someone of his stature.

"Senator Zaporowski, Not Guilty."

The assembly erupted. First, there was applause, but it was quickly drowned out by boos.

The Chief Justice pounded on his gavel. *"Order! Order!"*

Buck sank into his chair.

The final count: 66 yea, 34 nay. That left the Senate one vote short of the two-thirds majority needed to convict the President.

President George "Daddy Longlegs" Wartmann was officially acquitted.

The worm had turned.

~ ~ ~

Washington traffic was the worst. Harvey gripped the wheel tightly. His knuckles were white.

He listened to Washington NPR on the radio. Pundits talked back and forth while the Senate voted.

It sounded like Daddy would be convicted.

I'll believe it when I see it.

Cars *blew* past him. BMWs and Mercedes with DC or Maryland license plates. *They must be doing ninety!*

He'd blow his horn when they maneuvered past and flip them off.

"Learn to drive, idiot!"

Take Exit 19B, US Route 50, to Washington, in five hundred feet, his phone GPS spoke. It was a female voice.

Welcome to Washington, District of Columbia, she said minutes later.

Soon, still on US 50, he was sitting in traffic. It was bumper to bumper.

"Oh, my," said the NPR host. "*That* was unexpected. Maryland Senator Kyle Cropper just voted 'Not Guilty.' That's a shocker."

"He's the first Democrat to break ranks," said one of the panelists.

"*Shocked* I say!" mocked Harvey. "Yeah, right."

Turn left onto 12th Avenue.

"I'm *trying!*" Harvey muttered. He couldn't turn left. He was on a bridge.

"What a stupid city!" he shouted.

The pundits droned on. Harvey tried to circle back. He seemed to be going in circles.

"And we have breaking news," the host announced. She got Harvey's attention again. "The last vote has been cast. 66 in favor of conviction 34 against. That is one vote shy of the two-thirds majority necessary for conviction. President Wartmann has been acquitted.”

“Oh, wow, that’s a stunner.”

“What’s a stunner is how dumb you are,” Harvey breathed.

Traffic was going nowhere. Harvey blew his horn.

“Go! Go!”

The pundits droned on.

“It would be a mistake by Democrats to think Daddy Longlegs is a lame duck President,” a guest said. “Republicans have the House, after all.”

“Yep. And World War Three is just around the corner!” Harvey snapped.

Traffic ahead was going nowhere. In fact, Harvey saw all kinds of police lights. There was a heavy security cordon extending for blocks from the Capitol Building.

And probably the White House.

He had gotten as close as he was going to get.

Tears started to trail down his face. By the time he got to the spot he had picked out on Google Maps—*if* he could get there—everything would be over.

His face broke. He shook his head. “I’m so sorry, Karen,” he wept.

I can just turn around.

When he got home, though, he would go to jail. And for a long time. Stealing explosives was a serious felony. In fact, it was *multiple* felonies.

“The rest of my life,” he cried. *The rest of my life in prison.*

“I can’t, I can’t.”

He shook his head. And then he saw it. A plaque on the wall of the building he sat beside:

‘Hart Senate Office Building’ it read.

Waist-high black ornate posts were lined up alongside the street to prevent vehicles from getting onto its grounds.

But an opening where "authorized vehicles only" could enter offered just enough space for him to wedge his box truck alongside the building. Not *right next* to the building, but he had enough explosives to do real damage.

And he was already close enough.

He nodded, with tears streaming.

"This is the spot," he sniffed. "Thank you."

He turned the wheel hard to the right and gunned it.

He slammed into a small tree, which toppled over, and pushed forward until his truck hit the edge of a wall.

His chest and shoulder slammed into the steering wheel. He bloodied his mouth.

But he was wedged in, just like he hoped.

He grabbed the detonator switch and hunkered down.

"You, in the truck, hands where I can see them!" a guard shouted.

Harvey could hear screams. They knew what was coming.

He flipped the switch and closed his eyes.

Dear God, I beg for your mercy.

He pushed the button.

~ ~ ~

Kyle sauntered into his office. The phone was ringing off the hook. "It's a lot of press," his secretary said. "From around the *world*. Also, a lot of calls from Maryland."

Kyle nodded. He was tired. "No calls. No visitors, either. Not even the Whip or Majority Leader." He went to his inner office and closed the door.

His office couch beckoned. He sank into it and undid his tie. He rubbed his face, then his temples.

He looked bleary-eyed around his office.

"Don't blame your mother and me for going into politics," his father had said.

"You knew what you wanted."

Kyle smiled. It was true.

He spotted *Maryland Magazine* on the coffee table. He was on the cover holding his surfboard, dressed in a suit. He had never read the darn thing.

He picked up the magazine and flipped to the article. There he was again, actually in the ocean, riding a wave. The pull quote in the middle of the article jumped out:

"Surfing clarifies things," Kyle said. "It strips everything down. There's no noise out there—just you, the water, and the next wave. You can't fake it."

Kyle raised his head and stared at the far wall.

"Make time for it," Daddy had said. *"It clarifies things."*

And then that laugh.

Kyle suddenly felt nauseated. He scampered for the wastebasket behind his desk, and dry heaved.

His heart pounded. He thought back to his visit to Norfolk Naval Hospital with Daddy Longlegs.

Was it all an act?

"No," he whispered. "Couldn't have been."

But was it?

Kyle plopped back onto the couch and laid back. He stared at the ceiling.

Was I played?

I voted my conscience, right?

It was the longest day of his life. The weight of it crashed in on him like a wave.

He closed his eyes and drifted away.

Then all hell broke loose.

~ ~ ~

The walls buckled and the office lurched beneath him.

Kyle was thrown to the floor.

Ceiling tiles fell and wiring dangled above him.

Dust and smoke clouded the room.

His office door was crooked from the buckling walls, but it swung open—and Kyle froze. He was still on the floor, propped up by his elbows.

The tall, lanky figure of Daddy Longlegs walked in.

He wore his signature grin. Light fixtures dangled from the ceiling in the main office behind him.

Alarms blared.

"Senator Cropper," Daddy said, "I just wanted to thank you."

Smoke curled up from Daddy's cuffs.

Kyle blinked.

A flicker of fire danced along the hem of his jacket.

"Sir," Kyle said, his eyes wide. *"Your jacket."*

"Never mind that, son," Daddy said. He was completely unfazed, even as the flame spread—slow and hungry—climbing upward, devouring cloth and flesh.

"Your vote," he said. Flames now danced on his shoulders.

"It clarifies things."

And then he laughed. It was that famous, mischievous laugh. He had laughed that very same laugh when they had visited Thew in the hospital.

His grin widened even as his skin blackened and cracked.

Then—he turned.

A raging inferno now, he walked out.

"It clarifies things!" he shouted, and laughed some more.

He left a trail of fire in his footsteps.

The smell of smoke and burning flesh filled Kyle's nose.

"Oh my God! Senator Cropper!"

Two of his young aids rushed in. Their clothes were torn, their faces dirty with soot.

"It was a bomb!" one of them exclaimed. *"We have to get you out of here!"*

"Sir?"

Kyle's eyes were glassy. His voice was raspy:

"We are not ready."

EPILOGUE

"It's a giant golf ball," Daddy said.

There were actually *two*—Daddy happened to be looking up at one of them.

They were two large, multi-sided white domes as large as ten-story buildings. They stood next to a smaller facility, a District Energy natural gas plant that powered much of the campus. Or, rather, it had *once* powered much of the campus.

The natural gas plant had been turned off. The two domes—known as Walmsley Domes—had taken over, and now produced enough electricity for all of Cambridge.

Harvard University's President explained how the new domes worked—and how they promised to transform energy production globally.

"It's a new renewable energy source. Experts think the Walmsley Dome will overtake solar and wind power combined within two or three years."

"So it's powered by *gravity*," Daddy said.

"Well, the weight of the atmosphere—but yes, it is gravity that gives the atmosphere its weight."

Daddy nodded, slowly.

Gas prices were coming down some, but they were still historically high. *But this—this was a game changer.*

And it hadn't come soon enough.

Martin Bauer approached the President.

"Sir, he's awake."

~ ~ ~

Kyle lay propped up in his bed. A surfboard stood in the corner, courtesy of his younger brother Jack, to "liven up the place."

His parents filled him in on what had happened.

"It was some *kook*, literally. Got so wrapped up in politics that he lost his friends, lost his job, and apparently lost his mind," his father said. "That's why I always told you to keep out of politics."

Kyle laughed.

The door swung open, and Daddy Longlegs entered.

"Whoa, look at him now!" he said. He bumped fists with Jack and shook hands with Kyle's father Chris. He hugged Kyle's mom, as well as Kyle's wife Michelle and Jack's wife Nataline.

"You all seem to know each other," Kyle said.

"He was here when we first got here," Jack said. "He's been back twice since, but you were still out of it."

"What's the prognosis?" Daddy asked.

"They want to keep him for observation for another day or two," Michelle answered, "but everything is good—all his vitals are strong."

"Very good," said Daddy. He looked to Kyle and was about to say more, but Kyle spoke first.

"Did you play me?"

The room went quiet. It was an awkward silence, but only for a moment. Everyone looked at Daddy as if to say: *Well, did you?*

"Mind if I have a moment with Kyle?" Daddy asked.

Everyone filed out of the room. Everyone but Chris.

Daddy looked at Chris. "He's a big boy now, Mr. Cropper."

"Go, Dad," Kyle said.

Chris looked back to Kyle and nodded. He patted Kyle's leg and stood.

Daddy watched him leave, then turned to Kyle when the door closed.

"Why would you ask that?"

"You used my quote from the magazine. In the hospital, when we visited that kid Thew."

Daddy sat in the chair where Chris was sitting.

"My wife Care found that article. She told me that you came across as a solid young man with a grounding—someone I could work with. And when I found that Thew was from Maryland—*Ocean City*, no less—I thought it was Divine Providence. It was an opportunity to meet you.

"I remembered the pull quote. *Surfing clarifies things.* It stuck with me.

"And guess what? Care was right. You voted your conscious. That's a brave thing to do around here. I came here to tell you that—and to thank you in person.

"That's the truth," Daddy said, and stood. "If you don't believe me, well, I can't help you."

He walked to the door.

"What do you mean 'someone you could work with'"? Kyle asked. "I'm a Democrat, remember?"

Daddy came back. "Yes, but a Democrat who doesn't tow the party line and does what he thinks is right. I need people like that—like you."

Daddy went to the window and looked out on the Bethesda campus of the Walter Reed Military Medical Center.

"The world has changed. Try as I might to get everything back to how it was just a couple of months ago, there is no going back.

"Europe is unraveling. ICE's capture of neighborhoods in Paris and elsewhere—it's the first non-European capture of European territory since the Ottomans moved into the Balkans in the 14th Century. And before that, you'd have to go back to the 700s when the Moors moved into modern-day Spain."

He looked back to Kyle.

"I can see the future, kid."

He shook his head.

"We're not ready."

A Note from the Author

Writing *The Compass Room* took me into difficult territory. To tell this story honestly, I had to grapple with right-wing politics in Europe — especially the fear of immigration. It was uncomfortable ground for me.

Immigration looks very different in Europe than in America. Europe lies much closer to unstable regions of the world, and waves of migration can feel like sudden shocks. At the same time, European leaders seem unwilling to slow immigration because of demographic realities — an aging population and the economic need for workers. That tension is part of what fuels unrest in the novel.

Rather than focusing on the human costs of conflict, my aim was to examine its geopolitical aftermath: the way wars can unsettle nations and unbalance the global order.

Thank you for joining me on this journey. If *The Compass Room* spoke to you in any way, I would be deeply grateful if you left a short review where you purchased your copy. Reviews are one of the best ways readers can support authors — they help others discover new stories, and they encourage writers to keep creating.

The Wartmann Series continues. To follow along, visit: www.authormarkjames.com and www.northarrowpress.com.

With gratitude,
Mark James

NORTH
ARROW
PRESS

www.ingramcontent.com/pod-product-compliance
Lightning Source LLC
Chambersburg PA
CBHW021141310726
48971CB00002B/431